SEDUCING
THE
SKEPTIC

Accidental Angel Series

Book One

Kathy Lyons

USA Today Bestselling Author

Book design by eBook Prep www.ebookprep.com
Cover by The Killion Group www.thekilliongroupinc.com

November, 2015
ISBN: 978-1-61417-781-4

ePublishing Works!
www.epublishingworks.com

ALSO BY KATHY LYONS

CONTEMPORARY ROMANCE

The Mistake Makeover

The Player Next Door

Two Week Seduction

One Night in the Spa

Night Studies

Dinner With a Bad Boy (novella)

PARANORMAL ROMANCE
writing as JADE LEE

Dragonborn

Dragonbound

A Magic King

Seduced by Crimson

Sexy Bites

CHAPTER 1

"I'm afraid you're just not cut out for this program, Miss Mason."

It took a moment for Janet Mason to hear Professor Jefferson's words over the growing scream in her brain. She was being kicked out of the PhD program. After all the work she'd done to get into the program and his lab, to get her future on track, he was throwing her out. "But you know I'm a good student. You know I work really hard."

"I know you were and you did." Again with the heavy sigh. "But you haven't been that stellar student for a long time now."

She stared at him, her mouth hanging open in shock. Do something, damn it! Even passing out would be preferable to this gray blankness of non-function. But all she could think was that she couldn't get kicked out. Where would she go? What would she do? Theoretical physicists only got jobs if they had a PhD. She was a part-time barista. That wasn't enough to pay rent much less food.

"Look," she said, scrambling for any option. "The problem's the thesis proposal, right? Let me work on it. Let me—"

"There isn't time."

"Of course there is. You know what I can do in just a week. Remember that paper on proton acceleration?" Probably wasn't the time to tell him her star paper had been written in a weekend. "I got really intense on that and—"

"That was undergrad. I think you need to accept the situation here. It gives me no pleasure to do this to you."

Bullshit. He was totally loving it. "There is time. I'll get you something else. In two weeks, I can—"

"Monday, Janet. I can hold off until Monday, but no longer."

She blinked. It was Friday. *Late* Friday afternoon. Hell, almost everyone had already left for the weekend even though they weren't supposed to skip until five.

"I can do it, sir," she said rushing her words just so he wouldn't interrupt her.

"You can't. No one could."

She gritted her teeth. "Just watch me." Then she stood up and left. She walked right out without so much as a goodbye. Or a clue.

She made it home by way of Espresso Royale. She made her favorite drink—a quad raspberry latte with extra whip (thank God for sugar and caffeine)—before dropping her shifts for the next two weeks. "Going into deep retreat mode," she told her manager.

Yes, she only had a weekend, but assuming she pulled her butt out of the fire, she'd need to haul ass to lock it in. If it were just the work, she'd have it down in a single all-nighter. She could whip out a paper in no time. But the problem wasn't her writing, it was her core idea. She hadn't a clue what to research and no interest in anything either. She was stumped.

She made it home slowly, mentally cudgeling herself with every step. It didn't help.

None of her housemates were home. They all had lives. Well, everyone except the medical student who spent every waking moment at the hospital. It didn't matter anyway, because Janet needed a brilliant physics idea. An engineer, a med student, and an architect were the beginning of a bar joke, not the kind of resources who could help her with advanced physics.

So she sat on her bed, drank her latte, and tried to be inspired. She ended up watching Tom Hiddleston videos instead. Inspiration of the wrong sort, obviously.

What the hell was wrong with her? Why had her entire life faded into a wash of gray?

She stared at her walls, which were bare. She had a couple pictures she wanted to hang, but she'd never gotten around to it. And since her father had once said menial labor helped him think, she decided to give it a try. Maybe she would become brilliant while hanging a picture of Einstein.

She had a hanging kit purchased almost a year ago, but she needed a hammer. Usually she'd grab a shoe, but nowadays she wore mostly flip flops or stiletto heels for the occasional date. Which meant...

Marty's room. The engineer had a zillion tools kept in pristine order, and she wouldn't care if Janet borrowed a hammer. Assuming, of course, she kept the thing clean and returned it to its anal-retentive spot in the tool belt. Just in case, she knocked on her friend's door.

"Marty?"

No one home—which she already knew—so she opened the door and went in, stepping around three foam-covered fake swords and designs for a medieval catapult. Marty was a LARPer. Live Action Role Play was her favorite hobby, because the internet-based MMORPG versions were just too lame according to her. Janet, of course, was more into "sit on the couch and name the plot holes," but to each her own.

"If I were a tool belt, where would I be?" she asked herself. When had she started talking to empty rooms? "Closet. Duh."

She opened the walk-in closet which was filled on one side with clothes and the other side with Marty's Container Store obsession. The tool belt was in one of these boxes. No it wasn't, it was hanging on a hook at the back, a mixture of cheapo student belt with cobbled-on Batman Velcro pouches. She knew that it held all sorts of cool stuff plus all the usual tools. She was just grabbing it when a blast of cold air chilled her to the bones. She looked up. Had someone just come home? But why would she feel the breeze in a closet?

"Hello?" she called.

"Praise Goddess *garble!*"

She frowned. Okay, that sounded like it came from deeper inside the closet, not from downstairs. Which was weird. And come to think of it, the breeze had been from there too.

Intrigued, Janet pushed forward. The back of the walk-in was where Marty stored her costumes. Brocaded tabards right next to vampire capes complete with spooky netting. She had to be careful when moving them aside, but she pushed and…

"Whoa." The coolest hologram ever. Brilliant sky, rocky cliff, and a creepy looking tree with a huge ass nest braced between three branches thicker than her thighs.

So this was Marty's secret project. But why the hell would she build it behind her costumes in the back of the closet? For secrecy, obviously, and because she was an uber Narnia geek, but damn…talk about a narrow workspace.

Another blast of cold air hit her, and she squinted against the bitter wind. There had to be a fan here somewhere. Nice effect, but annoying as hell, not to mention cold. But where was it coming from? She stepped closer and half-tripped over Marty's thigh-high sex boots. Which is when he showed up. Or rather rose up from the middle of the nest.

A blonde god of a man reminiscent of Thor. His broad chest was all golden bronze, stretched over well-defined muscles. She thought the scars were overdone, as were the streaks of blood on his cuts, not to mention a couple weird white splashes, but whatever. She could appreciate her roommate's taste even if it was more beach blonde sun-god than Tom Hiddleston evil chaos-god.

"Prithee angel, forsooth I am stuck fast."

Prithee? Seriously? Marty needed some better writing, but beyond that, this was way cool. She stepped to the very back of the closet and really felt like she was teetering on the edge of a giant abyss. She glanced down long enough to feel a wave of vertigo and had to grab onto a tabard to keep from falling.

"Angel, please. Can you unbind me?"

She looked up and focused on the man. The wind was carrying away half his words, but she understood him well enough which was very odd. First of all, she couldn't exactly hear over the howling wind and yet had a pretty good idea of what he was saying. Plus, she'd been looking straight at his mouth when he spoke. The words she heard didn't match the shape of his lips at all. Which meant there was probably some sort of sync problem between the video and audio. Unless she was just distracted by how pretty he was with that rippling chest and all.

"How is she doing this?" She looked around the edges of the closet, trying to see how this was being projected. There was nothing. No wires, no projection equipment or screen. Another blast of air hit her and she recoiled backwards, accidently tripping—again—over Marty's boots. "Ow!" she cursed, then kicked the nearest leather torture device aside. Those stilettos were sharp.

Then she watched in fascination as the boot did not bounce off of the back of the closet wall. No, it flew into the air—straight into the hologram—where the sun-god tried to catch it. He missed. Her kick was wide, and he apparently was stuck in the nest by that white stuff.

But how could Marty have programmed it to time with her kick? How did it sense when—and what—would be thrown?

She shook her head, trying to process just how this illusion was being generated. And then the guy spoke again. She seemed to hear him better when she didn't look so closely at his lips. He said something about "stuck" and "dissolve." Dissolve the white goo, she assumed, but she hadn't a clue how. And then "hammer."

"Hammer!" she cried. She held up Marty's tool belt and grinned. She ought to feel embarrassed that she was responding to a hologram as if it were real life, but whatever.

This was a game, and she was having fun. Something that hadn't happened for her in months. Except...

Damn. She had to work. In truth, she had her entire academic career to fix, so she gave the illusion a regretful sigh. "I'm sorry. I can't play today." Then she searched for the off switch. Had the thing been triggered when she turned on the closet light?

She was turning around when he spoke again. She couldn't even hear the words properly, but the plea in them was heartbreaking. It was insane that she could respond so clearly to something that wasn't real. She turned back, which just made everything worse. She saw desperation in his eyes and felt an echo in her own heart.

How long had she been like him, reaching for an answer—any answer—with no one to help her? She knew it wasn't real, and yet she couldn't walk away. It would take no time at all for her to give him the hammer. If she just played out the first level, then maybe it would free her subconscious to solve her academic problem.

She pulled out the tool, but when she reached forward—gripping the tabard—she couldn't quite connect with his hand. She could throw it, but she didn't want to damage whatever sophisticated equipment was hiding back here. She could probably just step out into the air, but she didn't want to break the illusion. Or more accurately, the illusion felt so real that the very idea of walking on air was giving her the heebie-jeebies. Fortunately, closer inspection showed her the game's intended pathway.

Far to the edge of the closet, there was an easy step to a branch. Clearly it was what the player was meant to use. It looked solid enough, but with the wind it seemed to bounce and sway. Well, what was a game without a challenge? So she took a moment to tie the tool belt about her waist, securing the hammer in its normal slot. Then she stepped to the edge.

It was harder than it should have been to let go of the tabard. The icy wind was making her shudder and her hands cramp. Also, the heavy brocade was warm and…

Warmth. Right. With a quick jerk of her hand, she drew on the tabard. It was like a too large, ornate poncho for the front and back. No sides which made it easier to access the tool belt. A sweater would have made much more sense, but she didn't want to take too long at this, especially since sun-god guy kept looking around in anxiety and making hurry up gestures with his free hand.

So this was awkward. She stepped from the closet to the thick branch, but flip-flops were not meant for tree climbing. With a grunt of frustration, she kicked them off, then set about branch-walking barefoot. Icy cold whipped over her toes, and the branch was none too toasty. More like smooth iron wood which made sense only in her brain. Plus the wind caught her hair and whipped it into her eyes. At least it was pulled back into a ponytail, but her bangs were too long and they kept teasing at the edge of her eyes.

She narrowed her eyes and took another step forward, leaning into the wind. If this were real, she'd be screwed for sure. No one could balance barefoot on a branch that bounced in the wind. Especially in a damned tabard that was warm—thank you—but only seemed to increase the wind's drag.

She cursed and grabbed the brocade about her waist. Then she decided that she would forego any attempt to tightrope walk. Still close enough to grab the edge of the closet, she dropped down to straddle the branch. She'd been a kid with time on her hands once. She could shimmy her way to the nest. It might not look cool, but she'd get there.

She did. Her fingers were numb by the time she made it to the nest, and *ewwww* what was that smell? Even in the biting wind it was foul.

Meanwhile, sun-god guy was reaching out with his free hand, helping her scramble into the massive nest. Well, not really massive. For a bird it was clearly huge, but for the big guy and her, it was like having two people maneuver in a circle-shaped crib. At least there were downy feathers at the bottom that gave welcome insulation to her freezing feet.

"Hurry," he said, as he looked over her shoulder. She started to turn, but then decided she didn't want to know. Marty was a huge fan of make-up artist shows, not to mention zombie flicks and vampire books (not the teen heartthrob kind). So she just focused on the problem at hand.

Our hero was encased in that white crap. And it really did look like crap. As if from a massive bird. He was trying to move, bunching his biceps as he tried to break his right arm free. She grabbed his fingers and tried to help, but the stuff was like concrete.

"Do you have a weapon?" he asked. The wind had died down enough that she could hear him clearly now. He had a nice voice if a bit gravelly. In truth, he sounded like he was on day three of a whiskey bender. And now that she got a closer look at him, his face was equally haggard. But both voice and three-day beard had a He-Man kind of appeal, so she grinned at him even as she grabbed Marty's hammer.

She hesitated a moment. After all, she was about to start clobbering a guy encased in concrete bird shit. "In for a penny," she muttered, then began to whack at the stuff on his forearm.

"Harder," he said.

She chuckled, knowing there was a bad joke in there somewhere, but too focused on freeing his arm to find it. She was whacking at the stuff, but she'd been trying to go delicately. This was a video game somehow, and she didn't want to break the equipment. But obviously this required real strength because she was getting nowhere. So she began to hammer in earnest, slamming down as hard as she could.

She glanced up at sun-god's face to see if he was wincing in pain. The heavier she hit, the more it had to hurt him. But he was scanning the horizon, so she went back to slamming her hammer into the crap.

Crack!

She saw the crack more than heard it, but there was a definite pop of sorts and a chunk of the stuff broke free. She flipped the hammer around, wedging the pronged ends into the crack. Then she tried to lever his arm up and away. It didn't work. Not until she put all her weight on the handle which was getting slippery with sweat despite the cold.

This time she did hear the crack. The white concrete gave way, but so did she as she fell sideways against the nest. Hero-guy steadied her, keeping her from flying out into a plummet of doom, but it didn't keep her from stepping sideways onto...*ewwww*. Egg. Well, broken egg, now. And it was sliming her foot.

Then *ewww* turned into *ow!* The stuff stung! She stabilized herself on her one foot as she wiped off the other on the feathers. But then the feathers just stuck to her foot so she wiped it on the concrete crap. Meanwhile, the big guy had picked up the hammer and was slamming it down on his legs. That was going to take a while though because he was really buried.

Or rather, he was until she started looking at the egg stuff. It seemed to be reacting with the white stuff. Acid maybe? Which did not bode well for her foot, but whatever. This was just a game, right?

She had a flash of nervousness, quickly suppressed. This was more realistic than any game she'd ever been in. The sensory details were perfect, even the uncomfortable ones. And the wind simply could not be generated from the back of a closet, but she didn't want to think about that. The present, complete with blonde god hero, was much more compelling.

Since the stud-muffin was using the hammer, she took out the wrench. With a mental apology to her roommate, she used the thing to start working on the concrete that had been coated by the egg ooze. Holy crap, it worked! The white stuff was softer now and she could scrape it away easily with the wrench.

Made a damned mess, but at least she was seeing thigh now. Thick, corded man-thigh, but that was part of the reward, right? What's a game without eye-candy? She leaned down and grabbed a handful of egg-slopped feathers. Totally gross, but she used them to smear slime over the rest of his legs. He saw what she was doing and grabbed a handful as well.

But there wasn't enough to go around. Not until he used her hammer—Marty's pristine gleaming hammer—to slam into two more eggs near his feet. She hadn't even seen them there, but they burst with a sickening crunch.

He started scooping up the ooze immediately, not even noticing that baby bird embryos also dropped out. Part of her mind catalogued exactly what level of development they were at. The other part was just repelled by the sight. Then she heard it: a screech. It might have been there for a while, but she'd discounted it as the wind. But even her powers of denial couldn't block out that sound. An eagle's screech was what her brain said, but in her mind, an eagle's cry was the bell-like call of a majestic beast. Not this. This was a mixture of pissed-off bird and truck brake squeal. It grated down her spine way worse than fingernails on a chalkboard and a thousand times more loud.

She looked at the big guy. He had to have heard it. But his eyes were narrowed in concentration on his legs as he slammed his hammer down again and again. Right. He had to get free.

The screech came again. Really loud this time, and she couldn't stop herself from looking. Holy shit, that was one big bird. Like a really huge bird with talons that could rip through a freaking car! They were extended as the thing...

Oh shit. It was coming in for a landing. It was probably Mommy, and they'd just killed her babies. But in their defense, mama bird had probably meant hero to be baby food.

"My sword!" he said as she stood transfixed by those damned talons.

"Aiiiiiieeeeeeee!" she squealed because that thing was coming in fast. She waved her wrench at it. It was the only thing she had in hand, somehow managing to clobber it on

the foot. How she avoided getting impaled she had no idea, but the thing screamed at her in response before flapping away.

"My sword!" he said, and this time he pointed at a mound in the corner. Except it wasn't a mound. It was a hilt extending from a lumpy thing that could be a backpack buried under softened concrete crap. Oh. *That* sword.

She lurched forward and grabbed hold, flashing on Arthur pulling the sword out of the stone. She didn't do anything so graceful as that. For one thing, the sword was lying on its side, not sticking upright. She had to chip away at it with her wrench before she could get it free. Marty's wrench was never going to be the same. And it couldn't possibly be doing any favors to the sword.

She heard the guy bellow and whip his arms around. She knew from the screech and the scary flapping of wings that the eagle thing had come in for another pass. Something pelted her in the face and she saw a small rock land in front of her feet. It was pretty—kind of a rose tone—and she wondered what sort of stone it was. Her mind focused on that question because it distracted her from the pain in her fingers as she managed to grip the sword and start hauling it free. Her back was straining, her fingers were bloody, and that bird thing—

Well, it was motivation. She'd give it that.

The sword came free with a jerk and she tumbled backwards, landing badly on sun-god guy. He grunted in a manly way, which in this case sounded more like a curse, before he pushed her off him. Not hard enough to hurt, but with enough force to make it expedient.

Then he grabbed the sword with one hand and started waving it around above their heads. Normally this would be cause for alarm, but she was already maxed out on adrenaline, and given that she knew the bird was coming back any second now, she was all kinds of good with him waving a pointy stick around.

Her job, she decided, was to get his feet free so he could

do more than sit there and wave the sword. He was mostly free of the crap. His thighs were goopy—and a little bloody she now realized—but they could move. A few moments of concentrated work and she got his feet out too. But his hips. Jesus, his hips and ass were still locked down hard.

She knew what to do and set about covering his privates in the egg goop. She even took a deep breath and broke open the last egg, ignoring the dying embryo in favor of scooping up slop and wiping it all over his hips and as much of his ass as she could get to. She didn't even have time to be embarrassed, though the hysterical part of her brain was busy making dick jokes. Thankfully, none of the lumps she chiseled and tossed away belonged to him, and finally he was able to shove himself upright.

There was a tearing sound. His clothes, she thought. But then he was standing tall and whipping his sword around as the bird came back at him. At them. At…

"Oh shit."

It was definitely coming in for a landing, but hero was there looking really godly with his sword and his rippling abs. She'd love to be sitting on a couch right now with a remote control in her hand. She'd slow down the play to fully appreciate his magnificence. But she wasn't, and he was bellowing at her.

"My pack! Grab the pack!"

Right. The lump beside the sword. Personally she was more about getting out of Dodge than recovering his spare set of tighty-whities, but she knew how these games worked. If you didn't bother to grab the pack, then you'd escape the demented bird only to starve to death in the forest. So she set about freeing the pack. Except it was in there good and there weren't any more eggs to break.

"Not. Happening," she gasped. Damn, she was winded. Hacking at cement with a wrench really took its toll. "We have to get out!"

He'd managed to scare off the bird for the moment, but it wouldn't last long. He must have known that too because he looked at her—all grim seriousness—and nodded. "Go angel. I will protect your retreat."

Protect her retreat? Whatever. "The closet's just over there. Come on!"

She grabbed his arm and started hauling him toward the branch. Somehow in her brain, this made sense. The closet meant safety. She'd step out and bring her sun-god with her. They'd order pizza and laugh about the scary bird then talk about physics. And maybe make some chemistry. That all flashed through her brain as she dragged him toward the branch.

Except a second later, she really looked at the closet. Or looked *for* the closet. Because it wasn't there. Had she gotten turned around? She had the world's worst sense of direction, but...but...

"Oh shit."

"Can't you make another door?" he asked.

Make another...? "Wait!" There was a ripple there, right where the closet should be. A wave in the air, like heat coming off asphalt. Except there was no asphalt here. Only a hundred mile plummet to death. She stared hard at it. She thought of Marty's closet and desperately willed those damned stripper boots to appear. And somewhere in the back of her head a pull started. A wrench and an agony. The beginning of what was going to be a killer migraine.

Then she heard something else. A scream that was higher in pitch but three times as pissed off. She spun around to look and saw two dark splotches circling the air, one distinctly bigger than the one they'd been fighting before.

"What's that?" she asked, not really wanting to know.

"The mother," he answered, looking grim. "They will coordinate their attack, so you must go, angel. Now."

"How are you going to fight them?"

He shook his head. "I won't."

"Meaning you'll run, right?"

He didn't answer. She turned to look back at her ripple in

the air. She could maybe get it open in time, if that was indeed what she'd been doing. She could also probably take the guess, leap into it, and pray that it was enough of a door for her. Though the 100 mile plummet didn't make that an appealing option. Plus, it would totally screw him.

Which meant she needed to think of something else. Or maybe, they just needed to run. "We have to get out of this tree!"

He shook his head as he braced himself, sword raised. "Not during their pass. They'll pick us up like surtar." She didn't think she'd heard him right. Somewhere her panicked mind translated "surtar" as "low hanging fruit." Either way, that didn't sound good.

"Okay. What do I do?"

"My pack," he said. "Can you get to it? There are stones inside."

Okay, great. How did that help? She didn't waste her breath asking but scrambled back up on the branch and into the nest. Her feet were freezing anyway, and if she were going to die by angry bird she might as well make her last seconds comfortable. She found the lump of his pack easily enough. She tugged on it, but just like before, there was no prayer that it was getting free. It was cemented in there good.

She'd managed to expose a side of it though. She scraped at that now, but the softening effect wasn't enough or had worn out or whatever. She did a quick scan, but she already knew there weren't any more eggs. Course she really didn't need the pack itself, just the stones, right? If she could rip it open...

It was too tough. Leather soaked in concrete didn't give way to her fingernails. If only...

Box-cutter. Duh.

She might have slapped herself for her stupidity but there wasn't time. She felt around the tool belt. It was hidden beneath the tabard, and she tried to find the cutter while jerking the heavy brocade out of the way. Not so easy given that she didn't have five hands. She found Marty's asthma inhaler, duct tape, and a drill set before she located the box-cutter.

"Got it!"

"Throw them at the birds!" he bellowed.

Oh. He thought she'd gotten the stones. Well, not so much, but she was working on it. She attacked the pack with the cutter, breaking the razor part, but managing to stab a hole into the pack nevertheless. She shoved her hand inside relieved to find that it was softer in there and not at all gross or sharp. Who knew what weapons he had in there? But mostly it was cloth and…

A cloth roll with lumpy stuff inside. Lumpy like stones. She hauled it out, but it was too late. The birds were already attacking. She really wished she couldn't hear their screech above the pounding of her heart.

She looked back at the stud muffin. He'd braced himself as best he could outside the nest. He was balanced on two branches with the edge of the nest right in front. The smaller bird was doing his fly-by. Her big hero was swinging his sword and screaming, some sort of incoherent warrior bellow. She'd always thought that a dumb thing to do. Why waste your breath on noise? But the sound took the edge off her terror. And frankly, to paraphrase Malcolm Reynolds, he was way too pretty to die.

She couldn't make sense of what happened next. Just grunts and feathers and flashing sword. It all went so fast. She quickly unrolled the cloth, praying that she wasn't just going to find a set of pretty warrior rings or something. Nope. Stones. And some crystals. Different sizes, different grains, some even with stripes. Okay. What were these supposed to do?

The second bird was attacking. This was the big mama, and she abruptly understood what he meant about them attacking in a coordinated circle. First one then, before she could catch her breath, the second would be coming in for a kill. Smart birds. Except she was not going to admit she was dumber than a couple of really big vultures.

"Throw. Them." Words which he didn't even have the breath to yell. It was more a grunt of effort.

Okay then. She grabbed the first two stones, pale blue ones that felt… Oy… Weird in her hand. Whatever. Mama bird was past, but the smaller one was coming in. She pulled her hand back, and thanked God for her summers in softball. Then she threw.

Well, she'd never been a pitcher.

She'd meant to hit the thing in the chest. Missed by a mile. Well, not really, but in bird terms, she'd plunked them harmlessly against a wing feather and it had passed right through. Well what did she expect? She wasn't chunking boulders at them. These were pebbles.

"Activate. It."

She whipped her head around to look at her hero. Well as much as she could see of him amid the flashes of his sword in the sunlight and the gray black bird feathers that were floating around. He was damned good with that sword, thank God. But his face and body were streaked with sweat. Oh shit. He was getting tired. She'd thought his face kind of haggard before. Now it was gray and…and really not happy.

But he kept the bird off of them for that pass.

Course now it was little one's turn, though they had maybe a five second breather. He used it to drop the tip of his sword to the edge of the nest as he took in big gulps of air.

"Activate," he said between gasps. "Magic."

Right. Activate the magic. "How?"

His face took on a sad cast. Not just sad, but drooping with exhaustion and the grim realization that they were going to die. Okay, so maybe she was projecting her emotions onto him, but she recognized that look. It was the I-am-so-screwed-and-there's-nothing-I-can-do-about-it look.

Well fuck that. "Tell me what to do!"

He shook his head. "Don't know. I just do it."

Out of time. Little bird was coming.

Teeth and claws and feathers, and she threw it.

Again, she missed. She could already see that it was going toward the wing not the chest. Fuck, she was awful at softball. But the moment it got near, the moment the pebble was going to glance uselessly against its wing, the thing exploded.

Well, not exploded. Explosions meant fireballs and smoke. This became a huge orb of blue light. Or force. Or something. The bird's wing was shoved down and the head snapped sideways. There was an audible crack and then...

It plummeted out of the sky.

Broken wing? Broken neck? She peered over the edge and saw it continue to fall. It wasn't recovering. A second later she watched it hit and bounce on the rocky cliff. Ouch.

One down, one to go. And lest she forget, the surviving bird released another scream of fury that had Janet's toes curling in terror. But they had the stones now. They could blue fire the big bitch too. She looked to her warrior, expecting to see a reflection of her own excitement in his eyes. After all, they weren't going to die by bird now. Except he wasn't looking up.

Oh shit.

He was wiped. Like down on one knee, head on the hilt of his sword down. The only sign of strength in him was the one hand that gripped the nest to keep him from falling off the branch. Oh shit.

He must have been the one to turn on the blue thing and now he was completely exhausted.

"Tell me how to do it!" she screamed. With the wind noise and that bird screech, she had to bellow to be heard. "How do you turn these things on?"

He didn't answer. He barely even moved except to breathe. But he'd already told her, hadn't he? He just did it. He didn't know how.

Mama bird was doing her pass. Janet barely had time to see the bitch beyond a massive dark shadow, but she shoved her hero flat and did her best to cover him with her body, draping herself half in and half out of the nest. It wasn't as selfless as she'd like to think. He was her only chance. If he died, she was beyond screwed. So she shoved him down, covered him as best she could, and screamed at the bitch as loud as she could.

She called it every filthy name in her repertoire and a few mangled Russian words because the language had always sounded mean to her. She felt more than heard her warrior grunt as his body jerked sideways. She kept him on the branch—or he did—but when she looked up she saw a bright streak of crimson along his back. Damn. He'd gotten a talon across the back. On the one hand, she was glad he hadn't gotten pierced through the side. On the other hand: talon across the back and it was bleeding. A dark red streak that went from shoulderblade to hip.

"Fire."

One word, barely audible above the wind. She angled back to him.

"What?"

"Red. Stone."

She quickly sorted through the roll of stones, spilling half of them until she came on one that was as close to red as she could find. It was more rosy mauve than red but whatever. She held it out to him but he just shook his head.

"What?" she asked.

He reached out, then with a backhanded gesture knocked the thing out of her hand. It landed somewhere into the depths of the feathered nest.

"Shit," she cursed, but when she went to grab for it, he held onto her.

"Come. Out." He tugged on her arm, pulling her out of the nest. Well, not really pulling because he had zero strength. But the meaning was clear, especially as he glanced up into the sky. Mama bird was back. She didn't even need to look.

Janet scrambled out of the nest, joining him on the teetering branch. He straightened up, but damn, he was too tired to even carry his sword. She grabbed it, wrapped an arm around his waist and wondered exactly how they were going to scramble down a tree like this. It was all she could do to keep him braced there against the nest.

Then he did something. She wouldn't have noticed if she hadn't been pressed so tight against him. It was like his chest was a solid wall of muscle and then it was smaller. He'd caved in. He drooped more. And his face—Jesus—she'd seen movie zombies with a healthier complexion.

"Not a problem," she lied. "We've got this. We can do this."

Bitch mama was back. They were in a better position to flatten up now. They dropped below the line of the nest and since mama apparently didn't want to shove her home down into the valley, her beaks and talons missed, though Janet was sure she'd just gotten a hair cut. Mama bird's claws were definitely razor sharp.

And sun god in her arms was still bleeding. His back was slick with blood and sweat, and she was going to have trouble holding onto him. Just in case, she glanced over to the closet. Or rather where the closet ought to be.

Nothing. Not even the ripple.

Well, fine. No cheats then.

"We're going to have to run," she said.

He nodded, and she felt him gather his strength. And while he was pushing himself upright, she smelled something acrid. Something really nasty. Overall, the nest had been nasty to begin with, but this was gross with an extra helping of…

Fire.

The nest was on fire.

That little red stone had nestled deep into those downy feathers, and now the whole thing was crackling toasty warm. Nice! Especially since the heat was welcome on her face.

Except then reality kicked in. They were in a tree. On a

cliff. Hanging suspended over a zillion mile drop. And the tree was on fire.

"We really have to go."

He didn't waste his breath answering. He straightened up and gently pushed her forward, away from the rapidly growing bonfire of a nest. She went, releasing him as soon as she was sure he could find his balance. It didn't matter if he couldn't. No way could she support him and climb down a tree at the same time. But she waited, and at his nod, she released him.

Then she started moving. The fire helped warm her fingers, and so she was able to scramble forward, grabbing handholds as best she could. The nest had been on a conjunction of branches, she now saw. It hadn't been the main trunk, and what the hell kind of tree was this? It was huge. Easily the size of a city block. Sadly, the needles were sparse, so they provided zero coverage and just stabbed her hands when she grabbed at them. And the sap…yuck. Now that they were closer toward the center of the tree, there was sap that stuck to her feet and hands.

"Careful," he grunted from behind her. "Sap."

"Yeah. Gross."

"Flammable."

"Naturally." This tree was going to go poof and in a really spectacular fireball kind of way. They really needed to get out of here. She couldn't move any faster than she already was, and rather than focus on her impending death, her mind chattered away about the genetic disadvantage of tree sap being flammable. Evolutionarily speaking, that was seriously stupid for any tree that hung out on the side of a cliff. Mama bird came swooping back twice. The first had been an aborted attack. She came flying in, but veered away when she must have seen the fire. Then she was screeching and howling—Janet hadn't thought a bird could howl, but this creature managed it—while hero kept pushing them doggedly forward.

Janet looked behind her once. She was checking on sun-god—who was looking stained-sweatshirt gray—but saw the flames behind him. Wow. The nest had gone up all pretty and red. And fire was now creeping up the branch.

"Shit." She picked up the pace while mentally listing all the possible mutations that would have made more sense. It was the only way to stave off the panic. Much more sense to have poisonous sap or razor sharp leaves. Why not bark with metal in it for extra strength? Hero grunted something, but she couldn't tell what. She wasn't really sure how the man was still standing, much less moving, but she was grateful. The branch was thick enough for her to scramble. She'd been looking forward to straightening up from her crouch, but other branches cut into her headspace. And arm space. And chest space. Now it was more a game of twist, shove, scramble and pray.

Her tabard got caught more than once, and she cursed the damn thing. She would have tossed it aside, but she didn't want to take the time. And besides, she used the front half to wrap around her hands. That made it easier to grip things.

Once the back half of it got snagged on something. A branch. A needle. Who the hell cared? She tried to rip it free but nearly choked herself in the process. Then he was there with his sword raised. With one downward swipe, he cut the thing away. But the momentum of his swing nearly pulled him off the tree.

"Oh no," she said as she grabbed for him. Her hands slid right off his cold, slick chest, but she found purchase in his pants. There was a rope there or a belt or just a thicker fold of fabric. Whatever, it caught and held even when her fingers poked through the cloth beneath. But did she have the balance to hold them both?

They stood poised for a couple seconds while she was too terrified to scream. But just when she thought they were both going to plummet to their deaths, but he managed to steady them with one hand, pulling her tight against the solid mass of his chest.

Phew.

And wow. His chest was pasty gray, but still hunky. Like Chris Hemsworth broad. Clearly, it was better to catalogue hot guy attributes than advantageous tree mutations. But as everything grew blistering hot, there was only so much distraction her mind could provide. She was a breath away from full-out hysteria.

"There," he said, gesturing with his chiseled chin. "Fast."

She looked, then did as she was told. He had indicated a pathway down the center of the tree, and she began to scramble and claw her way down it. Above them, the branches caught fire, the sap hissing and snapping with the heat.

They had maybe a minute. Probably less.

Faster, faster. Must go faster. Now was not the time to start muttering movie quotes but *Independence Day* did fit with her desperation. She half slid, half fell. And then, hallelujah, she hit dirt. Or rock. Whatever. It was ground, and she looked around for the best direction to run...

Fucking-A.

The entire cliff face was littered with nests.

And birds. Like a million damned killer birds.

And they were all looking at her.

CHAPTER 2

Prince Keeven Gudtundsdor stumbled to the ground, all but falling to his knees as they escaped the inferno behind them. He should be at the end of his strength. Indeed he was close, but the knowledge that the Goddess had seen fit to gift him with one of Her angels gave him renewed determination. He was the last leader of his people. He would not fail them when salvation finally appeared in the guise of one confused woman. Nay, not confused, but more ignorant. She was innocent of the ways of his world, and it was up to him to keep her safe until she could gift the realm with a powerful child. That was the way with angels.

They came, they blessed, and they gave a child when a babe was most needed.

But how could he see this thing accomplished? With an inferno behind and a colony of birdbeasts ahead, they were all but doomed. Any moment now, one of the flock would startle from the fire or decide the angel looked like prey. The answer here was the same as always: keep moving forward. One step, one swing, even one breath at a time. Even if all the effort in his body achieved nothing but a stalemate.

"Walk slowly," he said softly, trying to make his voice sound as much like a cooing fledgling as possible.

"Walk?" the angel squeaked. "We're about to be fried or eaten or—"

"Come angel. Walk as I do. Like a fledgling bird." He held

out his elbows, lifting them to the side like short wings, then he took wide awkward steps.

"Waddle, you mean," she said. "I can waddle." And she did, though she went too fast and her breath was too loud.

"Calm, angel. They may sense your feelings and attack."

"Oh," she said, a hysterical edge to her voice. "So, no pressure."

His lips curved into a smile. He didn't understand her words per se, but he did get the general meaning in his heartspace. It had startled him at first to know her words without understanding the sound, but she was a heavenly creature, so of course she would communicate in such a way. And his heartspace told him now that she too was at the edge of her strength—though not in body, more in mind. There was a jagged feel to her that had to be the result of being thrust so quickly into his world.

She was frightened, so he smiled warmly at her. He even dared to touch her gently as he aimed them in as straight a path as possible to the back of the colony. "You are doing very well," he said as he eyed the distance to the woods. At their pace, it would take a hundred slow beats just to make it far enough away from the fire not to be singed. Meanwhile, the angel kept speaking, her words obviously meant to soothe herself as much as him.

"I'm calm. I'm like a waddling baby bird looking for its mommy. Waddle waddle, even though these birds are as big as freaking planes. Jesus, look at that beak. It's like a really thick javelin with a hook on the end."

He did not know these words, but he knew that talking to raw recruits often helped them keep control. So he kept his tone conversational as they meandered an agonizing path through the creatures. "The weak and the outcast are forced to nest in trees. The stronger birdbeasts claim the more stable ground."

She glanced at him, her eyes wide with horror. "Oh goody. Nice to know that we barely survived a weak one. Jesus..." she muttered, though the sound ended as more of a squeak.

He didn't blame her. The birdbeasts nearest them had finally sensed the fire. They were rustling ominously in their nests and a few had already taken to the air with raucous cries.

"So are any of them going to be pissed we've just burned down their thousand-year-old tree?"

Good question. "It was not their tree. It was an outcast's tree."

"Oh. So they don't care?"

He shrugged. "I don't know. I hope not."

She swallowed. "You know, it's okay to lie to me. Tell me everything's going to be just fine."

He blinked, then dropped to one knee before her. It wasn't a purposeful move. He'd stepped on a rock and the uneven ground brought him down. After days trapped in that nest, he was weak from hunger and thirst. Worse, he'd used the last of his strength to activate the blue stones she'd thrown, so now he had to rest in the dirt like a child. Nothing but sleep and good food would replenish his magic.

But since he was already going down, he shifted his body such that it appeared purposeful. And then he added reverent words to give power to the lie. "I swear to keep you safe, angel. Until my dying breath, I shall give my all to keep you well until you can return to your heavenly realm."

She gaped at him, her expression so stunned that he was confused. Had she not expected devotion from any man who called on her for aid? Meanwhile, she scanned their surroundings nervously. "Do you really think now is the time to be swearing fealty?"

He looked about him. "The fledglings often stop to rest as they…waddle."

"Oh. So this wasn't…I mean…"

"Yes, angel, I pledge you my service and my soul. My honor and my—"

"God, stop. Just…stop. I'm barely keeping it together as it is. You on one knee is just going to flip my too-surreal switch and I'll start gibbering like a baboon."

He didn't know what she meant. His heartspace flashed him an image of a hairy long-armed creature that made no sense. So he simply gathered his strength before standing. He covered a wave of dizziness by pretending to a waddle, and while his head cleared, he prayed that no other creature would attack. He could not defend her like this. A second later, she was ambling at his side.

"Look," she said when they'd passed a birdbeast large enough to carry off full-grown cattle. "I don't need vows. I don't even need the truth. Trust me, I don't think I can handle the truth." She released a high-pitched giggle.

Worried, he gripped her elbow, hoping his touch would reassure her. And if it didn't, he would be able to subdue her. He hoped. Given how weak he felt, he wasn't sure he could do more than fall down on top of her.

"No, no," she said, as she took a few rapid, shallow breaths. "I'm okay. Really." Then she blanched. "I'm having a nervous breakdown, aren't I?"

His heartspace did not explain her word to him, only that she thought herself ill. He scanned her body but saw nothing unexpected. Could this world be damaging to her? "I will get you home as soon as I can."

"Yeah. Sure. Okay." She took another step and winced before limping another step. "God, why didn't I think to put on shoes before wandering through Marty's closet of horrors?"

He glanced down at her feet. They were covered in sap, which turned out to be a good thing. The sticky resin had picked up a collection of needles, stones, and dirt. It protected her feet from the worst of the environment, including the cold, but it wasn't nearly as good as a solid pair of boots.

"I will find you good footwear as soon as we are clear of the birdbeasts."

She nodded, then winced again at another rock. "My mama told me to never go out without shoes. Clearly this was why."

She was making another joke he did not understand. He caught the words, but not the reason it was funny. So he nodded then gestured with his elbow to the right. "That way."

She frowned, looking to the left. "But isn't that a cave over there? That dark smudge in the rock?" She looked nervously around her. "It'd give us a breather to regroup at least."

Poor angel. She truly knew nothing of the mundane world. Guilt hit him hard for taking her away from the blessed realm in which she abided. Meanwhile, he stepped in front of her, forcing her to turn away from the cave. "That would not be a wise place to rest."

"Why—" She pressed her lips together. "Never mind. I don't want to know what kind of goblin lurks in there. Okay. Onward through the fray."

He fell in a half-step behind her. It was the most protective position he could manage. This way, he would see everything that came at them from in front and would take the first blow if something came from behind. "It is called a colony, not a fray."

"Good to know," she said, her tone strangely light. "I'll make sure to remember that when I update the wiki page."

He sensed that she was making fun, but not in a malicious way. More in the teasing way of comrades, and he felt honored by her friendship. But lest he forget the difference in their stations, she turned back to him.

"Look, I'm just babbling. Don't take anything I say seriously, okay?"

Chastised, he dipped his head. "Of course, angel."

She stood there a moment, frowning. "What just happened? Why do you look all sad—" She gasped. "Oh shit, you're wounded. God, how could I forget?"

Wounded? Oh yes. The gashes on his back. He had forgotten in the general misery of his body. "I will still be able to protect you," he said. Then remembering his vow to complete honesty, he amended his statement. "Until my last breath."

She rolled her eyes. "No one's dying. Can you make to that cut in the rock there?"

That was their destination. It was water, roaring quick and swift down the cliff. But if they followed it deeper, there would be thick woods and safety from the birdbeasts. "We need to go just beyond that perhaps another thirty beats."

"I have no idea what that means," she said, "but I don't care. Look, you've got to be freezing without a shirt and all. You can wear the tabard." She made to take it off, but he shook his head. He could not take her raiment, no matter how frozen he was. It was not fitting.

"Angel, I cannot—"

But it was too late. She'd already drawn it off, her movements too quick. She'd gained the attention of one of the nearest birdbeasts. He glanced around them. They were mostly through the colony now, but that only meant that the nearby creatures were hungrier than the ones in the center.

"Slowly, angel. Put that back on slowly."

She immediately froze, then in creeping motions, slid the thing off. Underneath she was undeniably womanly. She wore dark blue pants and a white shirt with strange colors on the front in a design he could not read. But underneath that splash of color, her breasts were full and her nipples tight as they puckered in the cold.

Lust slammed into him, hard and fast. She was beautiful, this angel who had saved his life. And he was beast to be thinking so carnally about her body even as she offered to clothe him.

"I cannot," he rasped.

"Please," she drawled as she waddled over to him. "I know it's gross and heavy, but it's freezing out here. And you've lost a lot of blood."

Blood and sweat were the most wholesome of things that clung to skin. He was revolted by himself. He would not taint her clothing with it. Then she stretched up on her toes, and he gripped her arm to hold her back. "No, angel."

"Look. You either put that on or I flip it over your head."

"No," he said, his voice low. "That would surely catch the creatures' attention."

"Exactly my point. So buck up, macho-man. Put it on."

He knelt down again, his heart and mind at war. They were in serious danger. Even once past the colony, there were horrors in the woods. He was on his last strength, and they had no supplies. He should be focused on what they needed to live, and yet kneeling there in the dirt, he felt her attire settle about his shoulders. He smelled her scent and felt her heat. His heart began to soar at the wonder of it all. An angel had given him her token, and the awe of it left him mute with wonder. Then in the largest miracle of his life, she touched his cheek, drawing his gaze up to hers.

"Listen up. No macho stupidity. I need you alive so you can keep me alive, okay?"

"I vow it."

She rolled her eyes. "You could have just said okay."

"Okay." The word was strange on his tongue, but he spoke it as a holy word for indeed it was one.

She frowned. "I get the feeling we're not talking on the same wavelength here."

He swallowed. He didn't know what she meant, but his heartspace told him that she was just now realizing the differences between them. She truly was an innocent. He pushed up to his feet, taking her hand in his and noting how very cold it was. He would need to get them both warm soon. Somehow.

"Come, angel. We will walk to safety together."

She grinned at him and headed in the right direction. Her waddle had a definite swagger to it now, and beast that he was, he could not stop watching the way her bottom dipped and swayed. He felt his lust stir despite his fatigue until shame made him look away. They were at the edge of the colony now. Behind them, the ancient tree was still burning, but here the bother of it was too far away. The birdbeasts were roosting happily in their nests and so they had no need to stop the two waddling by.

Another fifty slow beats later, they made it to the cut. He turned to follow the water. A little upstream, and then to the east into the dark wood. The ground was rugged here. Hard enough in his crumbling boots. But she was barefoot and limping more with each step. He needed to find them a place to rest. And food. They needed food.

He had thought that she would keep talking. He'd expected that once the immediate danger was past, she would begin to chatter more freely. She had not been reticent before. But as the colony disappeared behind them, she became quiet. Her expression did not lighten, but grew more tight. He thought it might be pain, but she made no complaint nor other sound as she limped and stumbled across the thin dirt.

Once he reached out to her, offering his hand as her ankle turned beneath a rock. She caught herself on a tree, then cursed as she scraped her hand.

"I can help you—" he began, but she shook her head.

"You're the wounded one. I can manage. But let me know if you're going to collapse or something, okay?"

He nodded slowly. "Okay," he intoned, hoping he invested the word with the right amount of reverence.

She merely rolled her eyes in response, and they continued on.

He found a place to rest eventually. It wasn't ideal, but the ground was soft and defensible. The stream wasn't far, and game would be nearby if he had the strength to kill it. He had no way to make a fire, but raw game would still be food. So he guided her to the edge of the stream and helped her sit down upon a rock.

"Water. Oh good. I'm parched," she murmured. But she did not lean down to drink. She just sat on the stone and stared, her eyes flat and her body listless.

Well, he would need to wash himself anyway, he thought. Bracing himself, he pulled off her vestment, then stepped into the icy mountain stream. It would waterlog his boots, but he had a desperate need to wipe all remnants of the birdbeast vomit from his body. And though the water stung the slice along his back, the pain felt cleansing. It felt healing, as if the test was done and now he could progress to the next lesson in his lifepath.

It was a silly thought, he knew. They were far from safe and his mission was barely begun. But he had survived the birdbeasts and now he had an angel to aid him. What more proof did he need that he had the Goddess's favor?

So he ducked under the water, taking a moment to scrub his face and hair. And when he came up, he was dripping. His teeth were chattering, and he'd lost dexterity in his hands. But he felt holy enough to cup his hands and offer his angel a drink.

She was watching him, her eyes wide and her mouth slightly parted. He stepped forward, trying to hold the water steady in his hands. "Please, angel, drink."

She blinked. Once. Twice. Then she frowned at him. "What?"

He came to her side and lifted his cupped hands to her mouth. "Drink, angel. You are parched."

"Um, oh. Uh… Jeez, you didn't need…"

He was watching her, seeing that she was flustered, but not understanding why. "I regret that I have not cleansed as I should—"

"God, no. That's not what I mean." She bet her lip in clear frustration. "How's your back? Does it hurt?"

"Drink, angel." He watched her closely and saw the moment she gave in to his desire to serve her. He did not fool himself that she wanted to take sustenance this way or of so crude a thing as water. She no doubt was used to glorious nectar, but this was all he had and so he reminded himself that it made it a worthy offering.

Or it was until her lips touched his skin. At the first brush of her warm lips upon his flesh, he nearly lost himself to shame. His body jolted awake, his cock growing thick and hard despite the lingering chill of his crumbling pants. She reached up, cupping his hands with her smaller ones. She was so soft, this angel, and when her tongue slid over his fingers as she tilted the makeshift cup, he thought of the most immoral things.

He saw himself doing the most wanton, carnal things with her. And he wanted it with a hunger that screamed of depravity. He was not generally a lustful man. As a prince, his bedmates were carefully selected, screened for their discretion and watched for duplicity. It had been somewhat distasteful as a teen, but he'd been so randy he hadn't cared. But as he'd grown to full manhood, he'd learned the callousness of using a woman's body with no regard for her heartspace. And as such knowledge grew inside him, it became easier to turn away the courtesans and the harlots. More fun as well to linger with friends and worldly women who taught him well. Until he chose the path of knighthood and such princely pastimes ended completely.

Until now.

Now, he wanted to show her what he had learned so earnestly. Now he wanted to teach this innocent angel the wonders of her world body. And he wanted to lose himself to rutting with her like a beast in a field. He hungered for all those things, and the knowledge was shame to him even as he returned to the stream to bring her more water.

"I can do it myself," she said as she made to push off the rock.

"Prithee, let me care for you."

She blinked. "We're back to 'prithee' again?"

He frowned. Did she not like his formal speech? Then before he could answer, she waved it aside. "Look, you're being lovely and all. Really. And I swear, I'll get off this rock in a second and clean myself too. I just…" She sighed as she looked up at the trees overhead. They were away from the worst of the cliffs now, so the trees had leaves not needles. The ground was softer with fewer rocks. Soon he would find a way to make her warm and comfortable. But he could not do that if she did not tell him what she needed.

"Angel, please tell me what is wrong."

She chuckled then, but the sound held no humor. "Look, I'm not stupid and there's only so much denial a girl can manage. Marty's good, but she's not this good. And no one makes a full holographic display in a closet. Plus..." She put her hands to her face to rub at her eyes, but then grimaced at the mess there. Her palms were covered in sap and probably stung.

"Let me carry you to the water. I will clean your hands." He made to do just that, but she started to cry. The tears were fat and filthy, and they froze him in place as surely as if he were back in the nest held fast.

"Even on *Star Trek*, the holodeck is still just a room. They can make it look like anything you want. A nest hanging over a cliff—no problem. Demented birds with talons like steel spikes—par for the course. They can make it look like any of that, but at the end of the day, it's still a room. Which means if we waddle in one direction long enough, we're going to come to a wall."

He listened to her words. Indeed, he opened his heartspace as wide as he could make it, but he still had no understanding of what she said.

"This isn't a video game. It's not a holographic display. And it sure as hell isn't the inside of Marty's closet."

Ah. Now he understood. She was finally accepting that she had left heaven and was in his world. "No, angel, it is not. But surely, after some rest you can re-open the door. It is only that you are tired."

She shook her head. "I'm out of shape, and my feet have swollen to five times their normal size, but that's not the problem."

"Then what is?" he asked.

"I've had a breakdown. Not surprising, really, given the stress I've been under. I just didn't think delusions went this whole hog, you know?" She waved vaguely at the woods then let her hand drop dully into her lap. "Total Buffy in the mental ward, except I'm not there. I'm here in Lala land."

"This is Bodil land, not Lala," he said. "I know not where Lala is."

She looked at him and suddenly laughed. Not long. A single burst of sound and a curve of her lips. Enough to break her out of her misery. "Thank you. It's good when the delusion can make you laugh." He didn't think she meant it. He didn't understand her words, but it wasn't hard for him to guess her thoughts. She couldn't understand his world and was frightened of it. Why wouldn't she be? She had left heaven for this place filled with fire and pain.

"Angel," he began, but she cut him off.

"What's your name, anyway?"

He started. "My name?" Did she truly not know who she'd come here to save?

She shrugged. "I like being on a first name basis with all my psychotic breaks. I'm Janet, by the way."

"Janet," he said, trying out the shape of her name on his lips. "Angel Janet, I am Prince Keeven Gudtundsdor of the Askel people."

Her lips quirked, but not in a smile. "A prince. Of course you are."

He nodded. "I am, though as we are in Bodil land…"

"Oh. Super secret, huh?"

He nodded.

"And I bet you're on a quest."

So she did know some things. Thank the Goddess she had not come here completely ignorant of his task. "I am, Angel."

"Rescuing a princess, are you?"

"From an evil creature. The foulest evil known—"

"A dragon?"

He frowned. He did not know this word and what his heartspace showed him was confusing. A flying lizard that shot fire.

"The Magician has weapons of fire," he said slowly. "I do

not know if he commands a..." He struggled to form her strange word.

"Dragon. Yeah, doesn't matter. Kill the big bad, rescue the princess with a kiss, and then live happily ever after, right?"

A kiss? Well, that was usually what was involved before they had children, so he nodded, though he could tell that every second of their conversation made Angel Janet more distraught not less. "Angel—"

"Stop calling me that. I'm just Janet. Deluded, psychotic, unstable Janet. That's me."

He nodded slowly, a question forming in his mind. He had not thought of it before because of the way she appeared in response to his prayer. But now that she could not return to Heaven, the idea took root and he knelt down before her.

"Angel, do you know why you are here?"

She opened her mouth to answer, then slowly closed it as she began to think. "You're asking me why the delusion. After all, the mind has its own way of working, right? There's usually a reason behind the break."

"You are not insane—"

"Says the delusion." Then when he began to answer, she held up her hand. "I'm here because I couldn't face getting kicked out of school. Because facing the big bad world is..." She chuckled. "Well, I suppose it's big, bad, and scary."

"But I'm here to keep you safe," he reminded her.

"Again, says the delusion." She tilted her head back and looked at the leaves above them. "I'm here for a reason," she said softly. "I just have to figure it out."

He smiled. It was indeed what he thought. "Probably for the traditional reasons," he suggested gently.

Her lips quirked. "Rescue the princess, save the kingdom, that sort of thing?"

He hesitated. It was not his place to say her mission, but if it was a usual sort of visit from an angel, her path was clear. She was meant to mate with a man and gift the realm with a powerfully magical child. But he was not positive that was her path and suggesting it now might cause untold problems. After all, he could not do the deed. His holy vow prevented it. Even if he lusted to the point of madness, using an angel to break a vow was the height of blasphemy.

"How do you usually find an answer?" he asked softly.

"I think. A lot."

"Then you should perhaps do that again."

She shrugged. "Rely on a broken brain to solve the problem? Sure, what have I got to lose?"

He had no answer for that. In truth, there was little he could do to make the loss of her heavenly realm any less devastating. But he could wash her feet and her hands. He could make her as comfortable as possible now. So without another word, he strode forward and lifted her up.

In his weakened state, she was heavy to carry, but he felt almost none of it when she squeaked and threw her arms around him. She was soft and womanly, and her hair had a strange scent of citrus where it tickled his nose.

"I can walk. Seriously, I can—"

He set her down on the ground near the stream. Then he carefully rolled up her pants and set her feet into the stream. She gasped at the cold. It was bracing, but soon it would help. She must have realized the truth of that because after a moment she sighed. Then she leaned forward and set her hands in the water too.

And while she rubbed her hands together, he set about cleaning her feet. He tried to be gentle, but the sap was thick and some of the stones had embedded themselves deep into it. He pushed and rubbed, and after a moment, he heard her moan slightly. He looked up startled, but her eyes had drifted closed and she had a dreamy smile on her face.

"Angel?"

"You know, for psychotic break, you sure do give good foot rubs."

So she did enjoy worldly pleasures. He grinned. If this is what she needed, then he would give it to her every moment he could. He bent his head to his task and was soon rewarded with another low groan.

"Stop," she said, though she didn't sound like she meant it. "I'm going to be a wet noodle."

He wasn't sure he understood her words, but she probably meant she was wet and needed food. They both did. "Have you any of the stones left?" he asked, though he already knew the answer.

She stilled for a moment, then her eyes flew wide. "The roll. Oh crap." She hastily looked about herself. "Oh hell, I must have dropped them."

"It is no matter."

"Of course it is. We risked our lives to get those things, and I dropped them." She dropped her head backward against a tree trunk, and he winced at the impact. "The wrench is gone too. And the hammer."

"The hammer is in your belt."

She straightened up and checked her belt. There, hanging from its proper loop was the hammer she had loaned to him. "But how...?"

"I returned it to you. I would not steal your tools, An— Janet."

She stared at him, her mouth slightly ajar. "Of course you wouldn't. So in the middle of being attacked by demented birds, saving my life, and let's not forget setting fire to the tree, you remembered to put the hammer back on my belt."

He smiled. "You don't have to be careful with your own things. It is only when you borrow other people's tools that care is required."

She snorted. "Nice try, hero, but they're Marty's tools, not mine. And I'm going to owe her big time when..." She swallowed and her expression darkened. "Well, when I return to my senses, I'll just have to see what amends I need to make and to whom."

He let his hands caress her ankles, soothing her best he could. "You are not mad, Angel. You are in a different realm, that is all." She opened her mouth to correct him, but he cut her off. "I will not cease calling you Angel until you remember that you are in a different place. That life is different here. You will not be Janet unless you accept that it will take time for you to adjust to this place."

She flashed him an irritated look, but he thought there might be gratitude in there as well. Especially since her words were spoken in a gentle tone. "You're a very nice man, Prince Guy...um...uh..."

"Gudtundsdor."

"Gud-ten-door."

"Gudtundsdor."

"Gut-en... Oh hell. Prince G? Prince Guy?"

"Keeven." It was a liberty for him to request that she use his intimate name, but he hoped he had earned it.

She frowned at him. "That's not disrespectful? I mean, you're a prince."

"You're an angel."

"Yeah, yeah, I'm the fair maiden who smells like sunshine and roses—not. But..." Then she paused as she stared at him. "You really mean it, don't you? You really think I'm an angel from Heaven."

He looked at her closely, reading the shock and horror on her face, but he couldn't understand it. "You appeared in response to my prayers. The heavens opened up and you brought me the escape I needed."

"Oh no. I mean yeah, I can see how from your perspective you could think that. But Honest Injun, I am not an angel. I'm not anything close."

He stared at her. Was it possible? Was she some other heavenly creature? Or devilish one? His heartspace told him no. She was exactly what he thought: the answer to his prayers. Perhaps the term 'angel' was not appropriate, but she walked in the light with the Goddess. Of that he was certain.

"Really, Keeven. Don't start thinking—"

"It will be dark soon," he said as he stood up from the water.

His legs had cramped and he winced from the pain of straightening them. Weakness blew through him, making him teeter until he had to grip a tree branch to remain upright.

"Oh shit. You need rest and food. And heat."

He needed all those things, but… "Without my pack, I have no means to make us a fire, but I will catch us game—"

"I've got matches. I just… Well, I was never a good girl scout, and they didn't teach campfire building in Brownies."

He held up his hand stopping her flow of words. He was too dizzy at the moment to understand. "You can make a fire? You have a firestone?"

"Um, no." She rooted around in her tool belt, tearing a small fabric pouch open with a low zzzzrrrr sound. "Yeah. Right here with her emergency supplies. Inhaler, Powerbar, and…." She held up a small box. "Matches."

He just stared. He had no understanding of what she held.

"Look." Then she took a small stick out, turned the box on its side and flicked the one against the other. A flame shot out of the end with a hiss.

His eyes widened with delight. Goddess, he was thick at the moment. She had fire! He could make them a campfire, catch some food, and cook it for her. With the stream here, they had water. "I can provide for you tonight, then. I should not have doubted."

"Wait a moment, big guy. You promised me no macho man stuff. You're the wounded one. I can… Um…" She pushed to her feet, wincing as she stepped down. "I can gather firewood."

He shook his head, his joy at being able to adequately provide for her making him giddy. "No, Angel. Not on cut and bleeding feet, you cannot." Before she could argue, he swooped down and picked her up. She cried out, startled, but as before she wrapped her arms around his shoulders and pulled herself close.

"You're wounded, remember?" she said.

"I heal quickly."

"Liar."

He pulled back abruptly. He could tell by her voice that she had meant no insult. She had been teasing him, he guessed, but such a word could never be used in jest. At least not when spoken to him.

"Keeven?"

"I am a Knight of Askel. We do not lie, Angel. It is the gravest insult to suggest we do."

She swallowed and looked abashed. "I was...I mean...it was a joke."

He shook his head. "That is one of the rules of this place. You cannot call 'liar,' even in jest."

She bit her lip. "Ooo-kay. But you're still wounded. And you can't have healed in the couple hours it's been since your back got sliced open. So you started that particular jest by saying you heal fast."

He opened his mouth to argue, but then slowly shut it. She was right. His words had not been entirely truthful. He did heal fast, but his back still pulled and he was weak from a variety of wounds and hunger. He felt his face heat in shame. She had been right to name him a liar. "I beg pardon. I have fallen short of my stature." The words cut at him as he spoke them, especially because it was true most of the time. After all, he was a prince and a knight. For most people, his stature as akin to a god's. And yet, he knew all too well his constant failings.

"Hey," she said as she touched his cheek. Her fingers were warm, her caress gentle, and the ease with which she lifted his face to hers was like a balm to his soul. His heartspace warmed, and all his pains eased. "It was a joke. I think you're amazing. And I'm afraid that you're going to make being in this delusion too sweet for me to leave."

He swallowed. "You are not mad, Angel. You are merely displaced."

She chuckled. "Well, I've been called worse things. Today even."

And then she kissed him.

CHAPTER 3

She'd meant it to be just a kiss.

Janet tended to be spur-of-the-moment with her affections. Her friends were used to her spontaneous hugs, and her various boyfriends had always enjoyed her impulsive kisses. And unlike her mother, she never used physical expression as a means to an end. Well, except for her first disastrous high school experience, but she'd learned from her mistake and moved on. Which meant that the minute she'd finished with her high school idiocy, she never lost control of what she did and what she allowed. Impulsive, but within strict guidelines.

Until now.

She'd planned to just show appreciation. He'd been rubbing her feet and reassuring her that she wasn't insane. And now he was carrying her to save her abused feet. Yes, he was a delusion, but he was the best damned man she'd ever met, even in fantasy. Of course she was going to kiss him. And of course he was going tighten up in surprise because that's what honorable men did when ladies under their care became physically affectionate.

But she was in his arms, and her body was pressed against his. He couldn't hide his reaction from her even if he'd tried. She pressed her lips to his, he went still for a moment as she expected, and then everything changed.

His mouth slanted over hers, his body grew rock hard both

down below where her hip pressed against his groin, but also his torso against her breasts. She'd been about to tease his lips, stroking her tongue against them, but she never got the chance. He tightened his arms around her and then he thrust inside. He touched her everywhere: tongue, teeth, the roof of her mouth. He was a large man, and he seemed to keep pushing deeper into her.

She was shocked for a moment. This was a possession in the most carnal way. It was just her mouth. Just his tongue. And yet, she felt split wide and owned. She hadn't expected this. She certainly wouldn't have allowed it, even though she'd started it. And she never thought she'd love it, but she did.

Oh God, she did.

It was like this glorious man wanted to have her in every way possible. The way he held her and the way he stroked inside her said he longed for every part of her. She was that wonderful to him. And while her mind was scrambling to process the thrust of his tongue, the grip of his hands, and the intimate pulse of his groin, her body was already softening for him. She opened to his possession, she arched into his body, and she went liquid and hungry as she kissed him back.

Suddenly, her heart was pounding and her body was too hot. Her legs were held too tightly together, and she could not get enough of him. She put a hand on his shoulder, and used it to lever harder against him. Her other hand went into his wet hair, pulling him down to her and wishing he would just set her down. She wanted him on top of her. She wanted him inside her everywhere and every how. She wanted it so fiercely that it scared her. And him, apparently, because he abruptly broke off.

It was so fast a movement that he stumbled, and she nearly tumbled from his arms. But he held her safe even as he braced himself against a tree and closed his eyes, breathing hard.

She dropped her forehead to his cheek and did the same.

She still gripped him. She still pulled so tight against him that if he released her completely, her hold would keep her there for a while longer. And from this position, she felt their hearts pounding as if they beat for each other. A rapid tempo that echoed in her ears and in his rasping breath.

But he didn't return his mouth to hers, and he didn't let her press kisses to his jaw. When she tried, he flinched, his entire body gripping her before easing slowly open.

Really open. Oh hell, he was putting her down.

She reluctantly put her feet onto the soft dirt and then eventually, she stepped away from him.

"So, um," she said, needing to break the silence between them. "That was…amazing." She'd meant to discount it, saying something flippant. But even in jest, she couldn't make light of that kiss. "I've never been kissed like that before."

"Of course not, Angel," he said, his voice thick. "It was a crude thing I did—"

"Let's get something straight here," she said as she took a step back from him. "First off, I started it. Second, it was beyond great. Third, I have a wealth of experience to compare it to, so don't go saying I don't know what I'm talking about."

He stared at her a moment, then he straightened up to his full height. He looked first perplexed and then rather annoyed. "You have experienced kissing before?"

And a whole lot more. In fact, she'd lost her virginity in that disastrous high school experiment. But she decided that wasn't something he wanted to know. So she simply shrugged. "I told you I'm not an angel. I've never hung out on a cloud playing a harp, and God and I aren't exactly on speaking terms."

His head tilted. "You have a male divinity?"

That's what he took out of her whole speech? "Um, I guess so."

"I prayed to the Goddess for aid."

She didn't know what to say to that. As a rule, she was uncomfortable discussing religion. It was rude to suggest to anyone that their belief in a higher power was whole lot of donkey doo. Even if he was a delusion, she didn't want to insult him. So she simply shrugged and said what she usually said whenever her mother's friends bombarded her with religious crap.

"I think the universe is a lot more complicated than anyone can understand. I'll try to allow for your concepts, if you try to allow for mine."

He dipped his head in a half bow. "Wisely spoken, Angel Janet."

Well that was a lot more respect than she usually got for her canned words, and she wasn't entirely comfortable with it. So she shook her head. "Not an angel, okay? Just Janet." She barely resisted adding, "Damn it." Though *Rocky Horror* seemed to fit in this surreal fantasy world of hers.

He didn't answer. Instead, he looked up at the sky. "It will be getting dark soon, and there is much to do." Then he closed the distance between them in single stride, took another split second to pick her up, and soon he was walking in a steady path to higher ground. She wanted to object, but one look at his face and she knew he wasn't open to more discussion. Just as well. She was feeling a bit unsettled herself. Between the kiss and his insistence that she was his divine aid, she wasn't sure which way was up. But that was a delusion for you, she thought glumly. It obeyed its own rules and she just needed to ride it out.

Unless, of course, she found a way out of her delusion. Which was her current plan. Sadly, making out with a prince did not appear to be on the solution list, more's the pity. Fortunately, he seemed intent on going off to do manly campfire things, so she would take the time to figure out a solution.

She settled obediently on the rock he found in a clearing. He wrapped her in the remains of the tabard, telling her he'd be back soon with firewood. She nodded because he seemed to want her too, and then while he was gone, she tried to think of a way out.

She took a moment to try meditating herself out. She closed her eyes, took deep breaths and searched for her zen. She didn't find it, but when she got as close as she was going to get, she slowly opened her eyes willing herself to see Marty's closet.

Forest. Trees.

Okay, something else then. After a few more very silly minutes, she decided the whole "Abracadabra, wake up!" wasn't going to work. She'd also suffered enough pain in her feet to know that pinching herself wasn't going to do it either. So what was next?

She hadn't a clue.

So she busied herself by taking stock of her toolbelt. That took all of five seconds. The hammer was there, as was a super bright halogen flashlight. On another day she would have played with making shadow animals, but she'd never been very good with anything but the dog. Next were measuring tape, inhaler, wire cutters and two screwdrivers—flat and Phillips heads. The matches had fallen inside the roll of duct tape which was wedged against a diet bar and a stubby pencil. All in all, not that exciting for a woman in theoretical physics who had never been on a construction site in her life. She tucked away everything because she'd decided to be heroic and save the diet bar for Keeven. No sense in tempting herself with the sight of compressed protein. Next she set about inspecting her surroundings without getting up off her rock. Another minute.

Then she got off her rock, took one step, and realized she needed shoes.

Well, duh. She looked around, deciding she was a clever girl. She had tools and brains. Between the two she should be able to fashion something.

Twenty minutes later, she'd managed to tie some broad leaves around her feet with some vines. It looked stupid and worked even worse, but it passed the time until he came back with firewood which he stacked in a precise pattern.

"Wait a second," she said. "Teach me that."

"What?"

"How to make a fire."

He looked like he was about to object, but then thought better of it. Good. Because she had no intention of remaining helpless, even in a delusion. So she hobbled over to him and squatted down.

He made no comment about her bad attempt at shoes, for which she was grateful. And fifteen minutes later, they had a roaring fire. Now if only they had some marshmallows. Or chocolate. Or forget s'mores. She wanted a steak, and her stomach rumbled in agreement.

"There aren't any berries growing around here somewhere?" she asked hopefully.

He shook his head gravely. "I will provide for you."

She cast him a weak smile. "I'm sure you will. And to that end..." She fixed her smile in place then zipped open the pouch on her toolbelt. Sacrifice was good for the soul, right? It better be, because she was about to do the most selfless act of her entire life. She held out the Atkins diet bar. "This is for you. Something to tide you over until we come across a cheeseburger tree."

He took the bar, his expression confused. "My thanks."

Lord, he had no idea what it was. She took it back from him and ripped it open. The thing didn't really have a scent. Compressed protein rarely did, at least not in her experience. But she would swear she could smell a four course turkey dinner in that one pasty brown bar. She offered it back to him. "It's food. I know it looks gross, but it's good for you."

He better take it quick before she changed her mind. Selflessness wasn't her usual style. But ever the gentleman, he pressed it back on her. "You should eat it. I can wait until after I catch—"

"You're the wounded one, remember? Besides, I already had one," she lied. After all, she hadn't sworn any oath of honesty. "And it's simple logic. You're planning on going out and killing us some dinner, right?"

He nodded. "I expect to find something quickly."

"I'm sure you do. So eat up, get some strength, and go catch me a T-bone."

He frowned for a moment, his face taking on that slightly distant abstract look when she said something he didn't understand. "Angel…" he began but she shook her head.

"Don't try to figure me out. Most of what I say is nonsense. But eat, will ya? I think I'm going to catch a nap. All that learning how to make fire stuff is exhausting. Not to mention battling evil birds before waddling through their colony."

"I will stay close to guard your rest."

She chuckled. "You will eat that bar and then probably go drink half the river because those things are thick. Then you'll catch and clean us some dinner, because if you think I'm bad at making fires, I'm ten times worse at making dinner. Go on. I'll be fine."

He hesitated a moment, but she busied herself with folding up the tabard for a pillow and curling herself close enough to the fire to be toasty without getting burned. She closed her eyes and did her best to look relaxed and content while praying that her stomach didn't rumble. Then she waited for him to leave.

And waited.

When she couldn't stand it anymore, she cracked an eye, ready to blast him for hovering, but he wasn't anywhere nearby. She rolled over, putting her back to the fire so that her eyes would adjust to the darkness. Still nothing. Just dark trees, rustling wind, and no stud muffin serving her sirloin cooked medium rare.

In the end she gave up and flopped onto her back. She'd pick out constellations to pass the time as she tried to think of a way out of her delusion.

Or not. Notnotnotnotnot.

She swallowed, trying to fight the panic.

None of the stars were in familiar patterns. That was bad enough. No Big Dipper, no Orion's belt, and definitely no Queen Cassiopeia. Those were her favorite constellations and her go-to when she wanted to stop thinking about her life and imagine life among the stars. But despite a whole Milky Way of stars, there wasn't a single grouping she recognized. And she looked really hard, especially around the *three moons*.

Her heart pounded hard in her throat, and she tried to reassure herself. This was a delusion, she reminded herself. It made sense that a world of birdbeasts and sword-wielding heroes would have a different type of sky. But those thoughts really weren't all that comforting. It just brought home to her exactly how far she'd slipped from reality.

This was bad, she decided, as she slammed her eyes closed.

Delusions. Three moons. Birdbeasts. All of it was bad.

So it was time for her to face the truth. She forced herself to open her eyes and inspect the three moons. One quarter moon, two of them closer to half, and all three of them fairly small. Well, at least she hadn't gotten the massive Vulcan red nightmare of a moon.

Then she bit her lip and decided to face the harder truth. All of this was an escape from re-working her thesis. It had to be. The idea of trying to out-Einstein Einstein had pushed her into a delusion with manageable monsters and a hero who was intent on taking care of her. Classic psychology, she thought, even though she'd never taken a psychology class in her life.

Okay, so she'd established what had happened. Now to address what to do about it. Well the answer was obvious, right? She had to face what had created the psychological break in the first place. And that meant thinking up a new thesis.

She pushed to a seated position. This was good, she thought, trying to find a bright side. All alone in the woods without internet or friends, she could focus exclusively on her task. No distractions. Just pure inspiration.

She didn't have paper or pen, but she had dirt and a stick. And since there were three moons above her, she decided to look for dualities—or tri-alities—between the different types of string theories. It was a silly process, something that needed a calculator, not to mention a super-computer. But she was in the realm of mathematics and physics, and it was relatively easy to lose herself in their confined, logical progressions.

Or it should have been.

Frankly, it was hard etching calculus into the dirt. Second, she was starving and there were a zillion unfamiliar noises all around her. She tried to think of them as soothing nature sounds, but she kept wondering if one of them was a birdbeast preparing to dive bomb her. Or something more likely in this wood: a mountain cat or a bear.

And why the hell was she looking for commonalities among three distinct theories anyway? Because there were three moons? Oy. She truly was mad if she thought she could find a unifying concept that no one else had ever been able to find. More importantly, for the first time in her life she really wondered why. Not why the strings were formed one way and not another, but why would anyone care? Why did she care? Because at the moment, she really wanted a pizza and socks. Not necessarily in that order.

Why had she ever thought physics was a good idea? Sure, at the lower levels it was all about looking at the rules of the world. Every action was not only predictable, but it was impossible for things to happen differently. You can't simply decide to not be affected by gravity. Everyone walked on the earth. No one floated around in space unless they really were in space.

Except at the graduate level you really had to work on disproving all those cherished laws. If you couldn't think of something amazing and new—and obviously she couldn't— then your work was all about proving how something she cherished was *not* true. Care to disprove Einstein's Theory of Relativity? Then come join our particle physics program.

But she didn't want to do that. So she was stuck trying to discover something new. Which involved *thinking* in new ways. Which she really didn't like doing at all. Which left her staring at marks in the dirt while her stomach rumbled and she flinched at every rustle.

"Is there a pathway for me to walk? I need to get to the fire."

Janet jumped, turning to see Keeven standing at the edge of the clearing. In his hands were...okay, she didn't really want to look at the bloody things in his hands. Skinned rabbits if she had to guess. But he was looking at her scratches in the dirt as if they were ancient hieroglyphs. Too bad she knew exactly how non-mystical they were.

"Oh, sorry. Just stomp over it all. It isn't important."

He looked at her like she was insane. "I cannot just walk on your magic."

"It's not magic. I promise." And to prove it, she took her stick and crossed out everything she could reach.

He stepped carefully, almost reverently over her crossed out calculus. "Were you praying?"

"To the God of Wasted Time," she quipped. But at his serious look, she sobered. "I have my own quest, Keeven. But I'm afraid that no matter how hard I try, it's just not going to work out for me."

"You have done all you've been asked?"

"To the best of my ability." She crossed out another set of computations. "I guess I'm not good enough." She said the words lightly. The fault lay in her chosen field, after all, not in herself. Because to disprove the work of physic's greats was the act of a heretic. And to set herself as someone who could discover bigger and better, well that was just arrogance. "And yet I continue to tilt at the windmill."

He didn't respond beyond a quick confused look. Then he set his attention to skewering the rabbits onto sticks before holding them above the fire. "There is honor in the attempt, no matter the outcome."

She looked at his face and couldn't tell if he really believed his words or not. He'd spoken them the way some of her friends recited mantras: by rote and as if he hoped it were true. "I'm not interested in honor," she said honestly. "I want a degree and a professorship worth about $150k a year."

He lifted his gaze to hers. "Is that a worthy goal?" He didn't have to say the next words. "For an angel" was implied by his very tone.

"I have no idea," she shot back, a little annoyed. "But it's mine, and I'm sticking to it."

He didn't respond at all, and she took his silence as judgment.

"Don't cop an attitude with me," she groused. "We can't all rescue princesses, you know."

He lifted his gaze to hers, his expression serious and slightly wounded. "My gravest apologies, Angel. I meant no disrespect."

Bull hockey. The very fact that he called her "Angel" meant that he was reminding her of her holy status. Which was ridiculous because she didn't have a holy status. And yet, sitting here with him made her feel guilty. After all, she was directing all her attention to the esoteric realms of pure science. Not a practical help-the-world thought in her head. But she liked it in the supremely predictable, math-as-god, logical place to live.

Even if she had somehow managed to escape into a delusion that kept trying to make her re-examine all the notions she held dear. Things like there was only one moon and demented birds with talons the size of javelins did not exist anywhere.

"I just need to work harder," she said to herself. That was her mantra and had been for years. Work harder. Eventually you'll be successful.

So she picked up her stick and tried to think again. A moment later, she held out her hand. "Give me a rabbit. No need for you to hold both our dinners."

"I can cook both—"

"Just shut up and give it to me. This is my first psychotic break, and it's made me cranky."

He wisely didn't argue. And so they passed the next hour in silence. She carefully cooked something that looked too much like it had once been a living thing. She'd never speak badly of cold cuts again. And when he pronounced it done, she ate the entire thing because she was ravenous. She never thought she could feel this hungry in a delusion, but apparently she could.

She ate every bite, buried the bones as he directed (even murmured thanks to the creature that nourished them and the ground that received them per his direction), then went to wash in the river. She was greasy from the food and filthy in general, and given her general irritable nature, she had no problem torturing Keeven with her wet and nearly naked body.

He stood watch, which was the heroic thing to do. She stripped to her underwear and plunged into the icy bath. Given that it was full dark and this was a mountain stream, it was a damned cold thing to do. Her breath escaped her body in a choked gasp, her toes went numb within a minute, and yet she stayed there to scrub her hair and squeeze her jeans and tee. Marty's tabard was a lost cause, so she left it in the dirt to serve as a pillow.

Fifteen minutes later, she'd pulled on the clothes because he said it was better to let them dry on her body—which made no sense—and because she was feeling embarrassed because he'd barely spared her two looks. She started scrambling up the bank, only to have him pick her up and carry her. Given that he was naked-chest warm, she didn't argue. In truth, she started to feel bad about being so moody, but the apology wouldn't come. This was *her* delusion. He was a figment of her broken psyche. She could be as rude to him as she wanted.

Except, apparently, she couldn't. Within a minute of getting warm by the fire, she fumbled her way through an apology. "Look, I'm sorry I'm grumpy. Thank you for getting dinner and generally being such a great guy."

He looked at her, his regard steady. "This transition is hard on you. I will try to make it easier."

"You're doing fine. And news flash, your humility is becoming annoying. If you won't fight back, then you're no good to me."

He frowned at her, and for a moment she thought he didn't understand her words. Then he leaned forward, bracing his elbows on his knees. "Do you want me to tell you that you pout like a small child? That you have no understanding of the proper way to do anything? And that I know you pranced about in the water to tempt me?"

Ouch. "Yeah. Say that," but her tone implied the exact opposite.

"Or should I say that you are a terrible liar? I know you gave me the last of your food. That whether devil or angel, you are vulnerable in a strange world. That you have the air of someone who is usually the one in control, and yet here you must rely on me for the simplest things."

"I'm not in control at home," she said honestly. "I just know the rules."

He nodded as if that was exactly what he meant. "And despite all this, you came to my aid when I would surely have died, you fought beasts that terrify the most seasoned warriors, and then you apologize when you are angry that your invocation to return home has not worked."

She blinked. "My invocation to what?"

He gestured at the remains of her scratched out calculations. "Was this not at attempt to return to your world?"

She opened her mouth to try and explain higher math and PhD programs, but then stopped. In the end, she had to agree. She had been trying to wake up from her delusion. And yet she was still here, nearly naked by a fire under the light of three moons.

"I don't know what to do," she said to a long scratch she'd made in the dirt.

"You have tried your usual methods," he asked.

She nodded.

"Then try something unusual."

Her gaze snapped up to his. "What?"

He shrugged. "I have no idea."

He said it so simply as if he had absolute faith that she would figure it out. What man in her life had ever done that? They usually were all about solving the problem for her. And frankly, she was good with that. She'd love to hand this particular problem over to someone else. But one couldn't ask the delusion to solve itself. So in the end, she simply laughed.

"I guess I'll have to figure out something else."

She said it, but her mind was frozen shut. And with her belly full and the heat on her face, she was feeling wiped out. She had no idea what time it was in the real world. Here it was well past dark, and so she decided to give herself a break. It was time to sleep, and maybe she'd wake up back under a one-moon sky in the morning. Most likely in a mental ward, but at least it would be home.

"I don't want to close my eyes," she said even as she stretched out onto the ground. "I'm afraid you won't be here when I wake up."

"I have vowed never to abandon you," he said softly.

Could a delusion really abandon anything? Wasn't it usually the other way around? "Some things might not be under your control."

"True," he said sadly. "But I will remain here nevertheless. I will keep watch while you sleep."

She cracked an eye, seeing that he'd settled down at the base of a tree, his back supported and his eyes facing away from the fire. He was preserving his night vision, she realized.

"When are you going to sleep?"

"Tomorrow during the day. You are not able to travel until your feet heal more. We will be safe here for a while."

Oh goody. No bears or mountain cats. He hadn't exactly mentioned those creatures, but she decided not to press for details. "Okay," she finally said. "But if we're safe, we're safe enough for you to sleep too."

That didn't exactly track, but she was going to feel really guilty if he didn't get some shut eye. He was the wounded one, after all. And she was wholly dependant upon him. Which meant...

Ugh. She pushed up and forced her eyes open. "I'll keep watch. You need your rest so you can carry me in the morning."

"I—"

"You promised not to be stupidly macho, remember?"

He looked at her, his expression serious. She forced herself to look awake and in earnest. In the end, he nodded. "I will set some traps around us. Be careful where you walk."

"Traps?"

"In case a beast wanders too close. They will not protect us against a clever man or a lucky creature, but—"

"How far are we from clever men?"

"Very far," he said, then shrugged. "As much as I am aware, at least."

"Well, lucky beasts will be lucky no matter what, so set the traps and then come sleep."

He nodded and disappeared into the woods. His last words were, "I will not be long."

She smiled. Famous last words. So she stretched out and prepared to wait for him. She meant to. She tried to. But in the end, her eyes drifted shut and she slept.

Keeven settled on the ground near the angel. Unable to resist, he touched the curls that lay across her forehead. She was a beauty, his lost angel, and lust slammed into him again. It had barely eased from their kiss—or her bath in the stream—but he was a man of discipline. He could ignore it.

He had to ignore it because he could not father her child. His wife had already been selected for him, the bonds already made, the holy vows spoken not one week before. He was married, and this angel was not for him. And yet, he searched for a way out.

As a prince, he was honor bound to do what was best for his people. That meant fathering children who had the best chance of aiding in defense of the realm. Janet's child would be a demi-angel and a potential savior. History was filled with great children of angels, and he could make sure that such a child was raised with a true understanding of his or her destiny.

Janet was willing. Her kiss had shown him that much. And the lust that pounded through his blood added credence to this Goddess-gift. Plus, they had escaped the birdbeasts when they should have died a thousand different ways. So here they were, safe in a clearing next to a warm fire in a place were neither man nor beast cared to wander. They were safe. That he was not right now pushing between her thighs would be called a sacrilege by the priests. An arrogant refusal of a divine gift.

And yet as a knight of Askel, he was bound to live his life with honor. That meant fulfilling his vows to create children with the princess and taking no other to his bed.

There was an easy solution, of course. He could resist Janet and give her to an honorable man. Their children would grow alongside his own. Two sets of parents, and a new generation of powerful people to defend the realm.

But his heart had no interest in giving Janet away. Nor did he have any desire to see her with another man.

He sighed as he looked to the heavens, trying to remind himself of all that his choices protected. He thought of the people who defended the Wall. It was only due to that barrier that the northern Gezan did not come down and rampage the realm. In his lifetime alone there had been two minor breeches, and one of them had cost the lives of his father and older brother. The maintenance of the Wall and the defense of the realm now fell to himself and his mother. And then, of course, to the next generation.

But he could not do it. The stones that powered the Wall were weak, and there were too few with his ability to restore them. One demi-angel could restore the Wall for a year. Two such children—one from himself and the princess, another from Janet and whoever she chose as a consort—could protect them for a decade.

That was the clear path. He had to honor his vows, and Janet would wed another. It was what had to happen.

Keeven stepped away, settling himself as far from her as possible. Then he closed his eyes and tried not to curse his deity for sending him a gift he could not open.

CHAPTER 4

Lust haunted Keeven all through the night. By morning, his foul mood allowed him to kill their breakfast with savage intent. And with every breath, he repeated his litany: he was a Knight of Askel. He would act honorably. He would not bed the angel no matter what she did or how much he lusted. Which worked as long as she slept. But the moment she woke, every part of him stirred to life.

He was waiting by the fire for her when she began to wake with mutters and winces as she rolled over on the hard ground. His brother woke much the same way, with curses and fierce expressions, and Keeven found the entire process charming.

Eventually, she cracked her eyes and focused on him. Or more specifically, first him, then the fire, then the woods around them, then back on him. And she groaned.

"Still camping. Still delusional. Perfect."

"I have caught some breakfast for us. Fish this morning."

"Ugh. Fish and morning. Two words that should never go together."

He grinned, knowing better than to take anything she said to heart. His brother used to call him all sorts of foul names before midday. "I find it most heartening," he said as he popped a morsel in his mouth. If she knew what he had gone through to catch the fish without rod or hook, she would be impressed. But she was not awake enough yet to understand how well he had provided for her.

"Oh God, I ache. Who the hell made the ground so freaking hard? Delusional dirt should be pillow soft. It's a rule."

He didn't answer. He didn't need to. Eventually she would get up, cursing the very air in this beautiful place, and then she would eat and feel better. Or maybe not as she rolled over and closed her eyes. But she didn't settle into sleep. Instead, she groaned again. "I have to... Oh crap."

She looked at him and he arched a brow in query.

"No bathroom. No Starbucks. This delusion sucks." Then she flopped onto her back and glared at him. "At least you're still here. That's something, I suppose."

"I told you I would not abandon you."

She waved a dismissive hand at him. "Abandon, smandon. I need coffee."

He shook his head. "I do not know what that is."

She sighed. "Do you know who the most addicted coffee drinkers are? Baristas. Cause we get it cheap. Do you know what I do when I'm not getting kicked out of PhD programs? I'm a barista. Which means I'm about an hour away from a killer headache. Which sucks for us both because when I'm caffeine-deprived, I'm a real bitch." Then she sighed. "More of a bitch. And that ought to scare you silly."

"We walked through a birdbeast colony unscathed. Nothing scares me this morning. Not even you."

She snorted. "Speak for yourself, big guy. My feet got cut up all to hell."

He leaned forward to look at her feet. They had been tucked tight to her body as she slept, but now she had stretched them out. In truth, they looked better than he'd feared. Scratched yes. Painful to walk on for any distance, most definitely. But there did not appear to be any infection.

She pushed herself upright with another fierce groan, then she pulled her hair out of its binding and shook it out. Auburn locks sparkling in the sunlight. He saw flashes of red and gold, but mostly he just saw beauty. Simple, innocent beauty.

"I'm going to take a shower...er...a frigid bath. That'll wake me up."

He stood up to carry her, but she held out her hand.

"I'll walk it. My feet aren't so bad, and I think I've got a solution anyway." Then she leaned forward and pulled a morsel of fish off his stick, popping it into her mouth. "Mmmm. Okay, so maybe fish isn't so bad first thing."

He was hard in an instant, his desire for her so strong that he nearly lunged for her. She was smiling at him, her expression filled with mischief as she pushed to her feet. She had no idea how powerful it was for a woman to eat off a man's plate. To do such a thing in public would declare her his intended. For her to do as such with a married man was the gravest breech. And yet he had no wish to stop her.

So he sat and let her head unprotected to the stream. At the moment, she was in more danger from him than any beast that wandered about. He would watch over her when he could walk without pain.

It took a long time.

He made it to her side in time to carry her back to the campsite. She was resting wet and laughing in his arms when she spoke again, her words filled with humor even through chattering teeth.

"I'm only l-letting you do this because you're b-bigger than me. And because I don't want to c-cover my feet in crap before I bind them."

He frowned. "You intend to bind your feet?"

She nodded as he set her down near the fire to dry. Her nipples were tight against her white shirt, the design doing nothing to hide the dark tips from view.

"I was trying to avoid it, but my guess is you've got places to go, people to see. A Magician to defeat. At a minimum, that means trucking out of these woods to civilization where I can buy some real shoes, right?"

"I am not entirely sure where we are, but I believe there is a village within a day's fast walk. Perhaps two."

"That's what I thought." She popped more of the white fish meat into her mouth, licking her fingers and giving him flashes of her pink tongue. Was he doomed to see everything she did as erotic? Apparently so, because after she'd feasted, she leaned back and tilted her face to the sun. He traced the curve of her neck and the pulse that beat just under her ear, and in his mind he was kissing along that line, licking the wet from her skin as she purred in delight. "Well I'm not sitting here for two days while you go out and come back, so that means I'm going to have to hoof it right along beside you."

"I can carry you—"

"Which is ridiculous. I mean you're strong and all, but after the first few hours, I'd start to feel guilty."

He smiled. "We will take frequent rests."

"I'm sure we will, big guy, because let's face it, I'm not a wilderness girl and I quit the Girl Scouts after my first summer camp. They had spiders in them there tents."

He didn't understand half of what she said, but he was smiling at the cadence in her voice, at the laughter in her tone, and the way she sprawled there in the sun completely at ease. No warrior did that. And no court lady either. But she was relaxed in his presence and as carefree as a displaced angel could be. So he was pleased to hear her chatter no matter what she said. And he was content to sit and listen despite the matters pressing him on all sides.

She was the one who broke the interlude. She grabbed the belt that she had laid aside and opened the pouch with the strange metal fastening. "I was hoping to avoid this, but it's become a necessity. There's only a little tape here, but it'll be better than nothing. I just shudder to think about ripping this stuff off once it's on."

He leaned forward, wondering at what she drew out. It was some sort of wide silver circle, except that when she started tugging at it he saw it was a kind of tape wound around itself. "What is that?"

"It's called duct tape, and we're going to wrap my feet in it. But first, would you mind cutting off a strip of Marty's tabard? I'm going to owe her big time when I wake up, but let's face it. That thing is better off in strips around my feet."

He held up the mantle that bespoke her rank among the heavens, or so he'd thought. The thing was thick and heavily embroidered which flashes of gold and silver thread worked in a miraculously straight and steady hand. "You wish me to tear this up?"

"It's butt ugly, so yes, I want you to tear it up. I'm just glad I have a good excuse."

He hesitated, looking at the rainbow tree on a field of gold. "This does not have special meaning?"

She shrugged. "I'm sure it does, but look at it. It's a psychedelic mushroom. It's begging to be sacrificed during a schizophrenic episode."

He didn't respond. It was all part of her belief that she was mad. She clearly found comfort in the idea that she was insane rather than displaced from the heavens. And he could not entirely blame her for the choice. So he cut two long strips off her attire and then helped her wind it about her feet before encircling it all with the sliver duct tape of Heaven. And when it was done, she took a few awkward steps about the camp and declared it, "good enough for government work."

So began their slow walk through the words. Normally he would have chaffed at the late start, her slow steps, or even the meandering path they took through the woods as he kept them close to the water. But he could not begrudge this time, especially as she chattered about her home life, telling him things that made no sense and yet pleased him nonetheless. As the day continued, her headache clearly began to pain her, but she made no complaint and he kept the pace slow so she could rest whenever she needed.

Which turned out to be lucky for him. She may not have become infected from their time with the birdbeasts, but he certainly had. His head throbbed and his joints ached more with every step. His back was on fire, and he knew a fever built in his body. But as he had no medicines to quiet the coming illness, his only hope came in finding a healer soon. Or at least people who would care for Angel Janet while he recovered from his sickness.

Hope appeared sooner than he expected. A road that was more of a cart track of packed dirt, but it was undeniably a path that would lead to people. He should have been happy, knowing as he did that somewhere along this way would be a farmer and his cart. Or a homestead with food and attire for sale. The amenities of life that he was anxious to give his angel.

But with people would come questions and a return to his duties. And the more others could aid Janet, the less he could tarry by her side. His men needed him. His country required his duty. And his own wishes meant nothing against that.

So he regretted every step that brought them closer to the time he would have to leave.

Janet had to find a way out of this delusion. Her head was killing her. It throbbed with every step of her abused feet. And contrary to her hopes, duct tape over quilted cotton was not the same as a good pair of hiking boots. Still she kept up a running babble of chatter because it distracted her and kept her from whimpering like a two-year-old. It also seemed to please Keeven, Mr. Stoic Warrior Prince. When they'd first started walking, he'd smiled at her whenever she said something silly. And those rare moments when he actually laughed? Well, it was like the sun coming out on a rainy day. His entire body seemed to lighten. His shoulders straightened, his head lifted, and even his golden blonde hair seemed to grow brighter.

But as the day wore on, her lack-of-caffeine headache was moving toward migraine territory. She'd run out of chatter, was tired of asking him questions about how to survive in the wild, and couldn't really be bothered with the basics of anything except putting one step in front of the other. And if her mood soured, his completely tanked. He seemed to get more dour with every step. Even finding the road—such as it was—didn't seem to help. He grew more grim by the second, while she limped and stumbled her way down the dirt track.

Please God, let there be a rest stop somewhere close. A gas station. A friendly oasis with a Starbucks. Or even better—as long as she was wishing for the stars—a spa with perfumed soap and a hot tub. Now that would be a mirage worth hallucinating.

Nope. What she got was the heavy rumble of an Amish guy with his horse and cart loaded up with…pigs? Was that a cart full of pigs? Wow. And she thought the birdbeasts had smelled bad.

Keeven turned to her with a reassuring smile. "Sometimes the local people are touchy. It would be best—"

"I won't say a word. I swear."

He arched a brow, his doubt obvious and she chuckled. It was as close as he'd come to a joke in the last two hours.

"Okay, okay. I'll do my best to be silent until I'm sure I can follow your lead. That's the best offer you're likely to get, so I suggest you smile and do your thing."

He pasted on a too-wide smile that made her crack up even more. It also highlighted just how handsome the man was when he wasn't glowering at the innocent dirt road for some mysterious reason. "What thing am I supposed to do?" he asked.

She dropped down onto the nearest bit of patchy grass. "Get us a ride. My feet are killing me." Then she extended her duct tape encased feet and flopped onto her back. The ground was hard and lumpy, and there was a rock that dug into her side, but just stretching out felt wonderful. Clearly she was out of shape.

Meanwhile, the cart rumbled forward, the pig stench growing exponentially with every breeze. Janet told herself that she didn't care so long as she got a real bed tonight and normal shoes.

The donkey plodded forward. At least she thought it was a donkey. As large as a horse with thick shoulders and a long nose. But it also had a mane that went from between its ears all the way down its spine to the tail. It was rather pretty, actually, as someone had taken time to braid it. It looked like a long French braid all the way down the creature's body.

Definitely odd, but then genetics was not her field. Weird mutations like this were simply that: weird mutations. Far be it from her to argue with a hairy donkey.

"Greetings, sir," Keeven said as he stepped out onto the track. "Pray, will you aid us? I have magic to offer in trade."

Janet narrowed her eyes. Magic to trade? Wasn't he supposed to be super-honest or something? What magic could he offer? Unless he had skill in sleight-of-hand or something. It was possible, she supposed.

Then the farmer answered. His voice was deep, almost rumbly, but his words were clear enough. Clear in the sense that she could tell that there were words there but spoken in a language she didn't recognize.

So that was odd. She wasn't great with languages but she had the basics. She knew if something was Russian or Asian. Spanish vs. German was fairly clear. And she'd even heard some Navajo, thanks to her first roommate in college. This was nothing like that. In truth, some of the sounds were so guttural—like a burp with shape—she was surprised that the human body could form it into a word.

"We were picked up by the birdbeasts." Keeven said. Then he lifted his arms. "We need everything."

Obviously Keeven understood the farmer. He crossed to the side of the cart. "I have some small magics. I also have a strong back. We can pay for what we need."

The farmer answered back in his strange language, and even without knowledge of his words, Janet heard the universal tone of shopping. Clearly the farmer wanted something.

Janet smiled, feeling more at ease than she had been all day. At least relief was in sight, though she shuddered at the thought of slopping pigs in return for their supper. She pushed herself upright, brushing off her pants as she gained her feet. First thing she wanted was a pizza with—

Her thoughts stopped cold. When she'd been on the ground, her main view was of the cart wheels and the bizarre donkey with the pretty French braid. Now that she was standing, she got a good look at the farmer beneath his big floppy hat.

He had frog skin. That's all she could think. Mottled green and slightly shimmery, it looked exactly like frog skin.

She must have made a sound. A choke or something. Or maybe they'd just noticed her as she stood up. Either way, both men turned to look at her in curiosity. Which is when she realized the farmer had...well, his eyes were... Oh My God...they were bulbous. Frog eyes. She had seen them before but she thought that with the floppy hat and all, the shadows had confused her. Or perhaps she just couldn't deal with it, so she'd focused on the skin.

But now he tipped his hat back and the sun fell full on his big, slit-iris, green eyes and she felt dizzy with the bizarreness of it all.

"Angel?" Keeven asked, stepping closer to her.

She gaped at him, then at the farmer. Was it a mask? Was this Halloween? A movie set?

No, no, this was a delusion. A simple madness that she'd come to accept as real-ish. She'd been so mired in her caffeine headache and her aching feet that she'd forgotten this was a delusion. But now her broken brain had dreamt up something to remind her. After all, she'd started this psychotic break with man-eating pigeons. Why not a frog as farmer?

She pressed a hand to her mouth to keep in her scream. She was insane. It was okay.

Keeven took hold of her arm, holding her steady. "Janet, what is wrong?"

She swallowed. She wanted to scream, he's a freaking

frog! But that would be rude. And God knew, she didn't want to be rude in her own delusion. But...

"I...I..."

"Heaven doesn't have the Freerik people, does it?"

She blinked. Is that what frog people were called? "Freerik?"

"Him," he said, speaking low as he gestured to the farmer. "The green skin and unusual eyes. He is normal here, Angel. And he can help us."

She nodded, her head bobbling up and down without control. "Oh. Okay. Boots and food and maybe a jacket for you. It's pretty cold and your chest probably gets tired of being all ripply gorgeous all the time."

Holy crap, she needed to shut up right now. She closed her eyes and slammed her mouth shut. She could be quiet. She could be under control. She was not insane. Well, she was, but she didn't have to go around telling everyone.

"Angel?"

"I'm fine. Just...I'm just going to stay here with my eyes closed. I'm going to breathe the..." Well, she was going to say fresh mountain air, but that clearly wasn't true. So she focused on something else: she sat down. She sat down with her eyes closed and rested her pounding head on her forearms. "I'll wait right here." She didn't intend to move until she figured out—one way or another—if she was delusional or...or...

She swallowed. She couldn't even think it.

Could she really be somewhere that wasn't Earth?

Keveen didn't stop her, though she knew his expression was tight with concern. And then the farmer hopped down from his seat. She heard him land—*thud*—in the dirt, and she had a sudden vision of him crouching on all fours like a frog.

She didn't want to look, but she couldn't stop herself. Her eyes opened and...he walked like a man. A normal man with regular shifts of hips and arms, more or less. Phew. That was a relief. Until he tugged off his gloves, and Janet saw he had webbed hands.

Oh wow. Not webbed all the way up to his fingertips, but webbed to about mid-finger on his green-skinned hand. And he was coming closer to her.

She slammed her eyes shut and tried not to squeak in alarm.

"My lady is distraught," Keveen was saying. For her part, she thought distraught was a better then saying completely bonkers. "She is not used to the...the area here. And the birdbeasts frightened her."

Birdbeasts. Frog men. Lord, she was such a weenie. Who was she to discriminate against frog-people just because their eyes were weird? He probably thought duct tape shoes were weird. Besides, hiding her face from her own delusion was ridiculous. And if this wasn't a delusion, then she would have to face it one way or another. So she took a deep breath, mentally throttled her *but-this-can't-be* braincells, and lifted her head.

"It's okay, Keveen. I can handle this." She gave a self-conscious laugh. "I just hate it when I don't understand a language." So she pasted on a smile even though it probably looked manic, and tried to keep her voice casual. "So, um, what language is that anyway?"

He frowned at her. "It is our language. The same language we all speak."

She blinked. "Noooo," she said slowly. "You're speaking English."

He opened his mouth to answer, but then slowly shut it as he looked at her. A flash of pity crossed his features. What the farmer thought, she didn't know. It's not like she could read frog micro-expressions. So she took a deep breath.

"I can tell I'm not going to like the answer," she said, doing her best to hold it together. "So I'll just go back to...to waiting."

Keveen's expression grew even worse, from her

perspective. It went from pity to talking-to-a-child. "I will make all the arrangements, Angel. But in the meantime, can you try to listen very hard to my words? Can you hear with your ears as well as your heart?"

"My heart doesn't hear," she retorted automatically. It was a cranky thing to say, so she immediately snapped her mouth shut. She was not going to say another thing until life sorted itself out. That was her plan, and she was sticking to it.

She was…

Truly…

Until she really started listening to Keeven and the frog-man. They had set about negotiations, bartering in the way of all good shoppers in third-world countries. She hadn't thought of Prince Keeven as a man who would get into haggling, but it was clear that he negotiated like a pro.

And then something truly bizarre happened. The farmer reached into his belt and pulled out a stone. This one was greenish colored, but in general it seemed like exactly the same type of stone that Keeven had used to whack the birdbeast. She wasn't looking closely, of course.

But then again, yes she was, because the farmer handed it to Keeven who held it in his outstretched hand. He just held it and stared hard. She felt his breathing deepen, though she was at least three feet away. She also knew that his shoulders tensed, his eyes drifted shut, and there was an air of taut knowing about him. Like if she stepped closer into the circle, she would have all the answers she sought, clear as day.

Perversely, she didn't move. Some things she just wasn't prepared to see. Not yet. So she sat and watched intently as whatever Keeven did became thicker. It was a circle of energy so powerful, she could almost see it. But she couldn't. And yet it was as real to her as the wagon cart. Then it began to contract. It became tighter and harder.

It was a strain for him. His breath was labored now and his face scrunched tight. And all the while, the field shrank. Smaller and smaller until it seemed to fall straight into the stone.

Boom.

There was no sound, but she heard it nonetheless. *Boom,* with a resonance all around her. And then Keeven took a deep breath before handing the farmer back his stone.

The man looked skeptical. No wonder. Janet had just seen the whole thing, and she was completely doubtful of every bit. But the farmer took the stone and scrambled back onto his seat. No hopping like a frog, but there was a springy leap that gave him easy clearance into his dray. She decided the man was especially spry for his age—which frankly could be anywhere from twenty to two hundred. Frog skin didn't appear to wrinkle.

The frogman set the stone in a slot on the back of his seat, murmured something that did not sound like a croak, and Janet was flopped back onto the ground by an explosion of air that wasn't air. That made no sense, but she'd felt a push against her, and as she'd been rocking back on her bottom anyway, she toppled.

"Angel!" Keeven rushed to her side.

She stared at him. Then she stared at the cart and the frogman. And lastly, she looked at the glowing green stone. No wait, it wasn't glowing. It was just normal colored. And yet she felt its power, for lack of a better word. It was strong and steady, a barrier that seemed to stretch along the back seat of the dray.

"What is that?" she asked. Though she really wanted to ask, What did you do?

"The blue crystals create an invisible wall."

She said nothing to that because force fields hadn't been invented yet. Keeven waited a moment then huffed out a breath.

"Smell the air."

She frowned and sniffed. Nothing. Just sweet mountain breezes, though to be honest, she was rather rank.

Keeven took her hand and gently pulled her to her feet. Then he walked her around to the edge of the dray, back where the pig-like things were snuffling. There were only eight of them, milling about in the back. And whoa—they reeked! Enough to make her eyes water.

Wait a moment. Back here, behind the seat divider, she was practically faint from the noxious, ammonia-like smell. But a step further up, in front of the stone, and bam...nothing but sweet mountain air.

She gaped, not believing her own nose. She stepped forward and backward two more times while Keeven and the farmer watched her with a clear amusement. Then she stopped walking. She closed her eyes and all but clicked her heels while she repeated her incantation. "It's a delusion. It's a delusion. Anything can happen in a delusion. It's a—"

"Why would you rather think yourself insane than simply in a different place?"

She cracked an eye at Keeven. "My world has rules. My *universe* has rules like gravity and electrical current. Magic air fresheners don't fit with any of that." It was one thing to think she was in another world. She'd almost gotten herself to that thought. But to make it a world of magic? Where the physics of airflow and smelly pigs went completely bonkers? That was too much. That meant she wasn't even in her same universe.

Ergo, she was insane.

Keeven didn't comment. He didn't need to. He simply looked at her and waited for her to come to a rational conclusion. But there was no rationality here, and so she shook her head.

"I'm tired and caffeine-deprived. I'm just not going to think about this now, okay?"

He shrugged. "Then let us be on our way." He held out his hand and she took it without thinking. The solid warmth of his calloused fingers as they wrapped around hers steadied her as nothing else could. And when he helped her climb up into the front of the dray, she didn't even wince at sliding in next to Farmer Frog. And when Keeven settled in beside her, she leaned against him. Not hard, but enough that he extended his arm behind her and pulled her tight to his side.

She knew he was tired. Whatever he'd done with the stone had added lines to his face which she actually found reassuring. She twisted on the bench and stroked a thumb between his brows to soothe the tension there.

"This is really hard for me," she whispered, "but I'm trying." Whatever possessed her to say that, she had no clue. But the words came out unbidden and her voice cracked on the last one.

His face eased, and he took hold of her fingers before pressing them to his mouth. "I know, Angel," he said against her palm. "Were our situations reversed, I would not be half so capable as you."

She almost called him a liar, but remembered at the last second to have care with that word. So she settled on squeezing her fingers around his and tugging him against her though they were already as close on this bench as it was possible to get.

"Lean on me, big guy. I know you're tired. Might as well rest on me."

"I could not—"

"No macho-crap, remember? Rest. I'll be quiet."

He chuckled as he settled onto the bench. She felt him slump a bit, but not with his full weight. And certainly not against her though what she felt of him was hot and manly. Emphasis on hot. Wow, the guy was a furnace.

"Hey," she said as she mock punched him. "Are you suggesting that I can't shut up?"

He shook his head, though his eyes were shut. "Nothing about you is restful, Angel. And yet, when with you, I feel at ease."

She wanted to say something smart-ass in response. She was sure she had a host of them somewhere. But no one had ever said anything so nice about her before. She eased his troubles. That was…well, that was the stuff of songs. So she tugged him a little harder against her, and she did her best to bear up silently as his weight settled heavier against her.

In time, he slept.

She didn't.

She wanted to. She really wanted to, but every time her eyes drifted shut, she saw him putting that power into a stone. She might as well think the word: magic. She saw him putting magic into the stone. And when she didn't want to see that anymore, she popped open her lids and looked about her.

She didn't want to look at the farmer's hands. He'd left his gloves off, so she had a good view of his dark green skin and the webbing between his fingers. Instead, she let her eyes see other things. The trees, the landscape, the little animals that darted beneath the trees. Even some of the insects and a couple large butterflies that flitted past. They were all lovely. And not a one of them looked familiar.

She hadn't paid attention in the woods. After all, one tree looked like every other tree when she was trying to skirt around it without stabbing another stick into her foot. But she wasn't walking now, and she had her promised silence to keep her from chattering as a distraction.

She was looking now, and though everything she saw fit into the general pattern of her knowledge—tree, squirrel, pig, butterfly—the particulars looked strange. She didn't know enough biology to say what was weird. Maybe the way a creature moved, maybe the shape of the leaves on the tree, or perhaps it was the paleness of the grass that looked more lime than the rich emerald of spring. New grass, she supposed, and yet it didn't look that new.

Everything felt a little off, and she grew more unsettled the more she saw. And when the farmer started to sing—a rich baritone that was punctuated by a rhythmic croak—she felt her heart begin to crumble inside her.

This was no delusion.

She wasn't experienced with psychotic breaks, but she was sure that manic-depressives in the middle of a manic phase truly believed they could fly. And delusional people thought they were making sense, right? They looked at frog-people and wondered how to add them to their just-now-formed rock band.

That wasn't what she was doing. That wasn't anything like what she was thinking.

But if this wasn't a delusion, then how could she have gone from Marty's closet to sitting in Farmer Frog's dray behind the donkey with a French braid? How could this be real? And yet, how could it not?

By the time they turned off the dirt track to an even more uneven patch of grass, Janet had come to a conclusion. Well, not a conclusion as much as a decision. But for her to fully embrace her choice, she needed Keeven to wake up.

"Keeven?" She nudged him. "Come on big guy," she murmured to him. Then she started shaking him. Which is when—to her total horror—she realized that Keeven wasn't asleep. He was unconscious.

"Keeven!"

CHAPTER 5

"...frogs."

Keeven existed in the twilight of weakness. An abominable place that he needed to escape, but there was a simplicity here. He knew shadows and the vaguest impression of touch. Sound was a distant memory, but sometimes words penetrated the fog. More and more now. Enough that he took comfort from them.

"...cute..."

"...three..."

"...swallow."

That last one was an order. And as something was stroking his throat, he did as he was told. Not really consciously, but because she wanted it.

"He did it!"

There was such enthusiasm in her voice that he did it again. Or perhaps not, because he felt something dribble along his cheek.

"Come on, Keeven. Swallow."

This time he heard all the words. And this time he knew he obeyed because he felt hot broth slide down his parched throat.

And so it continued. He never opened his eyes. He hadn't the strength. But he felt her touch, heard her words, and did as she bid. He ate, and she was pleased.

He slept.

* * *

"Bath time, dude. I know, it's embarrassing for you, but I've become somewhat fond of it. If you don't like it, then wake the fuck up. That's your mission, you know. To wake up."

There was a pause, then the words began, like fresh water from a stream.

"You never listen to me. Fine. I've managed to get hot water for you since your fever's broken. Or at least as hot as we can make things. Apparently frogs don't like hot water nearly as much as I do, but they tolerate my oddities, for which I'm grateful. And I really like them—the family, not the bath. Well, yes, the bath too. Anyway, the baby is adorable. She's more like a toddler, except there is no toddling to be had. Hopping. That part of their froggy genetics is really clear at this age. Anyway, she's adorable even if I can't pronounce her name. And she does seem determined to get into everything. And I do mean everything."

Keeven still hadn't opened his eyes, but he heard everything now. The steady stream of her words. She filled his heartspace with her chatter, and he was profoundly grateful. He heard the splash of water, the steady caress of cloth, and her. Always her as she stroked over every part of him.

His hand, held with care.

His chest, stroked slowly and with a patter of words that felt more like a caress.

Then he felt the covering pulled off, and he lurched awake. It was an instinctive response. The rapid drag of his eyes open as he moved a hand to cover himself. Or so he thought. But with the sunlight flooding his eyes, his mind stuttered at the light, and he realized he had barely shifted his fingers.

I can manage myself, he tried to say. He heard something more like "Ungh."

"Keeven!"

He felt her fingers on his cheek. He shifted toward it like a babe rooting for a teat. Her fingers extended and he felt her palm pressing against him. And when he inhaled, he smelled her.

"No, no, don't go back to sleep yet, big guy. We need to get some food into you first." Then she twisted and called to someone else. "Soup!"

He smiled, pleased beyond measure because the word had been spoken in his language, not hers. His thoughts were not entirely clear, but he knew that was important, and he was happy.

"Yeah, yeah. You keep smiling there, big guy. Just so long as you open and swallow when I tell you."

So he did. And by the time she'd finished scooping thick broth into him, he had enough strength to open his eyes.

"There you are, Keeven. I knew you were in there somewhere." She spoke brusquely, but he heard the relief in her tone. He also had enough strength to really look at her.

Her hair was neatened back into her customary tail and her face was slightly reddened by the sun, giving a vitality to her that he had not seen before. But he also noted the red in her eyes and the simple relief in her body as she looked at him. And he saw her smile.

"You're on the mend, which is good, but we're not going to push it, okay? Bed rest and nourishing broth." Then she leaned forward. "And no video games no matter how much you beg."

"Knights of Askel do not beg," he said. His voice was a hoarse croak but she understood him. Her smile widened, and she arched her brows at him.

"We'll see about that. These people are really nice here, but their diet is somewhat monotonous. You get the broth. I've had my choice of that and eggs. That's it. All day, every day. Not a latte in sight. Don't even get me started on chocolate. I've been having dreams about a hot fudge sundae that makes me weep."

He raised his hand. It was a massive undertaking, and he

was appalled by how frail he had become. But he still did it, lifting his fingers to her cheek. She helped him when he was only part way. She entwined his fingers with hers and brought them to her lips.

"Angel," he said, awe in his tone.

She rolled her eyes. "Hardly. And certainly not given the curse words I've been using lately. Please tell me that people have modern plumbing elsewhere. That there are houses and bathrooms and all sorts of things like that. Not this..." She looked around her. "This open air shit. It's like you've taken camping to a whole new level."

He didn't answer. A look around told him that this was a farm as was typical in Bodil. Since they were Freerik people, their homestead likely encircled a pond. Meals were over campfires, sleeping areas were under the stars while animals were penned nearby. Protection from weather came from their stones and the magic within. That his bedroll rested under the beautiful canopy of a pair of entwined trees told him that the farmer had given him a place of honor to recover. He would need to show his gratitude before they departed.

Meanwhile, Janet was prattling on, talking about running water and flush toilets, none of which made sense to him. In the end, he settled into the rhythm of her words, letting the meaningless sounds soothe him into sleep.

Janet watched his eyes drift closed and waited patiently for his breathing to settle into the deeper rhythms of sleep. Over the past few days, she'd made a study of his breathing. This was the healing kind: slow steady breaths with a slack jaw and a relaxed face. But there had been the faster, tighter pants of his fever, and the more disturbing ones tied to his dreams. Probably of the birdbeasts, because those vicious overgrown pigeons had certainly featured in hers.

She leaned back in her chair and lifted her head to the sky. Odd how a few days ago, everything in her had been focused on finding a way out of this nightmare. But one collapsed prince later, and suddenly she was surprisingly content. For the first time in her life, there was nothing to strive for except Keeven's continued improvement.

Her basic needs were met. The farmer's family had provided everything. She had food, boring as it was. Clothing was given to her: a basic tunic over leggings. And she'd even gotten boots—a sturdy leather pair that fit her like a dream. She was starting to learn the language here and at least understand the rhythms of the compound.

There was only one thing disrupting her patience. One tiny, niggling detail that messed with her contentment: magic. The very word gave her the heebie-jeebies. If only she could understand the basic electromagnetic or atomic principles behind the magic stones, then everything would be right with the world...er, universe. So in the long boring times while Keeven dozed, Janet dedicated herself to learning more about their seemingly simple little rocks.

It began with the weather. Right now, it was overcast and would rain soon. She knew that not because she could feel it in the air but because the farmer had come and activated the stones that kept the rain off. He'd told her with hand gestures and smiles that because of the stones, the rain would slide harmlessly past them to water the ground. Having now seen it happen once before, she believed him. The blue stones were a kind of force field that allowed the breeze and some insects through, but not the rain. Not branches tossed about by a storm. And not the hopping toddler unless she told the child it was okay. Well, she said *oyan* which apparently meant "enter."

That was the effect of the stone. But how did it work? She was still clueless despite hours of contemplation and a little experimentation.

She was staring at the force field and mentally thinking of all the tests she wanted to run on the stones when the farmer's eldest son walked by, his strides long and fast as he sought out his wife. The woman in question was a petite girl of dark hair and an only slight tinge of green to her skin. But if there was any doubt that she was of their race, her webbed fingers gave her away. As did the open lust in her eyes whenever her husband came by.

Janet waved to him, and he smiled back, but he wouldn't stop. He had come in from working the fields, would dive into the pond that was the center of their family community, and then he would take his wife to bed. That had been one of the first things she'd learned about them: that they were an open family. They lived without walls, without privacy, and had no embarrassment about any biological function including sex. And once she'd gotten over her shock, she'd enjoyed the lustful displays. They had such enthusiasm for everything they did—sex, work, eating, everything—that she couldn't help but smile at every part of it.

She envied their uncomplicated a life. There were no thesis papers, no running to the grocery store, and no counting pennies to see if she had enough for peanut butter. There was education here. She'd seen one of the oldest generation helping a younger one with a book, and it had been a real book complete with pictures and a language she'd never seen before. Plus the daily education of how to farm, how to catch fish for dinner, and how to activate the magic rocks that were part of their daily life.

That had been Janet's mission once Keeven had shown that he was going to recover. She'd spent every moment she could with that book, trying to learn about their magic while fitting it into a framework she understood. So far her results had been spectacular failures. Despite working on the simplest stones—a training stone that grew bright—she'd gotten nowhere. But she wasn't discouraged. There had to be more erudite texts on the magic somewhere. She would study those when she could. But first, of course, she had to learn the language. So she'd applied herself to that as well.

That's how she passed the three days since Keeven had collapsed.

She looked to her tablet and chalk. Not the computerized tablet, of course, but an actual square slate and a piece of white chalk. She'd spent some time toying with new dissertation ideas, but as time wore on, she came to accept her situation. She was in a new place, a new world, potentially a new dimension. It sucked, but there it was. She was pretty sure no delusion had hours and hours of sitting and watching Keeven sweat from fever. Nor would she ever imagine the language of this world. It was like a mix of computer code and belches, though she might be exaggerating a bit.

Worse, she knew that if time worked the same way here as it did on Earth, she'd missed her Monday deadline. She was out of the PhD program, and part of her really didn't care. The other part—the I've-got-to-make-a-living-somehow part—really hoped that time worked differently in this dimension and she'd go back only to learn that she'd been gone overnight. Or for five minutes. Because, honestly, she didn't want to learn how to cook fish over an open flame to survive. Don't mention trying to catch that fish in the first place.

"You are not being restful," Keeven said from the bed.

She started, her gaze hopping to him. "I thought you were asleep."

"How can I sleep with you sighing and moaning like that?"

"I was not moaning."

"You were keening then. And I cannot sleep when a woman keens."

She frowned at him. "I don't even know what that means," she answered.

"It means come lie with me, Angel. Let us rest together."

She smiled at him. Did he know that she'd slept tucked against him every night? Did he know that she woke every morning with a desire to do exactly what the farmer and his wife did after the baby fell asleep each night?

"I'm supposed to practice turning on your magic stone."

He frowned, obviously confused, so she held it up for him to see. It was a simple piece of granite, as far as she could

Kathy Lyons

tell. But when the others held it—even the little toddler—it suddenly sprang to life like a mini-halogen light. There was no magic word except for the little girl belched a little when she did it. But no matter what Janet did, she couldn't figure out how to make it turn on.

"That's a child's learning stone," he said.

She rolled her eye. "Sure, make me feel special ed."

He let his eyes drift close. "There is no shame in learning something new."

She knew that was true, but she'd spent her life measuring herself by other people's success. It was the only standard she had for behavior, since her mother had been all over the place. At least with academia, one knew exactly what was good (an A), what was average (a C), and what was unacceptable (anything else). This damned stone put her decidedly in the "else" category.

"I keep working at it, but I just don't know the magic word." She held it between her hands and tried to will it to light. Nothing happened. "See. Nothing," she said. Okay, she might have made a keening sound.

"Just make it bright."

"Hey you. Just sprout wings and fly."

"I cannot do that."

"Well, I cannot make a piece of rock suddenly glow."

His lips curved and he stretched out his arm. "You will," he said. "Now come rest beside me. You keep the bad dreams away."

She knew for a fact that it wasn't true, but she appreciated the lie nonetheless. Then she remembered that he didn't lie, and she smiled. Okay, so maybe she couldn't light a rock, but she could help an exhausted knight sleep. Worked for her.

She set aside the rock and clamored onto the pallet with him. They didn't even need a blanket because he was Mr. Furnace. Not like Feverish Furnace, but perfectly warm. "Better?" she asked as she snuggled tight to his side.

"Much."

And then the rain began. She heard the patter of the rain on the leaves and the deeper tap as it hit the force field and slid to the ground. No fzssssst as if it were being zapped, no ping like it bounced off. Just a tap like rain on a roof that didn't have enough insulation to muffle the sound.

"Cool," she whispered.

"Then come closer," he answered as he tucked her tight beside him.

That wasn't what she meant, but she didn't argue.

She slept.

Keeven woke with the most wonderful feeling of heat and woman against him. She was soft and smelled like a ripe citrus fruit—tart and spicy amid the sweetness. He moved without thinking, settling her heavily against his cock, her rounded bottom begging him to cleave into her.

He didn't. Even half asleep, he was not a man to take merely because he wanted. But his cock was unwilling to be patient as it stretched and throbbed against her backside. He began nuzzling her shoulder, pressing his lips to her skin, licking the spice from her neck.

"Mmmm," she murmured. "I guess you're awake."

He didn't use words to answer. He was too deeply enmeshed in the taste of her. But his cock, ever eager, pulsed in response.

She stretched against him, feline in her movements, effectively killing any possibility of thought as her bottom and his cock grew more acquainted.

Meanwhile, his hands started moving, stroking across her belly, slipping under her tight shirt to find the fullness of her breasts. They were unbound beneath her attire—which was unusual—but he was grateful for it as his palm found the tight point of her nipple, rolling it in a circle as his fingers lifted and stroked her breast.

She sighed into his caresses, and he took that as encouragement to do more. He pulled at her nipple, squeezing it until he heard her moan. But when his hand slid lower on her belly, she stopped him. A quick press of her hand as she held him against her flat stomach.

"Not that I'm opposed, Keeven, but unless you have a condom, we're not going farther."

It was his name on her lips that brought him to full awareness. Or perhaps he was fully aware before, but not conscious of the meaning of anything he did. She was a willing woman, he was a man waking in the full flush of his morning needs. But at her words he remembered who he was and what they'd been about to do.

And so he stilled against her, and his breath stuttered out in a rush.

"Let me guess," she said. "No condom."

His heartspace showed him a sheath around his organ to prevent pregnancy. "None."

"Well that sucks." Then she twisted in his arms, her eyes flashing mischief in the dappled sunlight. "So we can't go whole hog, but..." She let her words drift off suggestively.

Again, it took too long for his thoughts to solidify. There was so much confusion with her shifting against him. Even the lift of her chest as she breathed brushed her breast against his arm and begged him to forget everything but what his cock demanded.

So he focused on the easiest of his questions. "So you understand pleasure? Of the body?"

She snorted. "I was born at night, Keeven, but not *last* night. Of course I understand it. And let me tell you, living here for the last few days has been an education all its own. There's no modesty here."

He dropped his forehead against her shoulder feeling the weight of his responsibilities as never before. "The rules here are complicated, Angel. I do not know what is right." Or more accurately, he guessed what the right path was—the path of celibacy where it came to her—but had no wish to walk it.

She twisted in his arms. He tried to prevent it, but she insisted and short of wrestling her into stillness, he could not stop her. Soon she was facing him, her eyes concerned.

"That sounded a lot more serious than—"

"You know pleasure, correct?"

She blinked. "I...um...well, it's been a while, but—"

"I cannot think with you so close," he said. Then he stroked the hair from her face and heard the sounds of the Freerik family waking. There was no subtly in the sounds of what they were doing. They were copulating as loudly and enthusiastically as he wished to do with her.

"Do you want me to go away?" she asked.

"No, I want—" He strangled his words for to say his hunger aloud would give it that much more power. His cock was throbbing with need, his body lusting to the point of madness. This was a divine command. It was the urge to create a demi-angel, and he was quickly losing the fight to remain himself against such a demand.

Then she kissed him, soft and sweet, a press of their lips before she added a teasing lick just as she pulled back. "Look, we don't have to do anything. I'm just not opposed, is all." Then she smiled. "So you know about condoms. You have those here?"

The sheaths to prevent disease and pregnancy were well known to him. He was a prince of the realm, after all. He had been taught pleasure at a young age but also the responsibility to not create a child before it was time.

"Angel," he breathed against her, giving in—a little—to the need thrumming inside him. He was a prince, after all, his marriage one of politics and children. So long as he did not father a child, what he wanted was allowed. "Turn back around. Let me show you how much joy can be found in this realm."

"But—"

"This is the only way. Please, Angel."

"If you're too tired or sick—"

"Nymph of Anachat, turn around!"

She chuckled, the vibration of her laughter nearly unraveling all his control. "I'm going to assume that's a good thing."

He didn't answer as she finally allowed him to push her over. He fitted her back against his cock, and then he possessed her breasts. He didn't just stroke them, he employed all the skills learned from countless courtesans. He pleasured her breasts, he teased her nipples, and he nearly brought her to fullness from that alone. But he did not want this moment to end so quickly.

So he eased his hand lower. And when she would have reached for him, he used the bulk of his arm to pin her still.

"Hey big guy," she said. "Don't I get to play too?"

His breath was coming hot and hard, but he swallowed and tried to explain. "If you touch me, I will lose control."

"That's okay—"

"Do you want a child?" he asked. "Tell me it must be *my* child and I will do anything you wish." If she said yes, he would throw away everything. He would toss aside his sworn oath to the princess, he would ignore the commands of his knighthood, and he would give in to the divine impulse. The Goddess had given him this angel to father a demi-angel. He knew this, and yet how could he be a man of honor if he ignored his vows?

Her breath caught. "No," she said softly. "No baby."

"Then do not move, Angel." He allowed himself a smile. "Except in that you must."

"That sounds rather cocky," she teased. His hand slipped beneath the small scrap of fabric covering her privacy and she gasped.

She was made as all women. This reassured him as he pressed his middle finger into her slick folds. She shuddered against him, and he nearly lost himself. But he was too interested in exploring her. In sliding across the places that made her gasp, in thrusting his finger deep inside where his cock ached to go. He opened and pleased this angel in his arms as she writhed against him.

It was fortunate he was a big man compared to her. Fortunate that he could restrain her movements with his chest while his fingers stroked across her before penetrating deep. He felt her tighten when he pushed inside. He knew the quivering in her belly and the arch of her back. And he fitted himself between the cheeks of her bottom and allowed the pleasure to build in his own body and mind.

She was a wonder, his angel. Her moans were stuttered, as if she did not want to make noise but could not stop herself. Her body flexed and her scent enveloped him in a citrus madness.

And when she was at the edge, her breath caught and held. He knew what was coming, so he thrust two fingers inside her. He wanted to know the grasp of her body, the draw of her flesh. And he thumbed her nexus one last time.

She cried out, her face buried in his arm to muffle the sound. But there was no restraining the explosion in her body as she gripped him. The pull on his fingers was more than enough. He thrust against her backside once more and released. His seed erupted from him in a rush that emptied his thoughts and drained his body.

And in this way, he denied a goddess's call.

He rested against her, his breath hard and deep. Eventually, they both quieted. In time, his breath stilled to a slow rhythm. He was just dancing along the edge of sleep when she twisted against him and he came back to himself. Then the slick wetness between them recalled him to his duty.

"Don't move," he said against her back. "Let me clean you."

"You don't need—"

"Let me," he begged. "I...I have something I must tell you."

She sighed as she rolled forward so he could find basin and

cloth. "And here I thought girls were the ones who always wanted to talk afterwards."

He found what he was looking for easily enough. He cleaned her as one might wash a new babe or a cherished holy relic. He stroked her skin and poured the water with as much reverence as he could manage. And when he was done, he finally found the strength to tell her the truth.

"I cannot father the demi-angel. I am sworn to the princess and must not break that faith. But I know many fine men who will serve in my stead. You have merely to ask and I will see that he performs his duty by you with honor and respect."

She pushed up from the pallet, her eyes narrowed and her head tilted to the side. Her hair draped enticingly down her shoulder, but her expression was guarded.

"Slow down, Keeven. What the hell are you talking about?"

He helped her rise until she sat on the pallet facing him. Her tight tunic had slipped to cover her once again though her breasts bounced in such a way that he momentarily lost his thoughts.

"Keeven?"

He looked back in her eyes, feeling sorrow in every word he uttered. "I cannot father your child."

She frowned. "What child? Didn't I just make it clear that I don't want one?"

He nodded, realizing with dismay that she was ignorant of the dictates of the Goddess. Not surprising since she worshiped a male deity, but the lust between them proved that it was his own goddess who had brought her here. "I prayed to the Goddess for aid. You appeared and..." He swallowed.

She folded her arms across her chest. "Don't stop now. What are you trying to tell me?"

"It is the nature of the Goddess to have her angels bear a child while they yet reside in the mundane world."

She blinked, her mouth slipping open. A moment later, she spoke, though her words were slow. "There's so many things wrong with that statement, I don't know where to begin."

He nodded. "You are confused in this realm, but—"

"I'm not having a baby, Keeven. Not with you, not with anyone."

He nodded, seeing her earnest desire in this. Then he gestured to the bed. "There are men in your realm, yes?"

"Yeah. What of it?"

"Do you usually...do you allow them to touch you as I did? Especially on such short acquaintance?"

"Jesus, no! I—You're..." She rubbed a hand over her face. "God, I miss coffee."

"Angel—"

"No, Keeven. Just shut up and listen, okay? This has been an odd few days for me. And this morning, you were all hot and manly and I've been listening to the others doing their thing for days now."

"The Freerik are a lusty lot."

She winced. "Yeah, I noticed. And you're recovered, obviously, and I was happy and feeling good all tucked up next to you. So...so there's nothing wrong with what we did."

"It is the way of the Goddess," he pressed. "To couple an angel with a man—"

"Jesus, Keeven, you're a hot guy and we had some fun. Don't make more of this—"

"Has it ever felt that good before? Has your body sung so sweetly for anyone else before?"

"Yeah, of cou—" she bit off her words. "Well, okay, maybe not quite like... Look, you're good at it. That's all."

"It is the Goddess," he pressed. "She has selected you to birth the next demi-angel."

She closed her eyes. "You're whacked, you know that, right?"

"But," he continued, "it cannot be me to sire the child. I am gravely sorry for the insult, Angel. You cannot know how sorry."

She took a breath, then released it without words. Then she looked at him. "Okay, we'll go with that for the moment. Why can't it be you? If you believe it's the Goddess's will and all that rot, then by extension, you'd be the one meant to be the father, right? I mean, I don't see any other guys hanging around. Cause I'm not giving birth to a tadpole."

He dipped his chin. "The Freerik do not mate with us. They are quiet people who treat us with respect as we honor them. But we do not mate with them."

"Groovy. So no frog babies." She pushed to her feet dropping her arms to her hips as she regarded him. "No babies at all."

"I am sworn to the princess."

She took a moment, her head tilted and her eyes narrowed. "Sworn to? Like betrothed?"

He took a moment, listening closely to his heartspace to be sure he understood her meaning. Then he shook his head.

"No, Angel. I am married."

CHAPTER 6

Jesus, she was an idiot. She'd taken a look at his rippling chest muscles and that big-ass sword, and she'd just fallen into his arms. Save a girl's life a time or three and she forgets to ask the obvious questions. Things like: are you married?

"What the hell, Keeven? You're married?"

He dipped his head, his expression one of deep shame. Well, he should! Jesus, married?

"Then why...?" She gestured to the bed, appalled at herself for having the best damn orgasm of her life with a married man. "How could you?"

"I told you I could not have a child with you." His cheeks flushed ruddy, clearly ashamed. "I understand if you prefer substance over pleasure. I will not touch you again."

"That's right you won't!" Then she took a breath, running over his words again in her head. "Wait. What?"

He didn't have a chance to respond as the farmer appeared at the door. Well, they didn't really have a door. After the night's rains, the frogman had to turn off the stones, so he went to the corner and shut it down. His expression was amiable, if somewhat wary. And when he spoke, he looked uncertainly between the two of them. The words were too fast for her to catch. She'd only learned a smattering of their language, but Keeven obviously understood.

"Yes, I am much better. Thank you for your generosity."

The farmer said more, probably asking about her because

he dipped his head in her direction.

"The Angel has realized that I cannot make a child with her. She is rightly furious with me."

Janet reared back. "That's not it at all, you dolt."

Meanwhile, the farmer brightened, and he abruptly rushed away, bellowing. This time she understood him. He was calling his children. At least…oh hell. She mentally ran through the names and realized he was calling his unmated children. Including the little ones. Not the toddler, but there was a grandchild who was certainly pre-pubescent.

"You can't be serious," she groaned. Hadn't Keeven just said that they don't mate across species? Apparently that didn't apply to angels because a moment later every single male in the compound ran, hopped, or swam to her location. Well, swam through the lake and then hopped. That was the youngest boy who hadn't quite grown into his land-legs yet.

She watched them file up, their expressions eager. And all the while, she had been shaking her head and muttering. "No, no, no, no, no." It wasn't her most eloquent response, but it was all she could manage.

And then the clear head of the family—Dotat was his name—approached speaking slowly and clearly in words she could follow. Or mostly.

"My children. Choose."

She shook her head. "I don't want…" Her voice stuttered off. She was speaking in English, and she knew they couldn't understand that. But the most she could handle in their language was "no." And maybe a "hell, no" that she'd learned from the toddler. Not the most diplomatic way to refuse to procreate.

She glared at Keeven. "Tell them please—politely—that I don't want a child. I have no desire to get pregnant. That all his descendants are fine men and I would be honored to…to… Hell you know. I'd be honored, but absolutely, positively not."

Keeven looked at her, his expression grave. "Are you sure?

They are all good people."

She threw up her hands. What would it take for him to understand? "Keeven! No children! No. Never. Nada. Nyet." That might be overstating her case. Actually, she'd like to have kids someday, but clearly she had to be emphatic to get through to them.

Meanwhile, Keeven turned to the farmer's family. "The angel is greatly impressed with your family and their strength but she is under divine geas and cannot be swayed from her path. I have pleaded on your behalf, but she regrets her inability to accept your fine lineage."

She glared at him. Divine geas? Whatever. If it got her out of sleeping with her host's progeny, she'd smile and accept it. But once she and Keeven were in private—if such a thing existed in this commune—then tall, blonde, and clueless was going to get an earful.

So she bowed respectfully to the family, feeling awkward as she pasted on a regretful face. It felt weird, but since most of them were in the process of bowing to her, she thought she ought to return the gesture.

Meanwhile, Keeven just kept talking. "We apologize for the insult. We will depart as soon as—"

"What?" she interrupted. She was furious with him, sure, but she didn't want to endanger his health by setting off too soon. "Your fever just broke yesterday. You can't possibly be healthy enough to—"

"How long have we been here?"

She frowned and thought back. "Three…no, four nights."

"That is one day too long—" he began, but the farmer interrupted. The words rolled too fast for her to follow, but in the end, Keeven bowed his thanks. "One more day, then. My thanks."

She smiled and nodded as well. "Thank you," she said in their language. At least she'd learned that much. Then she waited while they served her and Keeven breakfast. More eggs and green leaves in swamp water. Yum…not. But it was better than starving and they offered it to her with such smiles that she felt like an ass for grousing, even in the privacy of her own thoughts. They wouldn't allow her to help clean the dishes or anything. And when she tried to carry her plate to the side of the pond, the baby snatched it from her hands and hopped away.

So in the end, it was back to staring at Keeven who was looking a little pale after his exertions of the last hour.

"Jesus, sit down before you collapse," she said.

He frowned. "I do not understand why you call your deity for me to sit down."

"I didn't—" Oh right. She supposed she had. "Sorry. Keeven, please lie down before you collapse."

"You said sit before."

"Now I'm saying lie down before I knock you down," she huffed. "I'm still really ticked at you, but I'm beginning to think we have some basic cultural misunderstandings going on here. And I'm going to feel really bad if you collapse while I'm yelling at you."

He arched a brow—probably at her threat to knock him down—but then obligingly sat down on the pallet. "I will not collapse. You may begin yelling."

She took a deep breath, but then strangled her words before they were born. Telling her to start yelling sort of took the wind out of her sails. And then—as if he thought it would help—he softened his expression as he tried to apologize again.

"Angel, you have every right to be angry. I am your chosen one, and yet I cannot in honor father a child with you."

She held up her hand. "Stop right there!"

He pulled back slightly, but didn't speak.

"Number one, I'm not an angel. I know, I know, I showed up in mid-air while you were trapped by bird vomit, but I'm not an angel, okay? However I got here, I'm not divine."

His lips quirked at that, and she had a sudden urge to

strangle him. "What?" she demanded.

"Divine means from heaven, Angel." She opened her mouth to argue, but he continued. "And angel means someone who lives in the heavens."

Damn, he was being remarkably logical about this, which at the moment translated to: remarkably stubborn.

"Second," she continued, deciding to table the first issue for the moment, "why do you think you're my chosen one?" She almost choked on those words. He was pretty and all, but her chosen one?

"You came in response to my prayer, and I am the only one who understands your language, and you mine. That means we speak heartspace to heartspace. We are chosen for one another by the Goddess who sent you to me."

Right. To Mr. Married.

"Problem there, O Chosen One. You swore your vows to your goddess?" He nodded. "Then she'd know you were married and couldn't do the hanky panky with me." Clearly his heartspace had trouble understanding "hanky panky" so she gestured to the bed. "You can't in honor…blah, blah, blah."

He nodded. "Yes, I understood what you meant."

Oh.

"As I said, I am having difficulty seeing my path in this. I believe I am the one who is to help you chose the right father for the demi-angel."

And right there was the crux of the issue. Forget the half divine bull-shit. He wasn't going to believe she was normal any more than she wanted to believe there were frog people outside her tree room waiting to bed her. The real problem was this assumption of childbearing.

"Why exactly do you think I'm here to get impregnated? Why can't I have come here just to save you from the psycho birds?"

"Because you are still here."

Okay, so he had a point from a religious perspective. But

what about the scientific? "What if I'm here because…" Shit, it was hard to say aloud. Ridiculous to have the words clog her throat. She'd been thinking them for days now. "What if it was some fluke—divine or not—and I'm stuck here. No divine reason, just…oops, you got caught in a space-time eddy or something."

He blinked, clearly trying to sort through her words. In the end, he gave up. "I have no understanding of—"

"Right. No Sci-Fi channel here." She huffed as she dropped down on the foot of the pallet. "Okay, so let's go with your theory even though it's really, really wrong. I'm an angel…" She added a snort in case he missed her opinion of that. "I was sent by a deity to save you, and somehow I'm still here for some reason. Maybe it's to teach you modern plumbing. Let you experience the joys of a house with a roof and opaque walls. Maybe—"

"Do you think that's your purpose here?"

She threw up her hands. "It makes more sense than having a baby!"

He shook his head. Then when she would have scoffed he leaned forward and caught her hands. "The ways of the Goddess are mysterious, Angel Janet. All I can say is that our history has hundreds of examples of demi-angels born from a divine creature such as yourself and a man or woman."

She blinked. "You're kidding."

"They are the foundation of our race. The royal lines are the most purely divine of any who walk this land."

She didn't know what to say to that. He was so earnest, and she was…well…flummoxed. "Clearly this type of thing happens to you guys way more than it does to us."

"Angels used to walk constantly among us. Now it is the rare event. The last one was over fifty years ago and the woman he chose was unfit for the service. The child did not survive to be born."

There were so many questions bursting through her that

they got tangled up in her mind. All she managed was, "The woman was unfit?" That sounded like a cruel label just because the baby didn't make it to term.

"That is why I believe the Goddess sent a female angel this time. You can carry—"

"And we're back to me getting pregnant. No, Keeven. I don't care about your beliefs, I'm not planning on getting pregnant anytime soon."

He pressed his lips together, clearly refusing to argue. And so solid was his conviction that for a few minutes, she wondered. What if he was right? What if all she had to do to go home was to get pregnant and deliver a child. Then maybe the closet door would miraculously open, and she'd be able to prance through Marty's closet with a "Lucy, I'm home!" Except, of course, she wouldn't be prancing anywhere with her baby because the last thing Earth needed was another unwed mother. And apparently, here the babe would be revered as a demi-angel.

"No," she said to herself. "No matter what nuttiness brought me here, I'm still myself. I am not getting pregnant just to see if it's my ticket home." The very idea was repugnant, and she was appalled that she'd even thought it.

"We would be honored to have you abide in our world, Angel."

She took a moment. She had to take several moments of deep breaths. Then she said, "Here's what we're going to do. First off, you're going to stop calling me Angel."

"It is a term of respect. And whether you admit it or not, it is what you are here."

She waved it away. "Think what you want, but don't you dare say it again. If nothing else, it'll cut back on the hordes of men who will suddenly be chasing me." And wasn't that a bizarre thought? She'd never been chased at all, much less by hordes unless the birdbeasts counted. "Keeven, I need you to see me as a person, not a divine creature."

She could see him process that. In the end, he spoke gravely. "You are Janet." Score one for her. "Second, you're going to get better, and then you're going to start praying to send me home."

"I will not—"

"You will. Because, O Great Married Prince, when you prayed, you accidentally got the wrong girl. I was in my Marty's closet when I jumped into Narnia or whatever the hell this place is called."

"Bodil. This kingdom is called Bodil."

"And Marty would just get off on that. She's an engineer, re-enactor, and fantasy geek. She could teach you modern plumbing and may even be happy to pop out a kid or two. I don't know, you'd have to ask her. But she's from a huge Catholic family, so I'm pretty sure she's not averse to kids or religious dictates."

He frowned. "I do not believe the Goddess makes mistakes when she opens the path."

"Then you have more faith in her than I do." Obviously. "Doesn't matter, you're going to send me home."

"I haven't the strength. And my stones are lost."

"Too bad—Wait. What? What do the stones have to do with it?"

"Did you not see how I threw the first ones at the birdbeast and they did nothing?"

She tried to think back but it was all a blur. "I remember the blue one."

"Yes. That was in my pack and still strong. The ones I threw at the beginning were drained of all energy. I believe that is what the Goddess used to open the path."

Stones! Magic stones with power. And his prayers somehow activated them. This she could understand. In comparison to all the goddess stuff, this was almost scientific.

"How do we get more of those stones? How do we find one to open the door?"

He sighed. "There are no stones like that. Not in recent memory."

She pounced on the words she liked. "Recent memory? What about not-recent memory?"

"In ancient times, there was a vault of stones. A way to open the pathway between Bodil and heaven."

"And where is this vault?"

He looked at her with a mixture of apology and hope. It took her a moment to understand the expression, but when it hit, she was more convinced than ever that she was in a nightmare of her own twisted and broken psyche.

"It's in the dragon's castle, isn't it?"

"I do not understand this word of yours."

"Dragon. Monster. Whatever word you use for the fearsome beast who stole the princess." The very woman, she now realized, who was his *wife*.

He tried a few words, none of which translated in her brain. Until he said one that did.

"Monster." Which of course is what she'd said early, but whatever. "He resides in a castle to the south."

"So give me what details you have."

He nodded. "The night of my wedding—"

Ouch.

"The princess was stolen from her room. We think she fought with her captors and escaped."

Score one for the princess. "Then how—"

"She escaped to the castle where she is being held prisoner by a...*untranslatable*. I left my duties to rescue her, when I was caught by the birdbeasts and you found me."

More like she was called forth by his manly prayers and stupid her, she stepped through when she ought to have been figuring out her dissertation. But that was water under the bridge. "Let's talk a little bit more about that untranslatable word. What is holding the princess trapped in the castle?"

He tried a few other words. In the end, the best she could grab hold of was *demonic force*. "It's being sent by the big bad, right? The Magician."

"I believe so."

"So the plan is to bust in, kill the monster-thing, and raid the castle for a stone that sends me home." Oh yeah. Plus that other thing. "You can rescue your wife, too."

He blanched a little at that. Interesting. He really wasn't reacting how she expected a husband to act when one mentioned his wife. But she didn't have time to question him because he pressed for details. "Do you pledge to help me in any way you can to rescue the princess?"

This time she was the one to wince. "I'm not very useful, Keeven."

"Nevertheless."

She didn't think long about it. "I'm not going to willingly sacrifice life and limb, you know. Or sleep with someone just because you say so. But I promise to do what I can within reason to help you. I'll make it, I don't know, my number one priority short of getting out of this world."

"You must pledge to help me rescue the princess first before you depart this world. Unless I release you from your promise."

She barely spared the time to think about it. It's not like she had a lot of options here. He was her only means of escaping this world as far as she could tell. And if that meant helping him with his quest, then she could at least try.

"Fine," she said.

He smiled. "The bargain is acceptable to me, as well." Then he lifted his palm and sliced his fingernail across the fleshy side, creating a cut that welled bright red blood before extended it to her. Looking closer, she saw he had just dug under a callous and ripped himself open."What the hell are you doing?"

"I am offering my troth."

"Your what?"

"My bargain. My blood. This seals it."

"And what am I supposed to do with that?"

He lifted his hand to her mouth. "You lick it. You taste the magic of the promise, and it binds us."

"*Ewww!* I don't know where your blood's been." That's not exactly what she meant but those were the words that came out.

"It is the only way to seal a troth." Then when she stared at him, he changed his words. "To make the bargain binding."

"How very vampiric of you." She didn't need his frown to know that he didn't understand. "Wait…does that mean that I have to cut myself too?"

"Of course."

Easy for him to say. "What if I get infected?"

"Blood troths heal quickly and never infect." She arched her brow at that. "I have never heard of an infection from a blood troth."

"Oh come on…" she began, but she could tell he was not going to be swayed.

"Swear this troth in the magical way, Janet, and I will in return do all that I can to see you returned to your realm."

Well put like that, what was a little blood? Still, it's not like it was easy to slice open the skin on her hand. Oh wait, of course it was. He had his big ass sword.

"Fine," she said. "Blood oath it is." She just hoped her digestive juices were strong enough to kill whatever weird crap was in his blood that didn't jive with her system. She stood up and grabbed his sword and held it out to him.

He didn't understand. Of course not. He'd just flicked his skin open with his fingernail. She could already see that it had produced a jagged rip along his hand. Clearly, he'd done this before.

"Look, I'm not riddled with sword scars and callouses that are used to being ripped open. Just draw your man-blade and let me get a clean cut, okay?"

He nodded, though is lips twitched as he did it.

"Are you laughing at me?"

"Of course not," he said somberly. "I am merely pleased that you have ceased calling my sword an ass and progressed to a man. In truth, it is simply steel and stone as blessed as I can make it."

It took her some time to process his words. And when it finally translated in her brain, she also smiled, though she was sure there was a self-mocking twist to her lips. "Big-assed. Manly. Got it. I'm really going to have to work harder on learning your language. Wouldn't want to accidentally call someone a jackass when I really meant dirtbag."

There were other words that she'd wanted to use instead of jackass and dirtbag, but she really didn't want to freak out his heartspace. So instead, she gestured to him to draw his sword enough for her to cut up her hand.

With his help, she hurt herself. Not too deep, but not exactly shallow either. She had to stop herself from sucking on the wound herself. Odd how that was a natural reaction. Instead she offered her hand to his.

"I hope this quick-heal thing works."

He smiled and offered up his hand. "I bind myself to our bargain."

"Right. You get the princess, I get the portal stone. Deal." Then she frowned. "Er, I bind myself to it. Our bargain." She was going to fumble around for more words, but apparently he didn't think she needed more. He pressed his hands to her mouth while cupping hers in his other hand. And then together, they licked at each other's blood.

CHAPTER 7

Weight.
Duty.
Honor.
Responsibility.
Weight.
That's what she felt. It was a whole body experience, and it actually made her stumble. The words were concepts and threads intertwined, but the experience was capitol H heavy.

Her shoulders ached, her knees buckled, and her head bowed under the strain. But there was a strength there too. A pride that put power into her muscles, kept her from completely collapsing, and put a kind of joy in every breath.

She was equal to this weight. She was able to do all that was required...usually. Hopefully.

Then one last emotion hit her. It was a thin strand of melody that she heard when everything else was being crushed. An oboe of a sound, low and bittersweet. If she had a word for it, she'd choose *lonely*. But it was a quiet kind of loneliness, accepted because it didn't even acknowledge another possibility.

So perhaps the word *alone* was more appropriate, without judgment or longing. It was fact, and yet the melody made her heart ache.

And then it was gone.

It took a moment to return to the present. The feeling of

being crushed was so visceral that she was suffocating. Until it was gone. Until she was herself again, and she could take a deep breath and shake out her hands and feet. Jesus, they were tingling from blood loss.

"What the hell was that?" she gasped.

Then she looked at Keeven and did a doubletake.

He was kinked up. As in his head was down and shoved to one side, his knees were bent in weird angles, and his spine was contorted unnaturally. He looked like one of those mimes who gets trapped in a shrinking box, except he was a big guy and the box was much too small.

As she watched, he drew a deep, shuddering breath before dropping his hands forward onto his knees. His head rolled downward, and though he remained crouched, he quickly aligned his body while his breath went from shallow panic to slow and steady.

Janet lurched forward, terrified for him. He hadn't looked so ill since he'd been cemented in the birdnest.

"Keeven! Sit down. Just take a breath. Whoa..."

Her hands and feet were just coming back from numb, so she was clumsy as she gripped him. She wanted to pretend she was guiding him to the pallet, but it was more like they both collapsed down. She fell half sprawled on top of him, but he managed to catch her. It was awkward. She nearly beaned his chin with her forehead, but in a moment, they adjusted. A few breaths later, he was able to sit up straight and she could similarly balance herself enough to shake out her hands and feet some more.

"I don't think your blood agrees with me," she said, trying to lighten the mood.

"It is excellently compatible, as yours is for me. Did you not feel the power of the bind?"

"I felt crushed," she began, but then stopped herself. Once again, they were talking at cross purposes. "Tell me exactly what we just did. Last I knew we were licking each other's blood."

He nodded. "And if the compatibility is strong, then the magic reveals us to each other."

She took a breath. "One word at a time, big guy. Compatibility?"

"To have children."

Oh goody. They were back to that. "And that crushing feeling of...of being crushed?"

He frowned. "That is what you experienced of me?"

"It's what I felt. Wait, is that how you live? All the time? That's awful!"

He shook his head. "And you, twisted and shoved into tiny spaces where you cannot breathe? How is it that heaven is so small and ill-suited to you?"

She frowned. "I have no idea what you just said."

"That is what I experienced of you. Contorted into a misshapen spirit with only the tiniest space to live."

She stared at him, completely thrown. "What?"

Meanwhile, he was tilting his head and frowning at her. "You felt crushed? Perhaps you are correct. The magic was imperfect this time." She could tell by the way he said it that he didn't believe it, and yet he did not understand her feelings at all.

"So whenever you do the licking blood thing, the parties get a flashsense of the other?"

It took him a moment to understand her words, but in the end he nodded.

"And you've done this before?" she pressed.

"My mother the Queen has me blood bind to all our contracts. It is binding on the country and keeps her center mysterious."

In other words, Mama liked to keep her personality under wraps, but she had no problem exposing her son. "So what do people usually get from you?"

"Honor. Strength. That I will serve the country and the contract to the best of my ability."

She nodded. "Okay, I got that." She also got that the

weight of it was killing him, but she didn't say that aloud.

"And what of you, An—Janet? Why are you so twisted in your world?"

She reared back. "I'm not twisted!" Then when his eyes flew wide, she held up her hand. "I know you didn't mean twisted perverse." She huffed out a breath, not really wanting to think about what all this meant, but unable to stop herself from acknowledging a little bit of it. "I think I've been trying to twist this…" She gestured to the world at large. "Into my concept of reality. Of science and physics and a very non-magical world."

"But magic exists. You have experienced it many times now."

"Apparently so. And apparently it still doesn't fit well." Now there was an understatement. She took a deep breath. Her extremities had returned to their normal state. And now with the morning well advanced, she was wondering when she could get back to studying magic. "You should probably rest."

He shook his head. "No, I must repay the Freerik for their hospitality."

She tilted her head. "How? Like chopping wood or something? You're too weak."

The minute she said the word, she'd known it was a bad choice. "I am not weak!" he snapped, obviously insulted.

She held up her hands. "Of course not. But you have been sick."

"Just drained." He straightened his shoulders and twisted his head. His neck cracked loudly, but it was clearly a good thing because he was smiling. "But rest has restored my power, at least. I can repay them."

"I—" She shut her mouth. He was going to do whatever it was he intended to do. "Very well."

Then he smiled at her, obviously approving her uncharacteristic restraint. "Would you like to watch? I am instilling magic into their stones."

He had her at the word "magic," but she didn't want to confess that. So she shrugged and tried to appear casual. "Sure. Have at it, big guy."

He nodded, then pushed to his feet. "Then follow me."

Which is how she got a primer on recharging stones. It was actually very simple. Someone of royal blood—usually of the princess's line—laid a spell on the stone. Some stones were better suited to one spell or another, but in general, the stone was less important than the person shaping the purpose. They had stones for everything from starting a fire, to protecting them from the elements, to pretty ones that were kind of like fireworks or glowlights. There were the usual explosive ones, and ones like on the farmer's cart that blocked smell.

What Keeven did—and ones of his royal line—was charge the stones once they had a spell on top of it. Which, naturally, explained why he and the princess were now wed. A few pointed questions revealed that just about everything was about the child in this culture. His marriage to the princess was about giving birth to a kid—or a dozen kids— who could both lay on a spell and charge the rock. A combination power like that was rare among their kind. In fact, they hadn't seen a child like that in generations.

Which was all very fascinating to her. Now that she had someone who could explain things to her, she started asking question after question. It just didn't make scientific sense to her, these spells and the power that fueled them. But she wanted to know and so she pestered him all afternoon.

She would have happily done it for hours more. Probably years more, but they were attacked. Funny how suddenly being in fear for your life cuts off all curiosity in favor of violence.

It began quietly. The toddler had been playing in some reeds by the lake. Janet was sitting next to Keeven wishing for some basic physics instrumentation. He was recharging a fire stone—this world's equivalent of a Bic lighter—and she wanted to see exactly what was happening. Not with her eyes which detected nothing but how pretty his hair was in the sunshine and how his muscles had definition even when relaxed. But with an oscilloscope, to begin with. Five minutes of relaxed attention and she had a mental list as long as her arm of the various tests she'd like to perform on just that one rock. Which in no way diverted her attention from the way his chest lifted and lowered as he breathed.

And then the kid screamed.

She turned to look, seeing that the child had done an impressive leap into the center of the lake. She didn't worry too much about it. The child was a little like a spastic kitten, always poking into things and then squealing and jumping away. She didn't become worried until she saw a small gray thing skulking through the reeds.

She stood up, walking closer. It's not like she could help Keeven with what he was doing. Then she saw something out of her favorite computer game *Plants vs. Zombies*.

It was a little zombie complete with gray skin and bony legs. But it wasn't moving like a zombie. In fact, it was downright quick. If she hadn't been looking at the right time at the right spot, she probably would have missed it. And there was another. Maybe. Or something that looked like that with really sharp teeth.

She almost squealed "Protect your shins!" like in the game, but instead, she glanced back at Keeven who had finished his world. "Hey, do you have knee-high zombies in this world?"

He had the time to look up and frown. Obviously the word zombie didn't translate in his heartspace. But then she was overrun by the damned creatures.

Barely over a foot tall, three of the stupid things swarmed her. They were gray, had thin skin, but very sharp teeth and claws. And one of the bastards sunk his jaws into her leg. Thank God, she happened to be wearing her jeans or she'd have lost a piranha-sized hunk out of her leg.

She screamed and kicked, dislodging the one on her leg but rapidly getting attacked by two more. There wasn't time for terror. More of a stunned shock that she was living in a video game, plus a huge *ick* factor. She threw another off her, then watched as it bounced off a nearby tree only to hop back at her.

Fortunately, Keeven had faster reactions than she did. He went from cross-legged on the ground to roaring to the nearby farmers and fighting at her side in the time it took her to scream once. She was well into her third scream as he grabbed another zombie and squished it between his two hands.

Gross!

But at least it gave her time to throw off another, this time at the lake where she hoped it drowned. Sadly, three more had appeared from somewhere. Jesus, where the hell had they all come from?

She kicked and stomped and flailed, accomplishing very little against the zombie surge. Keeven was doing a little better, managing to kill a few by squishing them with his bare hands. *Ick.* The ones he tossed away were expertly thrown to land on the incoming gray zombie tide which she now saw originated from just beyond where the baby and done her squawk-hop thing.

There was one on Keeven's back, and she lurched forward, knocking it aside. Then she rapidly recalled every TV fight scene she could and managed a stroke of insight. They needed to protect each other's backs.

She quickly maneuvered herself so they were ass to ass. She saw him nod in approval before he set to catching another two zombies—one in each hand. She grabbed another pair coming at her, but her hands weren't large or strong enough to do his manly squish thing. Her weapon of choice was her kick boxing. Who'd ever thought those hours of Wii Fit would come in so handy?

Then it was kick, punch, gasp, gag in rapid order over and over. The last two were because those things smelled horrible, and even worse when squished into oblivion. They had to stop the things at the source, but she barely had time to think it as she fought nonstop.

Fortunately, there was help coming. She'd heard the farmer's croaking bellow and knew that his kids had responded. But they'd been on the opposite side of the lake. Even hopping at full speed, it would take too long for them to get here.

Keeven must have squished a plump one because suddenly noxious fumes had her doubling over. She dropped down onto her knee—flattening two of the damn things in the process—when she had enough space to look around her. Oh shit. There were like a hundred more of those things running at her.

"Find! Control!" Keeven bellowed.

Why, yes, my zen state is in my fanny pack, she thought back at him. She hadn't the breath to speak. But then he repeated it, this time more clearly.

"Controller! Find. Him."

The controller! As in some evil bastard with the zombie remote control? She shoved aside a few more of the creatures to look around her. Fortunately for her, the grey critters had determined Keeven was the bigger threat. So they were scrambling past her to get to him. This was not so good for Keeven, but it allowed her a moment to look for the bad guy in charge.

"There!" A big guy with a sack. As in a towering ogre with a rucksack the size of New Hampshire. And while she was pointing, another demon zombie hopped right out of the top of the sack.

They had to close that sack. She pushed to her feet, kicking the nearest little shit at the lake. She wanted to tell Keeven where the big ogre was. She'd pointed, but hadn't the breath to say more than her first exclamation.

But it didn't matter, she realized with dismay. Keeven was buried. As in covered in those damn critters. She was just shoving to her feet when she saw the farmer and his sons. They were coming full tilt, brandishing hoes and rakes and shovels. Whatever they could carry, and thankfully they were closer than she'd feared. Another fifteen or so seconds and the nearest one would be there to help Keeven. But the ogre and his rucksack of doom were in the opposite direction.

Damn.

Double, triple venti damn.

She was the only one who could reasonably start the attack on the evil ogre.

Best not to think about it, so she didn't. She just took off, remembering belatedly that all she had on her was her toolbelt. Maybe there was something in there she could use.

Her hands were slick. She told herself it was with sweat, not blood or zombie guts. And the first thing she grabbed was the box-cutter. Okay. Not going to help her *close* the sack. But as she was running forward, soccer kicking whatever was in her way, she noticed something else.

The ogre wore a choker. Not a pretty gold chain kind of necklace, but a dog collar with dark stones in it. Not something she'd usually notice, except the damn stones were glowing black. That had to be important. If only she knew the rules.

But there was no more time. She had to attack now.

It was a good thing she didn't have time to think about her next action. She performed it exactly as she'd done over a decade ago with her uncle. It had been her favorite game. Uncle Joey would lumber around pretending to be a big oaf, and she would jump on his back. She'd bang him on the head with her Nerf hammer, and he'd pretend to die but only after much roaring and bellowing. It usually ended in a tickling match on the floor and much fun was had by all.

They'd played it so often that she had the approach down perfect. Especially since it was exactly the same way she leaped off the diving board at the local pool. Step, step, step, *leap*.

Landed!

It wasn't exactly safely or even with any pretense to style, but she managed to catapult herself onto the thing's side. She grabbed onto its massive pack and wedged her knees and feet into whatever holds she could manage.

Ugh! Talk about stench. Her eyes were watering from the grossness of it all. Only on this guy it was more triple strength men's locker room than rotting meat which, all in all, was an improvement.

The thing bellowed and waved his arms around, but she was perched on its back and hauling on his hair. He wasn't able to reach her with his one fist, and the other was trapped around the opening to the rucksack.

Great! That gave her time to act. Well, not a lot of time as he started using the rucksack to bang at her. The heavy canvas landed with a thud against her leg, and she felt at least two little zombie critters go crunch on the inside.

Good. Let them die.

Meanwhile she did the only thing she could think of. She used the box-cutter blade to slice at his neck. The problem was that the blade wasn't all that long, his hide was tough as leather, and the damn dog collar kept stopping her. She wanted to reach around and get at his throat, but she couldn't grab hold. All she could do was tuck her fingers into the collar and swipe as best she could.

Until the damn blade broke.

Shit.

The ogre swung around, and she temporarily lost her footing. She probably would have fallen off, but she'd wedged her fingers in hard. Her fingers might be permanently mangled, but if she stopped the damned zombies, she'd count it worth the cost.

Then she scrambled back on. Or maybe she fell back onto the pack. Either way, she found another foothold, levered herself up, and pushed the box-cutter blade up another two notches. Thank God there was still more blade.

She started hacking away again. This time when the ogre bellowed, she felt the rumble of his throat like a super-powered vibrator against her arm.

Weird.

She had to get through the collar. Then she could really hurt the thing's neck. She made some progress, and the leather was starting to split. It helped, she supposed, that she'd gotten some of the creature's neck so bright red blood was soaking into the leather making it softer.

Ew, but she'd take it.

Which is when she realized the ogre wasn't fighting anymore.

She was still perched on its back sawing away, but the thing wasn't moving. It had dropped the rucksack, and was…

Aieeee!

Something ripped through her with the force of a lightning bolt. Something tight and electric that traveled up her fingers from the dog collar, straight through her bones, to zap every nerve in her body. She seized up, every muscle contracting in agony.

She fell off the backpack mid-arch. She hadn't even the breath to scream. She didn't feel when or where she landed, and it took a few more moments before she could even see. But when she could at least breathe through the pain and open her eyes, she realized she had an up close and personal view of the rucksack as it kept disgorging zombies.

Oh goody.

Time to get up. Get up and move. Come on body… It didn't matter how much she admonished her muscles, nothing was working. Her entire body was still arched tight as the electrical current seemed to zip and zing through her cells. All she could do was grit her teeth against the scream and watch in dread as the ogre put his massive hands to his collar. Two hands, bulging muscles, and a face that had red eyes and ugly, brown teeth.

He hauled on his collar.

The white hot pain was starting to fade, thank God. She could breathe without fearing she'd pass out, at least. And her eyes had stopped watering enough for her to see the ogre as he suddenly arched in his own pain.

Wait a moment. She knew that sudden agony. She'd just experienced it herself. And even if she wondered, the ogre spun around enough for her to see white hot bolts of electricity arching from the dog collar into his body. Bright enough that she could see the searing burns where the lightning detonated.

And it happened again.

And again.

That was one hell of a booby trap on the collar, and the ogre was doing it to himself.

Two more bolts flashed, one directly after the other. The impact was white, but the blood and muscles underneath definitely red. And the ogre's screams were the kind of nails-on-blackboard agony that had her every cell clenching in terror.

Until the collar ripped.

It was almost anti-climatic the way the thing popped off and was flung into the lake. There was no boom or burst of color. No sound beyond her own gasping breath and the ogre's rumbling growl as he collapsed onto his knees.

But he didn't leap up to attack her—which was good considering she was still lying flat on the ground. And more important—no more evil critters popped out of the sack.

She started to sit up. Her arms were weak and her bones burned, but she needed to defend herself from...

What the hell?

The ogre was back up, faster than she expected. Shit, the creature was hardy. He grabbed the sack and started running into the lake.

Escape?

She ought to follow it. She ought to stop it from whatever its next evil plan was, but she could barely stand much less attack. And she'd lost the damned box-cutter somewhere.

She glanced at Keeven and her heart lurched. All she saw was the farmer and his family practically buried beneath the zombies. Oh shit. Oh shitshitshitshit.

And then something weird happened.

The zombies started lurching. They'd never walked like zombies before, but now had bursts of speed only to stutter for a moment before bursting into speed again. And while she was still processing that, they stopped altogether.

They just stopped.

They didn't attack, didn't run forward or away. They just stopped. And that pause gave Keeven and the farmers time to flatten them.

She swallowed, her gaze hopping back to the ogre. It was standing hip deep in the lake, bent over as if he were holding something down. The rucksack? Was he drowning the things?

She shoved to her knees, not really sure what she intended. Good thing, because she was weaker than a wet noodle. At least she was awake, right?

She had no idea what the ogre was doing, but at least she knew the damned gray land piranhas were quiet. They may be dormant now, but she'd be damned if she let the things wake up.

So while she kept a wary eye on the ogre, she started kicking the gray critters into the lake. On closer inspection, they did appear to be breathing, so if she tossed them underwater, they'd probably drown, right?

Apparently the others thought so too because they were chucking the little shits in as fast as their bleeding arms could toss them.

Which is when the toddler started making noises again.

The kid had been the first one to alert her with its screeching leap into the lake. Now the toddler sat half in the water, one arm pointing to the ogre, the other pointing at the lake, while the munchkin kept screeching high, terrified words that Janet had no prayer of comprehending.

"What?" Janet managed to gasp. "What is she…saying?"

The Freerik were gasping for breath too and reeling from

the exertion of squishing all the zombies. It was Keeven, bleeding from a zillion cuts, who grimly started forward.

It took a few moments for Janet to figure out what he intended. She felt sick from the amount of blood that covered him everywhere. Sure a lot of it was zombie guts, but a lot was his.

Oh shit. Oh hell. He was going to take on the ogre. She could tell by the grim set to his shoulders, by the dark expression in his eyes, and the clenched ferocity in his jaw. He was both determined and pissed. A lethal combination, but shit, he was wounded by a thousand zombie bites.

"Keeven, you can't."

The man barely looked at her. It was a quick, thorough glance.

"I'm fine," she said, answering his unspoken question.

He grunted something that could have been, "Okay. Good." It could also have been, shut up woman while I kill me an ogre.

"At least get your sword!" She said the words, but they both knew the truth. His sword was back under their tree like two hundred yards away. No way would he let the ogre do whatever it was doing for that long.

"Keeven—"

And then they were out of time. The ogre straightened up with his own grunt. And the two faced off.

Shit.

CHAPTER 8

Keeven planted his feet and tried to center himself in his world and his power. It was difficult, and he felt himself weave on the marshy ground. It was the poison, he knew. Though each bite of the Aruckien had only a little poison in it, the cumulative effect was powerful.

But he could not leave Janet or the Freerik family alone to face the gool. He only prayed he could wound the thing enough for them to escape. The huge creature was strong and brutish, but usually not very intelligent. If Keeven could stay on his feet, he could prevail.

"No, Keeven," his angel called from the side. "You're bleeding from like a thousand bites."

"Get my sword," he said by way of answer. "Then help the others. They must drink plenty of water to flush out the poison."

"Poison?" she squeaked. He loved it when she tried to cut off her words and it came out more as a squawk. Especially since her next words were always layered with dark humor. "Of course there's poison. What would a zombie hoard be without poison?"

He grinned even as he took a step forward. The gool was huge and his steady regard showed him to be more intelligent than usual. But in water, the creature's greater size would not be as much of an asset. That gave Keeven a chance.

"Just wait a sec. I'm getting your sword," Janet said. From his peripheral vision, he saw her rush unsteadily toward their sleeping area. She was bitten in a dozen places, but not enough to kill her. Assuming, of course, that her angelic nature did not make her more susceptible.

He couldn't think about that now. What he had to do was in front of him: a huge ugly gool bent over as if drowning something. But what? It couldn't be the child, could it?

He quickly scanned the area, seeing the youngling held securely in her mother's arms. The Freerik family was recovering. Binding wounds, drinking water. None dead that he could see, but it was early yet. At least three of the sons would not survive the bites unless he found a solution quickly.

Which brought him back to the biggest threat as the gool slowly straightened up. The thing lifted the rucksack with him, holding it aloft with a furious bellow and shaking it in the air. By the Goddess, what was it doing? Then to his shock, the creature tore the magical sack to pieces and threw the torn threads in different directions.

The thing had just destroyed its only safety. It was through that sack that all his magic came. It was now defenseless. Or as defenseless as a gargantuan creature could be.

The gool took a step forward, and Keeven tensed. He could not let it get on land. Meanwhile, Janet made it back to his side. She was weaving on her feet, and her skin looked flushed with fever. Damn, he needed to get her some healing magic to counteract the poison soon.

She held out his sword and he took it easily, cursing when he realized how heavy it felt in his hands. He was weak. Too damned weak.

"Get back," he said Janet. "No," he corrected himself. "Run. As far as you can. I will not be able to defeat him." The words were bitter on his tongue, but he knew it was the truth. The poison was doing the job for the gool. He had to act now while he still could. Gritting his teeth, he lifted his sword though everything in him strained to do it.

The gool stopped. He stood there, his head cocked to one side. Then he lifted his chin and pointed to his neck.

"What's he doing?" Janet asked.

"I don't know."

"That's where his collar was. I...I cut off his collar. The thing with the black stones."

Keeven cursed under his breath. "That was his controlling collar. With it gone, the creature will run mad." Without direction, gools simply attacked without thought or reason. Except this one wasn't attacking.

"So it's on our side now?" Janet asked, hope clear in her voice.

"It's a beast."

"It doesn't look like a beast. I mean, sure it's ugly and all. But..." It was taking off its backpack now, slipping it from his shoulders with slow, efficient movements. "Um, what's in the backpack?" He glanced at her, but she was already answering her own question. "If we're lucky, it's a cheeseburger and a milkshake." He glanced at her in confusion in time to see her shrug. "A girl can dream, right? I'm starving. And frankly, he doesn't look so good."

Keeven narrowed his eyes. Was there a gray cast to the creature's skin? More so than usual? And was it...shrinking? He took a step forward to see more clearly while the gool started to open his pack. But then it stopped and held the bag aloft as if offering it to them.

And then Keeven went down. He didn't know if it was a magical attack or the poison was too thick in his blood. Whatever the cause, his knees buckled and he was soon crouching in the water. "Run," he rasped as his sword hit the water.

"Keeven!" his angel screamed, hauling him backwards onto land. It was wet ground, marshy and cold, but at least he wouldn't drown.

"Run," he repeated, his eyes on the gool. It was rushing forward, weaving and bobbing in the lake as if it were drunk.

But it knew a vulnerability and was coming straight for them.

Keeven tried to muster his strength. He managed to raise his sword a little, but he could not sustain it. His head spun and then his mind grappled with the shifting landscape. The world titled on its side, and he slowly realized he'd fallen sideways.

He'd failed. Even with the aid of an angel, he had failed.

Darkness claimed him.

"Oh bloody hell!" Janet had once read that curse in a historical romance, and it rapidly became her most powerful expletive word of choice. "Bloody, fracking, shitstorm hell!" Which, while satisfying, did nothing to help the current situation: Keeven unconscious on the grass and the big ugly whatchamacallit tromping straight for them.

She tried to drag Keeven back, but rapidly gave that up. He was just too damned big. She'd managed to get him out of the water, but that was about it. That meant she had to defend him from Gargantuan. So she tried to pick up Keeven's sword. She already knew she was too wussy to wield it—the thing weighed a ton—but at least she could keep the big thing from grabbing it.

Speaking of which, the big thing was looking decidedly less big. Ugly, to be sure, but he didn't seem like something she could possibly have leaped up onto not fifteen minutes ago. As for its neck, she hadn't been able to wrap her arm around it before, but it looked like she could get a good grip now. At least with her forearm. Which meant it really was shrinking.

It splashed forward, its steps none too steady. That gave her hope. Not only was the thing getting less intimidating by the second, but it was clearly sinking fast health-wise. Good. She hoped it drowned before it got to them.

No such luck. While she was still hovering anxiously over Keeven and looking for a weapon she could wield, it closed the distance between them and collapsed onto its knees near them. No attack, though she screamed at it as if she was a demented bird. She also ran full force at it, pummeling it for all she was worth. The thing didn't offer any resistance beyond a high pitched keen.

She slowed her attack, feeling rather stupid. After all, she'd done nothing to damage it as far as she could tell, and it wasn't offering up any resistance. Sort of like she'd just been kicking an ugly puppy.

She paused, staring down at it. Then it slowly lifted up his backpack to her. She stared at it. What the hell was she supposed to do now? Then it reached in and pulled out...

"Oh shit."

Vials. A roll of neatly packaged vials of some liquid. He pulled out one—not so easy given that his coordination was clearly off—and he offered it to her. And when she just stared at it, he popped the top and mimed drinking it. When she still didn't drink it, he grimaced at her. Yes, it was a real grimace and it looked especially ugly—before he downed the contents of the vial.

She waited anxiously, watching the effects. Oh double shit. He groaned loudly then keeled over, convulsing on the grass. Oddly enough, he seemed as surprised as she did, his eyes pulling wide and his mouth slipping open. Or maybe it was the convulsion. Hard to tell.

She looked at Keeven. He was out but still breathing, thank God. She looked to the farmer and his family, but they were busy binding each other's wounds and looking fearfully over at her. Great. Plus her legs and back burned from the damned zombie bites, her head throbbed as if with fever, and she really felt completely unequal to the task of anything. Certainly not...

The creature's back healed.

There was no other word for it. She wouldn't even have seen it if his convulsion hadn't flipped him onto his face. But he was more or less face down with his burned back facing upward to the sky. And while she watched, the skin seemed to raise up, the dark color soften, and...and new skin grew where there had been open wound before.

Okay. Magical healing. Great.

Which—if true—was exactly what Keeven needed right then. Unless the vial only worked on Gargantuan. And that assumed there was more.

She grabbed the roll of protected vials. A quick perusal showed that there were different types. Naturally. Couldn't all be healing potions, could they. Some might be acid for softening walls, some might be TNT. Who knew?

She did a quick comparison between vials, and grabbed one that looked like what big and ugly had drank. And then came decision time. The monster was effectively neutralized, but who knew how long that would last. Keeven might right now be dying or he might recover just fine if she didn't muck with him. There were too many questions, too many unknown variables. And only her to decide.

She took one last desperate glance at the farmer's family. Maybe they knew, but the stark fear on their faces told her that they were as clueless and terrified as she. And even if she could hand the decision to them, she had no way to understand the answer. She didn't speak enough of their language. Which meant...

"Bloody, fracking, goat-shit..." she continued to mutter curses while she did what she was going to do. After all, inaction was as much a decision as action. Might as well kill her only protector while trying to save his life than just sit there like a dumb potato. So she unstoppered the vial and poured what she could into his mouth. It wasn't easy. He was lying sideways and she had to turn his head. But then again, she'd been spoon feeding him soup for the last few days so she knew how to get most of it in.

She stroked his throat and was pleased when he swallowed. Then she poured a little more and waited. And waited.

His breath eased. She hadn't even realized he was wheezing until the sound was gone. Until his chest lifted and lowered with deeper, more healthy breaths. Okay. Magic healing it was.

She almost upended the rest of the vial in his mouth when she remembered that there were at least four more badly bitten frog-people to her right. Looking up, she called to them, lifting the vial up. The pre-pubescent boy hurried forward. He was limping slightly, a dark angry bite or three on his leg, but otherwise he seemed unhurt.

She handed him the vial and motioned that he should get his injured brothers to drink. Then she looked down at the roll of vials to see if there were more. No need. The boy exclaimed loudly, snatched up the other two vials and rushed back.

Now she felt really stupid. Instead of angsting over what to do, all she'd needed was to call one of the others over. Clearly they knew what a healing potion looked like. But now what? Keeven was doing better, but still very unconscious as was the big baddy. Turning to watch the others as they finished off the last of the potions, she saw an identical resignation on all their faces. Every one of them—including the toddler—had taken a wound of some kind. The men had the worst of it, it seemed, and all of them were stretched out unconscious. The women—including her—were weaving on their feet, and at least one of them sported bright spots of color in her cheeks that Janet guessed meant a fever. Much like her own hot, sweaty face. Chills would start next, and right on cue, a shudder racked her body.

But she couldn't give in to it. The men needed watching over. A steady drip of water into their mouths if they could take it, and someone had to make sure Gargantuan didn't rouse and kill them all. That meant her.

After all, she sincerely doubted any of this would have happened without her and Keeven descending on this little family grouping. If any of the family died because of them, Janet would never forgive herself. So as much as she wanted to just crawl away and hurl before passing out, she had to sit there and take watch. She'd be sentry over both Keeven and the big baddy.

Which is what she did. While shudders wracked her body,

she sat near the sword and tried to look fierce. The others did something similar, though the women did it while singing. Well, it was really more of a musical croak that she now thought was a kind of prayer. It haunted her fevered vigil, and in the end, she found it rather soothing.

And in such a way, they passed the rest of the day and into the night.

Which is when she must have fallen asleep.

She woke in their usual bed, but Keeven was no where to be seen. She groaned as she moved, her entire body one big ache, but at the sound the youngest boy abruptly popped up from a place near the ground.

"*Arieeeg,*" Janet said, proving that her normal verbal eloquence was at her usual sub-par. Fortunately, she didn't need real language. The kid hopped out of their little area under the tree and a few minutes later, Keeven appeared looking tired but much healthier than she felt. Nevertheless, she scanned him from head to toe, noting the lines of fatigue about his eyes as well as the pink healthy skin showing on his legs and arms.

"How are you feeling?" they both said at once.

She smiled, her headache seeming to ease with the gesture. "Better. I guess I fell asleep on watch." Then she gestured to their bedroom. "And I'm guessing you're the one who carried me here."

"I woke just before dawn, feeling stiff but much improved. Your fever was still hot, but not dangerously so." He cupped her face, his thumb doing a slow caress across her cheek. Lust slammed into her, but not so much that she couldn't close her eyes and just appreciate the sweetness of his touch. "The fever is gone," he said, relief in his tone. "But you should still drink a great deal of water before we leave."

"Yeah, I'm pretty thirsty," she said. And then her eyes popped open. "We're leaving?"

He nodded, his expression grim. "As soon as you are able to travel." Then he released her, the warmth of his fingers fading too quickly from her skin. A moment later he was offering her a bowl of water. It was, in fact, the same bowl she had used for his sponge baths.

She looked at him. "You want me to drink this?" The water was clear, but still...sponge baths.

"It is clean and you must drink all of this."

Right. She took the bowl and started to sip. But once on her lips, a roaring thirst claimed her. She gulped it down and was stunned that a few moments later, the entire bowl was empty. She set it down, a little bewildered, then focused back on the situation at hand.

"How is everybody?"

"They are all well, thanks to your quick thinking."

"Um...what quick thinking?"

"You gave them the potions."

She laughed. "Actually that was the kid. He knew exactly what to do."

"He said you told him to."

"Um...not really." And wasn't that terrifying? That both of them thought the other had a clue. *Eek.* "What about Gargantuan?"

At that, Keeven's expression turned serious. "What did you do to him?"

"Me? Nothing. He just drank the potion, started screaming, and then collapsed." She looked outside their tiny area, but couldn't see anything beyond the lake and a steadily growing pile of zombie bodies. The women were using big rakes and the like to drag the critters out of the water and pile them up, probably to burn. *Ew.* "I don't see him."

"When I woke, he was sitting beside us. Awake. Calm. Almost rational."

She blinked. "He spoke?"

"He acknowledged my orders and did as he was bid."

Really? "So...not violent?"

"Not violent. And his appearance has changed."

She pushed to her feet, barely wincing at the pull in her knees and ass. One thing was true, all this fighting for her life should give her buns of steel. "Where?"

He led her out and to the left. In the opposite direction of the family gathering place. There sat a large man. Like a really large man, well over six feet with a Neanderthal forehead and thick blonde hair. Not thick as in dense, thick as in really big hairs. His expression was bland, and his eyes were alert as she and Keevan approached. He was guarded by the eldest son, but he did no more than sit quietly inside a square pen of glowing blue rocks.

"Is that a cage?"

"He had the rocks in his pack. It keeps him in place." To demonstrate, Keeven put his hand up to the edge of an invisible wall. There were no sparks or anything, just a simple inability to push through. A moment later, Janet did the same thing, startled to note that the force field—or whatever it was—felt cool to her skin. In fact, if she pressed much longer or harder on it, she got the distinct idea that her hand would go numb.

So blue rocks = force field and blue rocks in a square = cage.

"That's amazing."

"It is," he said, but his gaze was on the man sitting so meditatively in the center of the force field. Though his eyes were open, he neither moved nor spoke. He just watched them.

"Have you fed him?" she asked.

"What does he eat?" Keeven countered.

He was asking her? A cow? Small dogs? "I have no idea. You know more about this than I do."

"Never has a gool become docile before. This is unprecedented." Then he looked at her as if she were the reason.

"Really, Keeven. I've got no clue."

"Really, Janet, you are the cause of much change in my world."

The use of her given name stopped her in her tracks. He'd

sworn he would never use her name until she'd accepted her situation. Well, duh. She was in Freaky World and everything she did had real consequences. Which meant no way was she offering advice because she had no idea what was going on. In the end, she just held up her hands in defeat. "What are you going to do with him?"

He arched his brows at her. "Normally, I would have killed him by now." At those words, the man's gaze flicked upward in alarm, but that was it. No other reaction beyond a quick dart of his gaze. Janet, on the other hand, struggled with such a cold-blooded reaction. She had a problem with capital punishment for the worst of the world's criminals. She could hardly sanction killing a man just because he was forced to carry a bag of zombies.

"Once that control collar thing was off of him, he's been nothing but helpful." That was perhaps a stretch, but it was all she had.

Meanwhile, Keeven breathed a heavy sigh. "When I woke, you were asleep and he was watching us."

"But he didn't attack, right? Because he's not being controlled by evil zombie guy." She frowned and looked around. "Shouldn't we be looking for evil zombie guy?"

He huffed out a breath and stared at her. Not angrily. More like very male frustration. "I know who the evil Magician is. What is a zombie?"

"Undead. Person who is dead then reanimated…never mind. Just call him Darth Vader."

Keeven stared at her, his brows furrowed in that expression he had when he was trying—and failing—to sort through her words.

"Okay, let's stick with Evil Magician. He's the one who sent Gargantuan, right? The one who nabbed your wife?"

He flinched. A horrible part of her liked seeing the way he winced every time she reminded him he was married. Or perhaps it was herself she was reminding. Either way, he nodded his head. "I believe so. The Magician's demonic force holds the Princess prisoner in the castle to the south. I believe he sent the Aruckien—the little things that bite—to aid that attack. Or perhaps distract us from rescuing her. Somehow, they have breached The Wall."

Cue drumbeats of doom. Clearly from the way he said this, he'd just told her something terrifying. But she had no reference points in this world. "Another brick in the wall, huh?" she said, quoting Pink Floyd.

He frowned at her. "Another chink in the Wall."

She burst out laughing. She knew it wasn't appropriate. She also knew that his actual word hadn't been in English, so he had no idea what he'd just said to her. But she couldn't stop herself. This was so bizarre. She felt like she'd been dropped into a bad fantasy movie and she was expected to take it seriously.

Not surprisingly, Keeven just stared at her, but before he could speak, she held up her hand. "Don't yell at me. I haven't a clue what your Wall is, brick or chink or otherwise. Keeven, I've got no clue what you're talking about except that you seem to think I know what to do with your prisoner. And I say again, I have no idea."

He huffed. "I must go to the Wall to repair the breach," he said, his words clear and crisp in the morning air. "He cannot stay here, trapped in a blue prison. I cannot set him free, it is too big a risk. And we cannot take him with us where he could cause terrible damage. And so I ask you, *Angel*, what do we do with him?"

She wanted to gape at him. She wanted to rage and kick and scream. She wasn't an angel, and she had no idea what to do with the guy. But she was here in this world, somehow she'd been labeled as a person with divine knowledge, and…and as much as she wanted to throw up her hands and refuse to answer, a man's life was at stake. She couldn't just abandon him or the responsibility Mr. Married Prince had given her.

"Ask him," she finally said.

"He does not speak."

"But he understands, right? He responded to your

commands?"

Keeven nodded slowly.

"So ask him what he wants to do."

Keeven gave her a look that screamed you-have-no-understanding-of-anything. She shot him an identical one back. And then with the air of a man humoring a lunatic, he spoke to the prisoner. "What do you want us to do with you?"

The gool opened his mouth, but no sound came out beyond a grunt. Then with a look of frustration, he put his hand to the grass and spelled out a word. It wasn't dirt, so Janet couldn't see the lines forming. And it certainly wasn't in English, so she had to look to Keeven for a translation. His face grew tighter and more grim with every stroke of the gool's finger.

"What is he saying?"

"I don't know."

"Liar."

He shot her a glare, but even knowing she'd just massively insulted the man, she didn't give in. He knew something.

"I don't know *exactly*," he ground out. "He wrote a word."

"I got that."

"In my language it means *revenge.*"

"In your language?"

"Or in his—the words of the Gezan—it could mean something else."

"Jeez, it's like pulling teeth with you. Something else what?"

Keeven folded his arms over his chest, his muscles bulging and his attitude dire. "Atone."

She frowned. An anthropologist would have a field day with the idea that two people had the same word for *revenge* and *atone*. But she wasn't so academically gifted as to understand exactly what that suggested about the two cultures. "So ask him," she pressed. "Which one does he mean?"

"Do you honestly believe he will tell the truth?"

"I honestly think that the more data we have, the better." It was a lie. She knew that his answer would be inconclusive without hard evidence. But it was the answer that all academics gave when they had no idea how to proceed. But in this she was surprised. The gool's answer was clear as day.

Keeven had barely posed the question, when the gool stood up. He pointed to the farmer, to the men still recovering by the water and the women painstakingly pulling the bodies of zombies out of their lake. And then he cried out. The sound was not just mournful, it was an agony of apology and pain. It was so heartfelt that tears sprang to her eyes and if she could, she would have turned off the stones immediately and given the thing a hug. And yet, when she looked at Keeven, his expression got even more grim.

"What?" she asked. "Can't you hear that he meant atone? He's in pain."

"Or he pretends to be," Keeven said flatly.

Well, there was no fighting a biased mind, was there? The prince—and the farmer too when she looked at him—were both grim-faced and determined to believe the worst. She rounded on Keeven, but he held up his hand.

"The Gezan are clever and their use of the gools is devious. He is not a typical beast, and so—"

"You mistrust him."

"We have learned to be cautious."

Cue: dire mood music again. Okay, so Keeven's mind was made up, but maybe she could convince Farmer Frog. She turned to the green-skinned man who so far had been nothing but a gracious and generous host. "Ask him," she said to Keeven. "Ask him if he will take charge of the gool. If he will let a victimized man atone for his crimes to this family in whatever way—"

"He will not," Keeven interrupted.

"You don't know that!" Janet huffed. "Just ask him."

So Keeven sighed and said the words in just the way she

had. Perhaps he could have been more earnest in selling the request, but generally speaking, Keeven did what she wanted. He posed the question to the farmer. He didn't even get halfway through before the man was shaking his head. His answer was curt and furious. He didn't even need to brandish his heavy ancient sword for emphasis.

Keeven turned to her. "He lists the damage done to his waters and his family—"

"I got it," she interrupted. "He said no." She looked to the gool who dipped his chin as if he expected such a thing and accepted it. That was even more heartbreaking than his agonizing cry from before. "That means we'll just have to take him with us."

"No."

She folded her arms. "I don't know what to tell you, *Prince*. You asked my angelic opinion, and I've given it to you. If you want to ignore me, then that's up to you. But I'm not changing my mind. He deserves a chance to prove himself."

"And who will pay the price if you are wrong? If he kills my people, damages our defenses, destroys—"

"And if he helps defend your Wall and gives aid to your people or rebuilds what was torn down?"

Keeven squared off with her. "It is too big a risk."

"Then make your decision. But don't look to me to support it."

He huffed. "You have no magic to help him? To restore what was lost to him? Or ensure his honesty?"

Was that what he'd been looking for? A divine truth serum? Godly compulsion? "Damn it, Keeven, I'm not an angel. I'm not a god. I don't have what you're looking for." She sighed. "I think I've told you that more than once."

She had, and she saw the acceptance of that settle on his shoulders. His face flattened out, his eyes looked from the gool to the women who were tediously gathering bodies out of the water. And then he made his decision.

"You will clean," he said to the gool.

The farmer voiced his objection in a low, menacing croak, but Janet could see that Keeven would not be overruled. Then the prince—because that's how he was acting just then—turned to her.

"You will guard him."

She swallowed. "I, uh, doubt that I'll be much of a deterrent..." She saw Keeven's eyes narrow, so she held up her hands to stop him. He wasn't killing the poor gool, so that was something. "I'll watch. I'll raise an alarm if he does anything hinky. I promise."

"You swear," he corrected.

"Uh, yeah. I swear."

He nodded, then started to stride away. The farmer, of course, gripped his rusty sword unearthed from God-only-knew-where and glared at her and the gool equally.

"Um, Keevan?"

"I have to make preparations. The transport will be here in a few hours."

Transport? Preparations? Not that she objected to any of that, but currently she was thinking words like "breakfast" and "transport to where?" Instead, she gestured to the stones. "How do I turn off the cage?"

He didn't even stop walking. He just waved his hand and the four blue glowing stones stopped glowing. Just like that, they turned off. The farmer released a grunt and lifted his sword. Janet—to her utter embarrassment—squeaked in alarm and jumped sideways away from the gool. And the prisoner? He just sat there. Then a few breaths later, he slowly, carefully, rose to his feet.

"Right," she said as she tried to control her rapidly thumping heart. "Now what?" She spoke to herself more than anyone else, but then the gool answered for her. He slowly raised his hand and pointed to the lake.

So that's what Keeven had meant by cleaning. She nodded and stepped back, gesturing to the lumbering creature to have at it. Likewise the farmer took a step back and after a sharp word to the women in the lake, he jerked his head at the gool.

The thing nodded and then walked forward with as much dignity as an XXXXXXL man-beast could. And he began lifting zombie bodies out of the water before throwing them into the extremely large and stinky pile.

And the whole time, Janet kept wondering, what next? What bizarre thing was going to happen to her next? She'd had the psychotic birds, the zombie attack, and the offer to spawn demi-angels. Was it time for the earth to erupt? How about acid rain? Or could she go really old school and anticipate a plague of locusts? But without a crystal ball, all she could do was wait and see.

CHAPTER 9

Keeven stomped away, showing his irritation along with—he hoped—a convincing amount of distraction. If the gool was to turn on them, he wanted the creature to do it now. And his plan was to give the creature every opportunity to strike while he pretended he was too busy to save anyone.

He had a weapon now. A rod he'd charged the second he'd seen it in the farmer's ancient cache of weapons. It shot tiny bullets of fire a very long distance, and it would pierce the gool's hide from well across the lake.

But nothing untoward happened. Though Keeven took pains to appear occupied and at a too far distance away, the gool did nothing more than angrily, vengefully, stack Aruckien bodies. And while Keeven waited in pretended nonchalance, he noticed something else: the creature was arranging the Aruckien bodies in such a way that they would burn most effectively.

He doubted that anyone else noticed, but Keeven had been attacked by the heinous creatures before. It was how the kingdom lost his brother and father. So he knew that the bodies burned best when arrayed in a rough spiral, one blighted creature setting fire to the next in an ever expanding wall of flame as set by a firestone in the center with more on the outside to burn inward.

This creature knew, and he set about creating the pyre with gleeful determination. As if what Angel Janet said were true:

the gool was a victim, bastardized by magic and set to a villainous task by his collar.

Maybe.

But he could not trust that she saw clearly. The angel was too innocent of the evils of this world to know the truth. And so it was set to him to watch and worry. Could the creature be turned to good use or was it a ruse set to blind them to a terrible danger?

Which brought him to the angel and the thought that she too might be an enemy. He did not want his thoughts to go there. He did not want to wonder why she appeared to him so easily after his prayers. But the Gezan were masters of witchcraft unfathomable to his people. What if the Magician sent her to him to bewitch him and undermine his rescue of the princess? What if she was sent to take him from his bride and the fathering of many children? What if everything she was…was a lie?

Angels were supposed to bring clarity, not questions. Janet brought endless questions wrapped in a body that made him thick with lust, thereby clouding his thoughts of anything but her.

If he were to think her evil.

He was never more grateful when the lieutenant circled the craft and landed. But the damned idiot planted the transport between him and Janet. Certainly the man had thought to separate the gool from the rest of the Freerik family, but he clearly missed that Janet was now blocked in with the gool. And Keeven had no line of sight with which to shoot his weapon.

Keeven roared at the idiot and took off running. It was no small thing to pass around a ship that carried food for a brigade, and with every second that passed as he ran, he thought of all the thousands of things the gool could do to Janet while he was too far away. Images spooled through his mind, each one more grisly than the last until he rounded the corner and saw…

Nothing. The gool continued his work, watched closely by

the Freerik father and Janet. Janet who stared open-mouthed at the transport while panic edged her features.

Damned stinking hell, not again.

He made it to her side in another thirty steps. He was breathless. He still had not fully recovered from yesterday's attack, and yet his sword was gripped tightly as he caught her arm.

"What is amiss?"

She swallowed, her eyes swiveling to him and then back to the transport. "So, um, did you expect that...um...thing to descend right there?"

He glanced at the ancient vehicle. "Yes. I sent for it."

"Really?" Her voice was high pitched with hysteria. "When?"

"My very first moment of consciousness, as soon as I had the strength. Long before the gool attacked."

She shot him an irritated look. "The zombies attacked. The gool was just—"

He cut her off with an irritated slash of his hand. "What is wrong with the transport? Why do you look at it like it is wrong somehow?"

"Like it's from freaking *Star Wars*? That's a...a shuttlecraft, you idiot! You fight with swords and have magic stones. What the hell are you doing with a *shuttlecraft*?"

He shook his head. "I do not understand your words. That is a transport vehicle. An ancient one created by our ancestors and treasured by the royals. It has served for generations, supplying the battalions as they preserve the Wall that saves us all."

"Your ancestors?" No no no no. She was on a magic world, not a technological one. And yet there it was, right in front of her eyes. "What is it made of?" she said, her voice sounding deceptively calm.

"A magic substance whose metalcraft has been lost."

"Uh-huh. How does it fly?"

"There are many stones that provide its magic, but they are powerful and nigh eternal."

"Uh-huh. And how long has it been…um…protected by your family?"

"Since the royal lineage began."

"Generations, Keeven. How many generations?"

He shook his head, but he stopped wondering at the things she did and did not know. "One hundred and forty-seven generations. I am to father the hundred and forty-eighth."

"A hundred and forty-seven," she muttered to herself. "Say twenty years per generation, that makes it something like three thousand years old. So for three millenia you've had that shuttlecraft zipping around—"

"It carries supplies to those—"

"At the Wall. Right. Okay, then. I think I want to see this Wall. Or wake up to the straight jacket and room with rubber walls. At this point, I'll take either."

He sighed. She was back to thinking herself insane so he gripped her chin and drew it to look at him. His nerves were pulled tight, part of his attention still watching the gool as he methodically placed bodies, the farmer as he watched the gool, and of course his men who were opening the doorway to wait in reverence for their prince. But the bulk of his attention focused on her. Always her, as he drew her frightened face to look at him.

"You are not mad, Angel Janet, and I am a thousand times tired of having this argument with you."

She swallowed, her eyes flashing as she shifted from terror to anger. "Well excuse me for freaking out when a transport from a galaxy far, far away lands in your sword-and-sorcery world."

"Adapt, angel. *Adapt.*"

Her jaw stiffened and he cursed himself for bellowing at a divine creature. But there was no more time. His interlude with her was ending, and that made him both furious and grateful. But mostly it made him frustrated.

With a groan, he dropped his forehead to hers. She met him quietly, with a strength in her spine that he'd always admired, even when she thought she was insane.

"There is no more time, Janet. My men are here. I must be a prince now, and you must be an angel. You cannot doubt your purpose; you cannot cry madness to the world. You simply cannot. Unless you want us to think you an enemy."

He felt her shudder, the motion transmitting from her body to his. Even without realizing it, he had pulled her into his arms and now her every shuddering breath felt like it was his own.

"Your world makes no sense."

"And yet, you must pretend it does."

"Or else?"

"Or else you might indeed be treated as a madwoman."

She froze, then slowly she lifted her head. He did the same, but he held her close in the circle of his arms. "And how—exactly—is a madwoman treated?"

"With medicines, naturally."

"In a locked up ward somewhere?"

He shook his head. "In a beautiful bed where she can bear her children in comfort. And where she has no choice in the selection of the babes' sires. And no contact with the children once they are born."

It took her a moment to understand his words. He could see her thinking, her breath catching and her body stilling before she took a slow step backwards.

"The medicines are to...to make her fertile?"

"They are to keep her docile as she gestates the next generation."

She blinked. "Right. And that's important to you. Not you personally, but as a culture. It's all about the babies, isn't it?"

He tilted his head. "It is important to me—personally— that you not be thought of as insane."

"Right. Because otherwise I'll be drugged and impregnated to spawn the next generation of babies."

"Demi-angels. Much needed and cherished demi-angels."

"Because I'm an angel."

He nodded. At last she understood.

Then suddenly her eyes widened, her breath caught and she took a horrified step back. "Is that what you were planning to do with your wife? Just use her as a breeding machine for the next royal?"

He could tell by her tone that she was horrified, but he did not understand the reason. "I have told you this is true. That is our responsibility as the purest blooded male and female in the kingdom. I am to sire, she is to birth and together—"

"Jesus, given that, she was probably grateful to be abducted!"

He froze, his heartspace growing so cold that he could no longer hear her words. He took a step back, his hands slipping away from her. She knew immediately that something had changed. Her eyes widened but her words were no less fierce. Sounds tumbled past his ears, words that he could no longer understand. All he heard was his name, spoken as a question.

"Keeven?" And then nonsense.

"You know nothing of this world," he finally spat. "Do not presume you understand."

Her words stopped—rather abruptly—and then she drew a breath. She was going to curse him for an idiot, she was going to point out loudly and in front of his men exactly how his thoughts were wrong. And she was not going to stop until she was heard.

Except he could not hear her. Nor could he let her—or anyone—realize the truth. His bride had run from him, choosing abduction rather than have him sire her child.

No one could know. Not even his angel with the fiery temper and the creeping fear of madness. Thank the Goddess that right now he was the only one who could understand her language. So he walked away, issuing orders as if she hadn't just revealed to all his greatest shame.

"Take the woman and the gool. We leave in ten minutes."

The lieutenant looked over Keeven's shoulder, frowning in confusion. "Take them?"

He regretted his next words. He knew they were wrong, but he had no choice. She needed to be silent until she could understand her danger, and this was the only way.

"Put them in chains."

Then he walked away.

"Keeven!" Janet screeched, but it did no good. The damned man kept walking away, his every stomp telling her she'd gone too far. Well, duh, but...wait... *chains*? "Like hell you're locking me up! You're going to listen to me!"

She ran at him, intending to grab Mr. Arrogant Prince and pummel him for the moron he was. But his men were quick and efficient. She'd no more than taken a step when she found herself whipped around, kicked behind her knees so that she dropped to the ground, and then felt heavy iron cuffs snapped onto her wrists.

"Keeven!" she screamed. No response. Not even by a ripple did the man react to her desperate bellow. She turned her eyes to the farmer, knowing that he at least would plead her case, but he took one look at her—his expression troubled—before hurrying after Keeven. Well, good. Maybe he'd make the idiot man see reason.

Except that did nothing to help her as one of the soldiers hauled her upright, turned her so that she could see his face, and spoke to her in clear, military accents. There was no sympathy in his tone. Neither was there any insolence. Just a calm explanation of she had no idea what. She could hear his tone, but the words meant nothing to her.

"I don't understand your language," she said clearly. But of course, they wouldn't understand her either.

The man's expression flattened out and he put a hand to his ear before slashing it flatly across his face. Was she supposed to understand that? She guessed it was either an order to stop talking or a comment that he couldn't understand her. Which she already knew.

So she tried gesturing, which was hard to do with her hands chained behind her back. She jerked her chin at Keeven and then...

And then he walked around her, took hold of the trailing edge of her chains, and pushed her toward the shuttlecraft. She stumbled. Not badly, but enough that she knew Keeven would have caught her arm to steady her. Not this guy. The most he would do was hold her chains harder so that her shoulders jerked painfully. Which told her without words that she would need to find her own balance.

To the side, she saw the gool being treated in a similar fashion. But unlike her, he had total command of his body even with his arms wrenched behind his back. She winced when she saw the tight cuffs against his bulging arms. Those had to be uncomfortably tight, but his expression was one of resigned acceptance. He didn't bellow or argue. He walked as he was directed, marching forward with her until they stood side by side outside the shuttlecraft.

That word made her mind stutter. She still couldn't believe it was there, but everyone else seemed to think it was perfectly normal to mix *Lord of the Rings* with *Battlestar Galactica*.

Meanwhile, Keeven had come back toward them. She turned to speak to him. In fact, she gave him quite a piece of her mind, but he didn't seem to hear her. It didn't matter how much she screeched or bellowed or simply sniveled, no one even seemed to notice. In fact...oh shit. That's what the soldier meant by his gesture. There was some sort of silencing on the cuffs. They really couldn't hear a thing she said.

Just to test it, she settled into silence. Then she waited until one of the soldiers came near enough for her to startle him. Or at least try to. She waited, picking a moment when she could see his face. Then she abruptly cried out. No word, just a sound that was loud and sharp, and watched closely to see if he flinched.

Nada. His eyes didn't even blink.

Crap.

She didn't know why she was surprised. They had magic stones to block smells, and stones to keep the water out from under the tree. Of course they had magic to block sounds.

Fine. She was silenced. And Keeven was a bastard. And...

Phoom!

Janet jumped sideways, the sound hitting her long before her brain said the word "explosion." Fortunately, she'd jerked toward the gool and he kept her upright. She wasn't even sure if it was out of solicitude or stoicism. The guy was just standing there—kinda dignified—without any obvious reaction to either the sudden burst of flames in front of them or the fact that she'd practically fallen on top of him.

It took a moment for her to process what had happened. The sound had come from the ship and the boom from the pile of zombie bodies which were now obliterated. All that remained was a tiny mushroom cloud of power. Obviously the shuttlecraft had weapons, and those weapons had just delivered a laser shot to the spiral of zombie bodies which were now sprinkling the air with fine ash. Hence the need to breathe something other than what was in the air.

Looking around, she saw a sort of satisfaction on everyone's faces, including the gool's. She had to admit to a kind of purging of her own now that those damned creatures were gone. Everyone, that is, except Keeven who had stepped into her sight. He was more grim-faced than usual as he barked out his commands.

It was the usual stuff of loading up and getting underway. She saw him express his gratitude to the farmer and his family. And she'd already seen that some supplies had been off-loaded presumably as a gift. Or, she realized as she climbed onto the craft, to make room for her and the gool.

"I guess this isn't *Star Trek*," she muttered to herself. No well appointed and spacious craft here. There weren't even seats, much less a carpet. It was all strange lead gray-colored plastic—or whatever this thing was made out of—and crates of supplies. One box near her was open, and she saw uniform pants inside. The rest were labeled in their strange script, except for the crate of onions and two caged chickens who were none to pleased to share their space.

She had no idea where she and the gool would fit, not to mention the two soldiers or Keeven. But a second later, she understood. One of the men shoved aside the double-stacked chickens to reveal two handlebars. First the gool, then she were uncuffed, her arms released from behind her back, thank God, before she was fastened to the bar above her head. So now she was dangling like a side of beef while Keeven stepped in, his expression still dark.

He gave one glance forward to where a pilot sat in a real chair and then did a double take. His eyes narrowed, and he shifted to see the man more fully. At which point, his chin dipped in a slow nod of acceptance. What he was accepting, she had no idea, but it was clear that the pilot was significant somehow.

Then Keeven looked to the soldiers standing guard over them. She opened her mouth to speak. It was an instinctive reaction to seeing a man she wanted to punch. But she saw his head shake in a negative. It wasn't an obvious move, but she was watching him closely.

What made him think that she was going to listen to a thing he wanted? She drew breath, but then saw a flash of utter despair cross his face. The movement was so quick— and so startling—that her words stuck in her throat. No one was going to hear her anyway, so why bellow at him? But more important, had she really seen what she thought? Had he looked completely defeated?

She didn't have time to wonder before he barked another order to her guards. "Treat her carefully. She's important."

Then he turned to the front of the craft and dropped down into the only other seat before speaking to the pilot. His words were too quiet to hear, but she was well able to see her two guards eyeing her speculatively. Because she was feeling petty, she stuck her tongue out at them, and then tried not to blush when they laughed uproariously at her.

Then suddenly they were airborne. She'd traveled before in airplanes, so that wasn't so much of a surprise. But there was no revving of the engines, no roar or push of rockets. The whole thing was completely soundless. She wouldn't even have realized that they'd taken off if she hadn't been looking out the front windshield. She could still see the dusky ash pile that had been the zombies. She saw the lake and then the road before the mountain peak of birdbeasts slipped into view. They banked to the right and she felt the tilt in the craft, but there was no engine noise whatsoever, which gave the whole experience a kind of amusement park ride feel. For all she knew, she was at Six Flags on the Spiderman ride.

She knew her eyes were wide with shock, and she absolutely heard the guards snicker at her. Whatever. They'd probably freak out at a game of laser tag, and she was a champion at that.

She glanced at the gool and saw that he was white-knuckled with horror. His eyes were riveted on the view out front, and his muscles were straining against his chains. She didn't know what he intended to do if he got free, but in this small container, boxed into the corner as they were, a psycho gool could be a bad thing. Fortunately, they were close enough for her to nudge him with her foot.

Once.

Again, a little harder this time.

Then a third time as a kind of kick that brought his gaze swiveling around to her. It also caught the guards' attention, which wasn't necessarily a bad thing. They called out to her, speaking harshly, but her focus was riveted on the gool.

She wanted to talk to him, tell him with the tone of her voice that everything was going to be fine. But he couldn't hear her, so she settled for a reassuring smile. She also took a deep and obvious breath. She expanded her ribcage and released it, exaggerating the motion as she still smiled at him.

It took a few more moments, but in the end he nodded. He visibly breathed, his grip on the chains eased, and whenever his gaze started to shift back to the front of the craft, she nudged him again. She wasn't going to let him look out front until he had better control of himself. Unfortunately, that meant she couldn't see anything either except the gool and the annoyed chicken right behind him.

Five minutes.

Ten.

Fifteen.

His shoulders eased. His gaze softened and he slowly dipped his chin to her. She thought he might have tried to smile, but it didn't really work. This time when his gaze shifted to the front, he didn't freak out. He tensed a little, but eventually relaxed. And with his ease, she was able to at last look forward again and nearly swallowed her tongue in surprise.

Jungle. They were flying over jungle.

There was no mistaking the canopy of a tropical rainforest. Jesus, how fast were they going? She had no way to judge. It all looked like trees slipping past at a rapid pace that could have been fifty miles per hour or five thousand. And while she was still gaping, Keeven pushed up from his seat. He was carrying a folded piece of paper in his hands, and he didn't give her more than a quick glance. It might have been a guilty glance, but she couldn't tell. Either way, he focused on the gool as he spread open the paper over the chicken crate.

"Do you know what this is?" he asked the gool.

The man frowned as he looked, shifting to peer closer. It took him a moment, but then he nodded.

"Where did you come through the Wall?"

So that was a map of the Wall. Janet shifted, doing her best to see around Keeven to the paper. He must have seen her, because he moved, letting her see the page clearly. Well, that was interesting.

She saw a lumpy peninsula, sort of like Italy only thicker in the middle. More like a dangling sack than a knee-high boot. And at the top where peninsula met continent was a straight-ish cut of a red line that went from water mass to water mass.

There were details etched around the red line. Notation for cliffs and a yellowish white bit at the edges for beaches. And then there were thinner, more wandering blue lines that she guessed meant rivers.

Meanwhile, Keeven put his finger on one edge of the red line. "Where did you come across?" he asked again as he slowly slid his finger all the way across the map.

Janet looked to the gool. There was total incomprehension on his face. A blank stare of I-have-no-idea. That could have meant: I don't understand what a map is. Or it maybe it was: I have no clue where I came across. Or even worse: I know but I'm not telling you, you frigging bastard. No way to tell, and she could see the same thought on Keeven's face.

Mr. High and Mighty Prince grimaced and rocked back on his heels. "Are you from the north?" he asked.

The gool nodded, then jerked his chin toward the map. Keeven put his finger above the red line and following the gool's direction, slid it up and to the right until it was off the map. So the creature...er, the man had been from the far north.

"How did you become a gool?"

The man looked up and glared and no wonder. It's not like he could answer with words and his hands were cuffed to a raised handlebar.

"You were captured?" Keeven continued.

The gool shrugged. He probably said something too—there was a clear opening of the mouth and a look of hatred—but in those cuffs, no sound came out.

"Enchanted?"

Another nod, only this time more vehement and truly angry.

"Controlled by the collar?"

Another yes.

"But how did you get across?"

The gool tried to gesture with his hands, but they were tied up. He did what he could with his elbows, but it clearly wasn't effective. So Keeven turned to the nearest guard.

"Take them off."

The guard protested. Something like, "But sir!" which is understandable in any language. Keeven obviously wasn't used to having his orders questioned because he didn't even move. He leveled the guard with a heavy stare, and the man scrambled to obey.

A moment later, one guard had uncuffed the gool while the other had stepped far enough back go give him room to shoot with his...um...blow gun? It was a hollowed out tube. That's it. Just a tube, but he held it like one would level a wand of death. And he didn't bring it to his lips, so it probably wasn't air-propelled. And a second later, the other guard had stepped back into a similar position with his little pea shooter pointed at the gool.

And what was the creature doing while the guards were looking all threatening? He was rolling out his shoulders and looking very calm.

"You go, guy," Janet muttered. She didn't care that he'd unleashed a sackful of zombies on them. The man was her co-prisoner, and she had some real sympathy for him.

"Well?" Keeven prompted. "How did you get across the Wall?"

The gool answered with hand gestures. He mimed going under the wall. And after a bit of questioning, they figured out it was a long tunnel that had come out next to a stream. Not a big river, but a stream that forked a little further south.

One of the guards said something. It was probably the name of the stream because a minute later, the man was pointing to a place on the map. Keeven nodded, and then he moved back to the front of the cabin.

The guard asked him something, gesturing to the gool. Keeven's answer was almost casual.

"Don't bother. We'll be there in a moment."

And sure enough, they were. As soon as Keeven got to the front and spoke with the pilot, the craft did another one of those steep banks, this time to the left. Janet was grateful that she could grip onto the chains, but the gool had no such luck. He shot his hands out, nearly breaking the slats of the chicken crate as he tried to stabilize himself.

The guards cried out, but they didn't shoot, thank God. And in a moment, the gool had himself properly balanced, though Janet was sure the chicken had shit himself. Great, now she had some sympathy for the poor chicken, too.

Two minutes later, they landed on a narrow stretch of land beside a fork in a stream. It was pretty, though the vegetation crowded close. She was sure they had crunched some trees as they descended through the canopy top.

And then Keeven was there again, pushing open the door to let in humid air that had to be about a hundred and ten in the shade.

He waited patiently as the guards hopped out followed by the gool. His instruction was short and sweet and not at all aimed at the guards. "Show them were you came through," he said, his tones clipped. "I will join you in a moment. And in case you wondered, we can kill you easily from the air."

The gool nodded, his expression showing nothing more than simple acceptance. No hatred, no fury. Unlike Janet who was still seething. Then he left while Keeven turned his attention to her.

"About damned time, you ass. Uncuff me," she said though she knew he couldn't hear her.

Fortunately, he did as she wanted, unlocking her cuffs with quick motions. No wait. He was unclipping her from the wall, not taking off the cuffs.

"What the hell?" she groused, trying to kick him when he got close. He didn't even avoid her, but took the blow to his shins stoically.

"Stop being a child and listen," he snapped at her, and she reared back at the harsh clip to his tone.

"Fuck off," she snapped, but he spoke right over her.

"I want you to meet Alenth. He's the pilot."

He took hold of her elbow, but she jerked it out of his grip. He let her go, but he blocked her exit out into the jungle heat. He simply waited until she'd gained her balance and lifted her cuffs up to him. "Take these off," she said emphatically. Apparently, she had a burning need to talk, cone of silence be damned.

"I know you want the cuffs off, but I can't risk having others hear you talk. They will know who you are, Janet. Or at least *what* you are."

He meant an angel. They would know, and so what?

"You have to trust me. It's dangerous."

She grimaced. She might have agreed with him, trusting to his greater understanding, but he'd made no secret of what she was in front of the Freerik family. They knew she was an angel. What was different about a few guards? Of course they were *armed* guards. And they were only part of a larger army that manned a Wall. And since he was a prince he probably had enemies, and there were always politics involved. Plus, if she were supposed to be this great angel to gestate the next group of little demi-angels, then perhaps...

She sighed. Okay, maybe what he said made sense. Didn't mean she was going to forgive him. She kept glaring at him, but in the end she dipped her chin.

"Good. You understand."

She stuck out her tongue at him. It was childish, but it got him to smile a little. A quirk of his lips as his expression lightened for a moment. Then he sobered.

"I want you to sit with Alenth. He's an honorable man, and he is my wife's cousin."

Wow. He'd almost said that in a normal tone. Almost. She caught the slight hesitation before the word "wife." It happened so often that, in her mind, the princess' name had a hesitation in front of it. She was called: Hesitation Wife. Janet was still thinking of that when he blindsided her with his next words.

"Alenth is the man I've chosen to mate with you."

CHAPTER 10

Smothering Hell, he was tired. Keeven strode forward toward his quarters near the center of Wall City, doing his best to appear vibrant and in control while every part of him drooped with fatigue. His list of tasks wasn't done yet. He still had to talk to Alenth, and that did not begin to address the question of Janet.

The very thought of her name sparked an ache so brutal it could have brought him to his knees. The hardest thing he'd ever done was to leave her with Alenth. But it was the right thing to do. He was not free, but Alenth was. And so he would keep his distance from Janet to give Alenth time to woo his angel in peace.

And yet, the very idea made his entire body roil with nausea. He didn't let it affect him, though he allowed himself a tiny sigh of weariness.

That sigh was a mistake. His lungs burned with the acid that was always underground, and that sigh nearly caused a cough. And once he started to hack and wheeze, he feared he'd never stop. Such was the way with the poison under the earth. Many a soul had died while his body spasmed, trying to cough out a restriction that was simple swelling of the tubes to the lungs. Coughing made the problem worse and yet the body's need to expel the burn was instinctive. So he held in his breath—and his sighs—as he fought the pain in his throat and made his way to the center of Wall City.

It had been a long day of searching out tunnels beneath the Wall. Already a dozen found and guarded while he painstakingly expanded the force downward further and further until the tunnels were cut off. The deepest had been into rock, more than a decan below the loamy surface. But they were closed now, every damn one of them, and he was so exhausted he could barely move.

Still he pushed onward, climbing through walkways and ladders to the center spot in the bivouac, high up in the largest tree, and the only opaque force field dwelling. He winced as always at the pompous display of privacy. If he could see every man, woman, and child in the encampment, then they should see that their leader had nothing to hide either. But it was hard to run an army without at least some secrecy. The opaque walls were more than simple ostentation.

He narrowed his eyes, peering through the force field to the people within in dwelling. As the ranking leader and the one who regularly powered the stones, he could see through the dull white to what was within. He saw Alenth first, reclining on the cushions as he told stories with his hands. It was a comical sight as the man mimed stirring a stew pot. Keeven knew the story of his young cousin-in-law's first attempt at cooking, and he smiled in memory of the boy's antics. But all the while, his gaze roved through the room looking for her.

There. Seated in a tiny corner of the room, her back to the cot. She had her arms wrapped around her updrawn legs and her chin plopped onto her knees. He couldn't see her clearly, but he knew by her very stillness that she was upset. Janet was a woman who liked to move. Her hands flitted about when she talked, her head and her feet bobbed as she ate. Even when she slept, her legs were restless and her back twitched. But always within a confined, tight distance from her body. As if every part of her tried to move beyond herself, but was stopped by an unseen force. She only grew content in her tiny space when she grieved.

Despite his vow to stay distant, he quickened his pace, but it didn't help. His third aide found him twenty-two steps from her side.

"Sir! Sir, we found another."

No other words could deter him, but these made his gut clench and his feet thud to a stop. He turned to the woman, her sweet freckled face serious and her riot of reddish brown curls tied ruthlessly back from her face. If Janet was constantly trying to break free of her restraints, Meaghan was always trying to keep contained.

"Sir," she repeated as she pulled out a neat folder, flipping it open to a detailed map of the Wall. "Right here. Another deep one."

She searched his face as she spoke, and for a moment, he allowed all his exhaustion to show.

"I cannot," he rasped. "Not one so deep." The poison would kill him for sure. "Set a watch—"

"I already have." Then she swallowed, seeing his throat work as he fought another cough. "Doctor Tefin wanted a word with you as soon as possible. He's waiting for you—"

"No, he's not." Just because he had taken a vow of honesty did not mean others had. She'd merely invented the request so that the physic would look into his throat and see the raw swelling there. "I don't need a doctor. Just rest."

She frowned. "How much time did you spend underground?"

He hadn't counted, which was unusual for him. And against regulations. "It was necessary."

"So you can prove that you're the biggest, baddest prince of them all?" she huffed.

No one else would be permitted to speak to him this way, but Meaghan was special. He liked her and she had no political affiliations whatsoever, which made her a rare gem. That she was also extremely efficient and dedicated to the protection of the realm had allowed her to rise in the ranks noticeably fast. People were beginning to wonder about their relationship, and yet even so, he couldn't bring himself to curb her. He appreciated her blunt speech too much.

"Because we haven't enough men to guard them all safely. Not from Aruckien."

There was more than enough moonlight to see her skin pale. Like him, she had lost family to the deadly imps. Like him, she had witnessed the carnage first hand and knew the horror of it.

"I understand," she said crisply. "The rest of the survey will be complete by morning—"

"Good."

"And all the royals have been accounted for save the four you already know about and three boys."

He winced. Four dead and three missing. "Which boys?"

She flipped a page on her clipboard and showed him the list of all those with royal blood on four tiny sheets. Beside each name was a neat scrawl of location and health except for the four who had been killed. A red line crossed them out. And there were three blank spaces for young men halfway through their teens. They were wild boys, resistant to the call of duty, and fast friends in their mischief. Not even the queen had been able to curb their antics.

"They're likely in a brothel somewhere."

Meaghan nodded. "It's what I thought, too. The parents are searching."

"With guards," he said firmly. He'd had more time to question the gool. He'd learned that at least a dozen of the evil creatures had slipped beneath the Wall with orders to find the people of power and kill them. It was a compulsion laid on the stone collar along with a draw to the nearest person of royal blood. They scented out the nearest soul like a wolf to a bloody child, then bid them open the damned sack to release the vermin. The Aruckien would do the rest.

Meanwhile, Meaghan was calculating in her head, a million tiny balance sheets of men and resources all tallied in silence. "We're stretched thin. I can pull a few from the Wall—"

"No royal is to walk without a guard," he repeated, his words so forceful that he set off his cough. It started as a simple hack, but the burn had him spasming more. Another half dozen coughs made his knees tremble and his throat thicken, threatening to cut off all breath completely. He had to get control of his body. Every cough made the swelling worse.

"Sir!"

Meaghan grabbed his arm, and he was too weak to throw her off. He couldn't allow his men to seem him debilitated. He had to get control now!

He grit his teeth and clenched his fists. It didn't help, but he still tightened every part of him until he was a rigid statue of dark will. He would not cough!

He didn't..

He waited.

When his eyes were beginning to spot from lack of air, he allowed the tiniest breath to slip down his burning throat. A taste. A bit.

In. Out. So shallow it would not be enough to keep him standing. But it worked for now. Until he could deepen it a bit more.

A bit more.

Until he could breathe as a man again.

He blinked the blurriness out of his eyes and focused back on Meaghan.

She was grim with anger. "You must see a doctor now."

He shook his head, his words barely audible since he would not spare the breath for volume. "They can do nothing."

It was true. Once the poison had seeped so firmly into the lungs, it was merely a race to see if the body healed faster than the cough destroyed. There were no medicines to help, no stones except those to set a man to sleep so he would die unconscious.

"I just need rest."

"Of course, sir." But instead of leaving his side as he expected, she kept pace with him. She didn't irritate him further with anxious looks at his face, but he knew the thought was there. She was babysitting him, fearing that he would die in the few steps it took him to make it to his door. Of course the walkway between the trees was wide enough to allow for two. Hell, it was wide enough for three because that's how frequently people came to his door.

He slowed his steps to look at her. He wanted to say something reassuring but knew she would reject any soft overture. For all that she took liberties with him, she allowed none in return. And then Alenth caught his eyes. Those inside could see out through the force field. He had just finished his story complete with a roll across the wood floor to lay sprawled half on, half off the cushions. Janet remained exactly as she'd been—arms wrapping her knees—but she might have given a smile. Perhaps. It was hard to see.

"Sir?"

Making a rapid decision, he gestured to his quarters. "Come inside. There's someone you must meet."

She stiffened even as she nodded. "The woman?"

There were undercurrents to the words she'd spoken. A hidden meaning or three that he did not understand. So he narrowed his eyes.

"What have you heard?"

"That you brought her here in chains and Alenth removed them, though kept her silent with a stone."

He nodded. That was as he'd expected. Alenth hated the sight of anyone in chains, much less a woman.

"That she is foreign."

He arched a brow, a silent question.

She shrugged. "She may dress like one of the Freerik, but we know there is something beneath the shirt. Something unusual."

Her toolbelt.

"Also she walks differently. Her hair is cut differently.

And she has never seen the sick."

He winced. "Alenth took her to the hospital?"

"Alenth took her everywhere. The Wall. The cook tent. The hospital. He treated her as an honored guest set to see everything we did here." She pursed her lips and made as if to spit at the leaves. She didn't, but he could tell she was disgusted. "As if she toured the sights."

Gawkers and camp followers were common, but they were not as despised as the wealthy few who wished to visit Wall City as a tourist come to see a war.

"She is special," he finally said. His throat had eased up enough that he could form full sentences again. "I need you to teach her our language."

Meaghan nodded. "Where is she from?"

He shot her an irritated look. "From someplace that does not speak like we do."

She took his rebuke in stride. "Is she your mistress?"

He was about to snap at her. His private affairs were his own, but there had been no censure in her tone. Little beyond a categorical question. As if she sought to label Janet to fit in her very organized mind and had no emotional attachment to whatever he answered. And yet, for all the flatness of her tone, he wondered what she thought.

"Is that what you think?"

"It is what everyone thinks. Except you brought her here in chains."

"Then how could she be my mistress?"

She looked at him long and hard. No words passed her throat, but the meaning blossomed in his mind in horror. His throat closed up for reasons other than the pain, and he felt his jaw drop in shock.

"I am a knight of Askel," he finally rasped. "I do not—"

She held up her hand to stop his words. "You do not chain or beat women for pleasure," she intoned. "And you certainly wouldn't parade her around for the perverse joy of it."

"So how—"

"They have no other explanation for her or your actions."

He wished they would all put as much focus into maintaining the Wall as they did the minutiae of his life. But he was the commander and the royal prince. Everyone watched him with intense interest.

He sighed, then jerked his chin to his quarters. "Meet her yourself." Three steps later, they passed together through the opening stones.

Alenth jumped to his feet the moment they entered. He'd always been quick, but there was an extra measure of fury in the movement. A narrowing of his eyes and a tightening of his shoulders. It was gone a moment later, but some of the aggression remained in his tense body posture.

Yet another person to manage in an already too full day. Keeven barely gave him more than a nod as his attention centered on Janet. At his entrance, she'd lifted her chin off her knees, but she didn't stand. Her gaze took in Meaghan, pausing for as much as a heartbeat before centering on him.

"Janet," he said, his voice thick. "How are you?"

She opened her mouth to answer, but no sound came out. Then she grimaced and pulled out the Silent Stone from her pocket.

He could have told her to set it aside, but he wanted the excuse to touch her. So he crossed to her and took the stone from her fingers. Their skin touched, hers cool compared to his. Odd. He must have another fever. The thought came and went, lost beneath the sight and scent of her. He knelt down before her, absently setting the stone aside.

"Are you hungry?"

She shook her head, her eyes wide and her mouth soft. So soft and pink.

He lost himself for a time just looking at her. Seeing the lines of strain around her mouth, and the slightly dazed focus of her eyes. He had seen the expression before on new recruits. Young men and women who had never seen the truth of a battlefield. Or in her case, the hospital.

"How many?" she asked.

He frowned, not understanding. "I—"

"How many do you lose to illness every year?"

In the background, he heard Meaghan gasp at the sound of Janet's language. She would guess fairly quickly the truth about his strange new companion. Especially as Janet touched his chin and drew him to look at her, haunted eyes and all.

"Give me a rough percentage."

"A tenth."

She winced. "Jesus. And this is a holding action, right? You've put up a force field above your entire nation. You're not pushing forward. You're just holding your border."

He nodded. There were many who desperately wanted to push deeper into Gezan territory, but they had no idea how thinly stretched their resources were. There was no way that his people could turn aggressor. Keeven nightly prayed that he would not be the man who lost the Wall and ended up ceding territory.

"But the force field can only be maintained by a royal, right? It's your family that powers the stones. The princess's family who lays down the pattern of the...the magic." She struggled with the word, but apparently was beginning to accept it.

"That's correct. Alenth's special skill is with the stones that fly—"

She waved him to silence. "How many royals are there?"

She had figured it out then. One day walking around—not even understanding the language—and she knew the truth.

"Keeven?"

"Two hundred and seven." But it might now be three less if they didn't find the boys.

She swallowed. "That's not enough, is it?" She dropped her head back against the cot. "You'd have to have royals thick here at The Wall. It's the only way to maintain it. But if a tenth of them die every year..." She shuddered.

He stroked her cheek, his thumb stroking gently across her skin. It wasn't wet. She hadn't cried yet. He could see she was beyond tears as she thought through the reality of their situation.

"We will survive."

"And the...the zombie things. They were sent to attack royals, weren't they?"

He didn't answer. Just a simple nod told her everything.

"How many came through? Except for the ones who attacked us, were there others?"

He nodded. "We lost four more that we're aware of."

Then he looked to Alenth, dreading what was to come next. Even without the benefit of Janet's words, the pilot knew he was about to hear the names of the dead. He braced himself, then nodded before Keeven quietly listed off the names. The royals were a small community. They all knew each other, some very well. One of the dead had been Alenth's childhood companion and best friend. A woman who would likely have been his bride.

He watched as Alenth paled, his hands gripping the nearby chair in reaction.

"I'm sorry," Keeven said, knowing that there was nothing else to say. Except perhaps, "She went quickly, we think. Overcome in seconds."

Alenth's eyes were wild with horror, and Keeven pushed to his feet to comfort the man, but he was gestured back. Janet too pushed to her feet, but Alenth shrank away.

"I'll just go..." he rasped. "I..." He swallowed.

"The transport has been readied for you," he said, glancing at Meaghan to see that it was true. She nodded. "Her parents would welcome you."

Alenth shoulders tightened but he didn't answer. He likely couldn't. They all dealt with loss up here at the Wall. But most expected that the ones at home were safe.

Keeven glanced at Meaghan. "Go with him. See that—"

"No," Alenth said. "I… No." He had no more words and so pushed out the opening.

Keeven glanced at Meaghan and after a quick nod, she left as well, following Alenth to make sure he did nothing foolish. Which left him alone with Janet.

He looked back to her, feeling the weight of his command as never before. A Wall to maintain and no strength to do it. Four red lines across the roster of royals due to his failure to see the tunnels. And the knowledge that more gools roved through the realm searching for his family and friends.

Then there was Janet. Beautiful, amazing Janet who could help them as no other. The mother of demi-angels who could make a measurable difference in their defense in just a few years. After all, he had begun work at the age of four, charging the Wall stones with his father and brother before his afternoon nap.

Which meant… He looked at the floor and forced the words out of his throat. "You should go to Alenth. He needs someone to talk to now." And maybe the comfort would grow to more. Perhaps even a child.

He heard her chuckle, though there was little humor in the sound. "I can't talk to him, remember?"

"There are other ways to speak."

"I'll stay here," she said firmly. She touched his face and firmly lifted it until he looked into her eyes. "I didn't understand before," she whispered. "I doubt I know the half of it now. But God, Keeven, what you're facing. Not just the country, but you. You're in charge of all of this and you…" She sighed. "I didn't get it before, but I do now."

His eyes widened, his body lifting with the joy of what she was saying. She knew. She would help. "You will stay? You will mate—"

She dropped a hand to his mouth, stopping his impulsive words. "I don't know what I'm going to do. Though I can tell you this," she said. "I'm not going to bed with Alenth."

He straightened, pulling away from her hand. "Alenth is an

honorable man. He treats women with gentleness and he laughs easily. He..." He was all the joyous things that Keeven as prince was not.

"He's not you," she said, as if that explained it all.

"I am married," he repeated, his words heavy with regret. What if they had met before his wedding? Before his choice had been determined by bloodlines and magic?

She tilted her head, her expression open. "I never thought I'd say this, Keeven. Ever. But you know what? I don't care. I know that's wrong of me, but it's true. You don't love her, do you?"

He snorted before he thought to moderate his reaction. In truth, he didn't even respect his wife, which for him was a thousand times worse than a lack of love.

"Does she love you?" Janet asked.

He shrugged. "Last time we spoke she called me a depressing wood slug with no thought in my head beyond what my mother put there."

Janet chuckled. "So she really doesn't know you at all."

"Worse. She's met my mother."

She smiled, obviously not having any understanding of his mother's personality. "Mom's not a gentle woman?"

"She is the Queen of Askel." He wanted to say more, but there was no way to express the difficulties inherent in that title. He bore only a fraction of the responsibilities that burdened his mother, and most days he felt crippled by the weight. And while he was struggling with the words, she tugged on his hand.

"It doesn't matter. I'll meet her if I meet her."

"But—"

"Come to bed, Keeven. You're about to collapse."

The temptation was strong. The immediate work was done for the day. His throat still burned, and rest was the only cure. But he hesitated, knowing full well the danger of going to bed with her while fatigue made him stupid and temptation could easily seduce him.

"I made a vow to my wife," he said, the words bitter on his tongue.

"What, exactly, was your vow?"

"To father children with her and no other. To honor her and to protect our young until my dying breath."

He felt her lips curve and felt stupid when she pointed out the obvious. "So nothing about loving her, being with her and no other?"

He shook his head. "This is a marriage for children."

"Then come to bed, Keeven. This is a bedding for entirely different reasons."

It took him a moment to see the promise in her eyes. To think of what she offered and to accept that she would lie with him and *not* make a child.

"You are an angel. You are here to have babies."

"Nope," she said, her tone light. "I'm just me, and I'm here for an entirely different reason."

He straightened. "What—"

"Don't know and don't care."

"But—"

"Come to bed Keeven." And then she took his hand and led him to bed.

CHAPTER 11

Janet had never seduced a man before, but that was her goal. She figured it was the best way to get past the have-her-mate-with-someone-else plan he had going. Plus, her heart just squeezed tight whenever she looked at him. He was everything she'd ever wanted in a man, except for the stick-up-the-ass honor thing. And even that made him uber-sexy.

So she was going to seduce him. If only she could get his clothes off, that is. And after he rested because he was obviously bone weary and breathing funny as well. She tugged at his tunic, trying to help him undress. He was more prone to serving others in everything. He served the kingdom as their prince, he served the Wall and his men as a knight, and he even served his princess, or would if he could find her. But when had anyone ever served him?

Probably not since he was a young boy. And not even then if he worked on the Wall while practically still in diapers.

"I keep thinking about the weight I felt," she said as she lifted his dirty tunic off his shoulders. "Back when we did the blood bond thing? I didn't understand it before, but I'm beginning to now."

He emerged from his shirt, his sculpted chest rippling as his shoulders slumped. She grabbed a washcloth, wetting it in the nearby basin. Her movements were efficient, but her body tingled with awareness. She knew he sat on the cot, too weary to argue with her as she began to clean his face.

"I should do that," he said, as he reached for the cloth.

She pushed his hand aside. "Tell me something. If you could lay down your burden, Keeven. If you could not be a knight or a prince or even a royal. If you were just a simple man with a farm—"

"I'm not."

She smiled. "We're playing my game now, pretend you are. What would you most want to do right now?"

He caught her hand then, turning it slowly in his fingers until the cloth slipped away into his other hand. Then he pressed his lips to her wrist. It was a simple gesture. Before that moment she would have said it wasn't even erotic. It was reverent, and yet as his rough lips pressed to the flesh there, she felt a shiver build inside her. It began at her toes, traveling with lightning speed up her spine until she arched with the power of it.

"Janet?"

She gasped and realized her eyes were closed. "You make me feel such things, Keeven," she whispered. She leaned into him, feeling his other hand large and supporting on her hip. The one at her wrist stroked gently with his thumb. She opened her eyes and looked into his. "What would you do if you could do anything?"

He sighed. "You ask me that as if I haven't told you a thousand different ways. I would have your belly grow round with my child. I would cherish the child that came and worship its mother. I would do all I could to see that you and our children lived long and very happy lives."

Her breath caught at the intensity of the emotion she saw in his face. He meant it. He wanted it. And he would do it if it took his very last breath.

She retrieved the washcloth and stroked it across his face, awed by the power he put into everything he did. "That's for another day, Keeven. What would you do now?"

He smiled against her wrist. "I would show you such

pleasure, Angel. I would set your heart on fire, and I would claim your body in such a way that you could not think of another man again. Ever."

She swallowed. "Keeven—"

"And in such a way, you would never leave me."

Oh the longing she heard, not just in his words, but in the cry of her heart. To have a man want her so powerfully was the wish of every woman. Except, of course, it wasn't her he wanted but her children. Even so, the need burned low in her belly, simmering with a hunger that made her knees week.

She leaned forward, cupped his cheeks and kissed him. A slow, drugging kiss that left her reeling. But when she lifted her head, her heart pounding and her breasts tight, he did not pursue her. His lips clung to hers, but when she pulled back, he did not draw her down for another.

"This is a child's game, Janet. I am a knight, and you are an angel. It does no good for us to pretend otherwise. You must choose a man—"

"You," she whispered.

He shook his head, though there was pain in the movement. "A man to father your children. You understand now how much we need them. We are few and growing fewer every day."

She sighed. He was a stubborn man. "Do you know," she said gently, "that in my world children are not so prized as they are here."

He jolted at that. Clearly he hadn't thought such a thing possible.

"My parents never married. That was probably a good thing. My mother was…" She shrugged. "Dramatic is a kind word. Unstable is a better one. She drove my father crazy and so eventually they split."

"But he had fathered a child. You."

"Two of us, actually. Myself and my younger sister. My brother has a different dad, but that's not important."

"How can your father not be important?"

She acknowledged the statement with a shrug. "He knew better than to give child support. Mom would have spent the money on jewelry or clothes to attract another man. Food and rent were secondary."

Keeven stiffened. "He did not provide for you?"

She smiled. "He did. He paid me for good grades. He's a history professor, you see. He valued education, and I liked that I had clear rules for praise. Mom ran hot and cold for no reason. It was a frightening, uncertain way to grow up. But with Dad? An A homework assignment got me a dollar. An A test got me five. And an A at the end of the semester? A hundred." She could tell that he didn't understand what she was saying, so she tried again. "He paid me to study, Keeven. My sister too. And we used the money to pay for our food and shelter."

"He should have taken you from your mother if she could not treat you properly."

How many times she had wished such a thing. "That would have been hard. My mother would have fought to keep us." But there was no point in trying to explain the legalities of child custody. "Here's the thing," she said, drawing his attention away from her broken home. "When everything in my life was uncertain, school was clear. The rules were simple and unchanging. So as soon as I got old enough, I ran there—to a PhD no less—simply because it made sense when everything else didn't."

"The world is not so clear a place," he said softly.

She chuckled. Trust Keeven to get it in one. "And then you prayed to your goddess, and I landed here. In that time, I've been attacked by demented birds and zombies, flown on a shuttlecraft to a force field, and gotten a first hand look at magic. The rules make no sense here at all."

"And so you want to leave," he said. It wasn't a question. It was a deduction.

She smiled, stroking her fingers across his lips. Feeling the heat of his breath and the gentle way his legs braced her as she stood between his knees. "I did. I still may. But Keeven,

I'm done with arbitrary rules. They don't make sense here, and I think they were getting a bit constrictive back home too."

He frowned. "That is why you felt contorted when we shared blood."

"Maybe. Okay, probably."

"So you want to stay?" There was no mistaking the hope in his voice.

"So having left one set of arbitrary rules, I'm not so keen on stepping into another."

He wanted to argue. She could see it in his expression, but she pressed her fingers to his mouth, stopping him.

"I don't know why I'm here in this world, Keeven, and neither do you. Maybe it's to fall in love and have babies. And maybe it's something else entirely. Here's what I know. I want to make love with you. I want to ease the burden you feel a little. I want to have some pleasure with you, Keeven, but not if it means having a baby."

She felt her words sink into him. It was a slow easing of his body. His shoulders dropped, his spine seemed to tightened then droop. As if he set down his burden. Or maybe she was being fanciful because a second later, she felt his fingers tighten on her hips. Nothing more. Just a tension that she felt throughout her whole body.

"Keeven?"

"May I draw off your tunic, Janet?"

She smiled. "Yes, you may, Keeven."

And so he did. He pulled it over her head then stroked a finger across her bra. It was a simple thing. She couldn't afford snazzy bras. But there was a little lace and a lot of elastic, and he touched it all with a strange look of wonder.

"You are so different, Angel," he murmured. "The clothes you wear, the way you speak and think—"

"I just want to be a woman now."

"And so it shall be."

She giggled. It wasn't the right time or the right mood, but he might as well said, "Make it so" or "so shall it be written, so shall it be done." He looked up at her, his eyes alight with humor. Had he purposely spoken so pompously? Just to make her laugh?

"I don't get you, Keeven," she said as she dropped a kiss on his nose. "But I like you."

His hands wrapped around her back and he unhooked the fastenings of her bra. She took a deep breath as the fabric loosened and he slid the thing forward and off her breasts.

"Nicely done," she said. "I didn't know if you'd know how."

"I studied it one night as you slept."

"Mmmm. Very thorough of you."

He began to kiss her breasts. She was standing before him, her bra dangling by her elbows, and he just leaned forward and began to suckle. His kiss was slow and seductive. A swirl of the tongue before a deep long pull. She shuddered at the exquisite feel of the flick of his tongue and the texture of his lips.

She let her arms drop from his shoulders and tossed aside her bra. He punished her inattention to him by nipping slightly on the nipple. She cried out in shock, and then he soothed her with his tongue.

Everything in her was liquid soft and she swayed forward, but he held her away. He abandoned the one nipple to kiss his way across to her other. It was the most leisurely lovemaking she'd ever experienced. He just held her hips away from him as he attended to her breasts.

God, he was good at that.

She touched his chest, needing to feel his hot flesh. She stroked his impressive muscles, brushed across some raised scars, and then she found the broad, flat disk of his nipples. She rubbed the edge of her nail across them, and he rumbled somewhere deep in his throat. It was an exquisitely manly sound—felt as much as heard—and she smiled even as her breath stuttered.

"I know you want to go slow," she said, doing her best not to sound so breathless. Didn't work. She was all but orgasming as it was. "But Keeven... Oh please...please do me now."

She felt him smile against her breast. Belatedly, she realized that he might not understand her slang, but it didn't matter. He gently shifted her to lay down on his cot. It wasn't big. In fact, she wondered just how a man his size managed to sleep on it. And then he helped her pull off her Freerik leggings.

They were ridiculously hot in this climate. Fortunately he had something that cooled his tent. Probably part of the same force field technology that... Oh. Oh my.

He'd pulled her clothes down—panties and all—and was kissing her belly. She'd been busy using her legs to strip out of the things, but the moment he began to lave her belly button, her entire body began to quiver. It tickled and it didn't. It made her mind spin out of control and her body gasp for breath. And yet every part of her stilled to appreciate his tongue on her lower abs. His fingers as he slowly widened her legs. And the brush of his thumb through her folds.

And then he abruptly stopped, lifting his chin to speak. "This place is protected from sound as well. No one can hear you if you cry out."

She frowned as she pulled her attention to the booming tree city around them. She could hear the noises of everyone around them. "One way sound, huh? You can hear them, but they can't hear you?"

He grinned. "Yes."

"Good. Because I'm going to make you scream. Now get naked."

He dipped his chin. "As you wish."

And she burst out laughing, thinking, "have fun storming the castle." And when he looked at her oddly, she just shook her head. "Some day I'm going to tell you all about movies. And we're going to watch them together. Every single silly, funny, wonderful, amazing…and um, you're not naked yet."

"Oh. Of course." He stood up and efficiently stripped out of his clothes. There was a moment when he sort of choked. It was as if he'd moved too fast and was about to cough. But he held it in. He held stock still as he breathed shallowly through his nose.

She sat up, looking at his face, but he gave her a quiet negative shake of his head. He was fine, he seemed to say. Which allowed her a moment to admire his physique. Broad shoulders, narrow waist. A light dusting of hair down to an impressive erection. Nice. She knew he had tight buns and strong, corded thighs, but her eyes were more on that enormous, clearly uncircumcised penis jutting up so proud. He was the only man she knew with a foreskin, so she reached out, needing to explore. He was breathing easier now, so he twisted slightly, bringing himself closer to her.

"Is this how you mate with—" he began.

"Yes."

"Have you ever seen a man before?"

"Not like this. Not like you." She didn't want to explain about cultural customs. She didn't even want to think about anything that she had seen or done before. It was all about him and his golden penis with the jutting mushroom head.

"Touch it," he urged. "You can take it firm—" His breath caught and she grinned. Clearly he hadn't expected her to be so bold as to grip him right off. "Yes," he said, his voice deepening to another low growl. "Yes, like that."

He was a handful all right. And as she stroked the foreskin down, his growl became a kind of purr. Nice.

She rolled her thumb across the pre-cum, wondering if it would taste as she expected. She glanced up at Keeven, seeing that his eyes had grown heavy and his chest expanded visibly with his breath. And then his eyes suddenly widened in surprise. Oh, right. She'd just licked her lips.

"Angel—" he began.

"Janet," she corrected. Talk about buzz kill. If anything

were to remind her that she was expected to be a divine broodmare, it was the way he said "Angel." His tone was reverent and worshipful, and all about planting the next Jesus or whatever. So she pulled back her hand and looked at him. She was still hot and hungry for him, but there was zero chance of her getting swept away right then. "Do you have a condom?"

His expression sobered. The reverence died and a dull flush crept up his cheeks. "You are both Janet and an angel to me. I meant no—"

She stood up, kicking aside her leggings as she did. They were both naked and facing each other. She took his face and gave him a kiss. Not just a press of the lips. Not just a easing tender press of the lips. She possessed his mouth in a raw, aching, hungry way. She jammed her lips against his, she all but levered his jaw open with her tongue, and she thrust herself inside him.

It was hard, powerful, and dominant, and she'd never done anything like it before. She possessed his mouth and he grabbed her to him with a growl that trapped his impressive erection against her belly. And she moved against it. She arched into him, she rubbed herself up and down, and she had herself so hot she almost came from the movements.

Then she stopped, pulling back with a gasping breath. "I am Janet. And I will take you as my lover but not if you keep thinking of me—"

He threw her down onto the cot. It was startling, not painful. She even bounced a bit and she was momentarily startled by how soft the thing was. Then he boldly walked over to a side table, pulled open a drawer before grabbing an envelope. She had no time to wonder what he was doing until she saw him draw out a condom.

Well, okay. No foiled pouch, no rolled and pre-lubricated—

He got it on just fine. And then he looked at her.

"I am a man and you are my woman."

He was going caveman on her and she kinda liked it. In

fact, she liked it a lot.

"Prepare yourself," he said.

She arched a brow. "Isn't that your job?"

He seemed to think about it for a second, and then nodded. So he dropped down to the floor beside the cot, grabbed one of her legs and threw it over his shoulder. Then he began to feast. It was quick and abrupt. She barely had time to gasp before she felt his fingers everywhere, his tongue lapping her, and when he sucked—oh God—stars appeared behind her eyes. She was orgasming before she had time to moan.

Her body arched off the cot, her legs tightened, and she writhed against him. She twisted and cried out, and still his tongue continued to take her. He thrust it inside her before licking a long stroke over her clit. And in time, he just stayed right there while her thrashing did the work for him.

And, oh God, it was good. So damned good.

Finally he let her rest. He pulled his face away as the contractions eased. And while she lay there languid, her breath slowing from a gasp to a pant, he shifted her legs to either side of his hips. He positioned himself at her entrance and he waited. He waited a very long time while she looked at him and wondered what he wanted. Why didn't he...

It didn't matter. Gathering her strength, she wrapped her legs around his backside. She arched her head back, and then she pulled him all the way in.

She meant to go fast, but he was very large. He also had the leverage to control what he did. So he entered her slowly. A single inevitable penetration while she expanded around him. She felt her insides pull wide, she felt how very solid he was, and she was surprised by how very much she liked it. She'd had sex before, but this was the big leagues. This was a big man marking her from the inside out. It made no logical sense, but that didn't change the feeling of being branded. As if the slow, steady push inside her was as permanent as hot iron. She was burned by him in all the best ways so that if anyone could look close, if anyone could see what was written on her body and soul, it would say: Keeven marks Janet as his own.

And then he began to thrust in earnest.

She was already sensitive. She'd just orgasmed for like half an hour. She wouldn't think he could ratchet her higher. But he set a pace designed to blow her mind. She already knew he was a disciplined man, but his control now was nothing short of godlike. He pulled back slowly, watching her face intently. Then he reversed, pushing inside a little faster, a little harder. Her eyes widened and her back arched. She couldn't stop herself from moving with him, against him. Big man, big push. And he went deeper inside.

Then he did it again. Always slow on the withdrawal. A little faster on the thrust. And so deep inside her.

Again. And again.

Soon she was crying out with every impact. Her legs were shaking with the force of gripping him. And every impalement sent sparks of need up her spine.

She was close. She was going to orgasm forever with this man.

Again. And again.

Her mind whited out. She was nothing but the rhythm of his thrust, the tightening in her belly, and the sparking flashes of ecstasy every time he embedded himself inside her.

She started babbling. She didn't even know she'd been speaking until she saw his eyes darken and his nostrils flare. Something about wanting him. Only him. Oh God, he was everything. And she meant it. She meant every word.

His breath grew ragged and his control shattered.

Suddenly he shoved his hands under her bottom, lifting her up so he could pound her deeper, harder, over and over without pause. The flashes up her spine became explosions. Tiny detonations that grew brighter and stronger.

Her orgasm hit her whole body at once. Everything contracted, then flew apart. She was the universe and he—

He was pouring himself into her. His face was fierce, his

expression pulled into a feral growl, and he pulsed inside her. Hard and thorough while she was everything that could take him in, that could welcome him into her.

Now she believed in magic. Now she knew that lovemaking could be divine because she felt it. She knew it.

And then he released. His body arched, his mouth opened, and his eyes flew wide. It was as though his soul opened and poured through him into her. And she was the pump that drew every drop inside herself. Pull. Pull. Because she had been created to take everything that he gave. Perfect.

So perfect that she wasn't even surprised when they realized the condom had broken.

CHAPTER 12

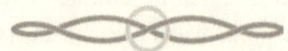

Keeven did not know the sheath had failed until he finally rolled off of her. The release had been the smallest of the surprises in their lovemaking. Never had he felt more connected, more joined with a soul as their bodies found pleasure. Never had the moment of release taken him so far outside of himself that he felt his heartspace merge with another's.

He did not know the sheath had failed, but he wasn't surprised. The Goddess had seen to it that despite Janet's wishes, she would carry the next generation of demi-angel. Still, he had to apologize to her. He had to find a way to atone for being the man who stole her independence against her will.

"Janet," he breathed, as he saw the mess of the split condom.

She had been lying in blissful relaxation, but something in his tone must have alerted her. She pushed up onto an elbow and looked. He saw the color drain from her face and a look of utter terror flash in her eyes. But a moment later, grim acceptance replaced the fear.

"Janet, I didn't plan this. I did not know—"

"Save it. Clearly something wants me barefoot and pregnant." She fell backwards onto his cot.

"It is possible that no child will be conceived," he offered, coming as close to a lie as he could.

"Yeah?" she said, her voice flat. "How often does a condom break in this world?"

He swallowed. "Never in my experience."

"Anyone else's?"

He thought back and sighed. "Of course I have heard of it. But...no. Not anyone I've ever known."

"Like I said. Barefoot and pregnant. Of all the ways I'm similar to my mother, I never thought it'd be this one. At least I'm older than seventeen. That's how old she was when I was conceived."

He reached forward, entwining his fingers with hers. He did not pull her arm off her eyes, but he tried to tell her with his touch how sorry he was. "I would not have done this to you. I know what it is to have no choice in one's life."

She was silent for a moment, then she brought her hand down from her face. She looked at him, her eyes somber as she studied him. "You had no choice in the princess, did you? No choice in spending your life in defense of the Wall. In fact, probably your only choice in life was to become a knight and give up lying."

"That's not true," he said softly. "I am a prince of the realm. I could choose nearly any life and any woman I wanted."

"Really?" She sounded skeptical.

"Really," he answered. "But I chose to live honorably."

"And so it's all laid out before you. Wife, Wall—"

"Life, Janet. Life in this small, vulnerable kingdom. I chose to live."

She smiled and tugged at his hand. "Very well then, honorable Sir Keeven. Come to bed. You look like you're about to collapse."

He arched a brow, but he could not argue with her. The knowledge that he had stolen her choices in this matter ate at him, but the thought that she was likely now nurturing his child lightened his heart as nothing else. That it was her child—his fierce angel Janet—made his soul sing with the possibilities of the demi-angel. He could not be happier.

So he settled onto the cot beside her. It was a small space, but they managed, wrapping themselves around each other to take what rest they could. But he could not sleep until he said one more thing.

"I will buy you all the shoes you could possibly want. A new one for every day of your life. You will never be barefoot unless you choose it."

She laughed then. A real laugh that eased them both. He could make her happy. In fact, he vowed it with every fiber of his being. He would make her happy. So he slept with her in his arms. And for a time he was content.

He woke late, his body cool and his arms empty. Outside, Wall City was alive with mid-morning activity. It was rare for him to wake so late, but Meaghan must have ordered him left alone. Whatever the cause, he was grateful as his gaze riveted on Janet. He could tell they would need time to talk in private.

He looked at her standing motionless in his room. She had her arms wrapped around her body and her gaze trained on something in the distance. He saw her in profile and knew from the morning sun that there was a trail of tears on her cheeks. And if he had any doubt, she reached up at that moment and wiped them away.

He pushed up onto his arms and called to her. Or he tried to. But the minute he tried to make a sound, his throat closed down on a cough. First one cough that burned in his throat, then a wheezing inhale that made everything worse.

"Keeven!" She was beside him in a moment, helping him sit upright. He knew what to do, so he pushed unsteadily to his feet and raised his arms above his head. He didn't even stand upright before the coughs had him doubling over, each hack more painful than the last. And the wheezing inhales grew harder and harder.

He looked up, meeting her eyes. He didn't want to die like this, gasping for air in front of his angel. She touched his cheeks, holding his gaze to hers. And he held his breath.

That was what saved him. The way he held his breath as he held her gaze. And then a slow sip of air while she looked at him. A slow exhale while she cradled his face. Ease in, easier out. Sip in, exhale—

He coughed up some phlegm and spit it into the trash. And with that things became easier still. In time he could take a breath, albeit not a deep one. But it was enough, and so he smiled at her as he stood upright like a man.

"Good morning, Janet," he said on a whisper.

"Is that a morning-after custom here?" she said, trying to tease him. "Greet your lover with the whooping cough?"

He smiled at her, but he could tell it wasn't a reassuring sight. "I am doing better now. Thank you."

"I didn't do anything. I didn't even call for help, which was massively dumb."

He gripped her arm. "Don't. I can't be seen like this."

"Ooo-kay," she said, drawing out the word. "Bad for morale. I get it. But shouldn't you call a doctor?"

He shook his head. Another cough was building, and so he spent his energy fighting it. She waited, watching him closely until his breath eased again.

"Is this because of the zombies?"

He shook his head then was surprised when the gesture didn't reassure her.

"It's the...the tropical disease that's killing everyone, isn't it?"

He rushed to reassure her. "No. Not that." Then his gaze shifted to the movements outside his room. There were guards set there as sentry, and Meaghan as well. As he watched, someone approached. Another lieutenant, but Meaghan stopped him, recording everything he said on her clipboard before sending the man away. He wondered how long she'd been there, protecting his sleep. He wondered too if she'd gotten any herself.

"Keeven, quit hiding from me. Tell me what's going on."

"There is a poison in the ground that burns the lungs," he

said. "I breathed too much of it yesterday."

"Closing the tunnels?"

He nodded. "It will heal in time."

"Assuming you don't go back down there. Assuming you don't push yourself too hard. And assuming you don't catch whatever dread disease or evil monster this whacko world throws at you."

He smiled at that. His heartspace could not translate everything she said, but he was well versed at understanding her meaning and not her words. He needed to distract her. He needed her attention on something that could be fixed and not the precariousness of his breath. "Why were you crying?"

She blinked, clearly startled by the rapid shift in conversation. And when she would have stepped away from him, he grabbed her hands and kept her close. He could tell she wanted to deflect him. Her gaze was hopping about the room, but he tightened his grip.

"It is rare for me to be left alone, Janet. We will not have privacy for long. You must tell me now what has upset you."

She turned to him with an arched look. "You mean other than losing my entire planet? Other than landing in a world with magic and evil attack zombies, not to mention a lover who is married to someone else?"

He held her gaze. "Yes. What else?"

"That selfsame lover woken by trying to hack up a lung?"

"You were crying before I woke."

She made a face and looked away from him, but a moment later her expression sobered. He knew if he waited long enough, she would tell him. He just prayed that he had the time to wait.

"I was thinking about junior."

"What is..." His heartspace showed him an image of a perfect baby, and he smiled. He couldn't stop himself. He set his hand on her belly and gave a silent prayer of thanks. "So you know already—"

"What? No! I have no idea, but...I was thinking about it. About him or her. What if things. What would I do if..." She sighed and put her hand over his. "If there is a baby."

He frowned. "What do you mean what would you do? You will be honored and cared for throughout the pregnancy. The child will be hailed as—"

"The hope of a new generation. Yeah, I heard all that. Quite a burden to put on a kid who isn't more than sixteen cells right now."

He straightened away from her. "The child is important."

"The child is a kid. No. The child is a conglomeration of cells that doesn't have to *become* at all."

He didn't understand her words. But when his heartspace showed him what she meant, he pulled back horrified. She couldn't possible mean... He felt his entire body go rigid with shock. He didn't have the words to express his total revulsion except... "*No!*"

She jolted at his word, jumping back from him not so much in fear as in surprise. He caught her. He would always catch her. And he held her wrist in a firm grip.

"You cannot do such a thing! Janet, I cannot allow you to even think it!"

She looked at him, her jaw going from slack to gritted in the blink of an eye. "First off, you can't control what I think."

His hands tightened and he saw her wince before he realized he was likely bruising her arm. Still, it was an act of will to make himself release her. If she tried to run from him, he didn't know what he would do. He could not let her leave. Fortunately, she remained right where she was, her eyes awash with tears of frustration or fury, he didn't know which.

"How can I make you understand?" he rasped. "You cannot—"

"I'm not going to!" She took a breath while he held his. He would say nothing right now that would risk her changing her mind. "You have to understand," she continued. "There are a lot of unwanted children where I'm from."

His mind reeled at that. "How can a child be unwanted?"

She stared at him, then she gestured with a quick flick of her wrist. "I'm not going to try to answer that. Not in the time we have. Just take it on faith that it's true."

"Faith? What kind of heaven allows a child—"

"Because I'm not from freaking heaven!" She took a deep breath, then released it on a huff. "Look, I'm not going to abort. I was just naming options."

"That is not an option."

"Yeah, I got your opinion, thank you."

It took him a moment to process her tone. More specifically, for him to realize exactly what she meant by "opinion." And when he did, he took another breath to calm himself, but in the end his words vibrated with a kind of fury that he'd rarely felt in all his life. Not when he was nearly dead from the birdbeasts. Not when his father was killed by the Aruckien. Not ever, except for when she implied that he had no voice over his own child.

"Janet, please answer me very carefully," he said quietly. "Do you acknowledge that you carry my child?"

"It's *our* child, Keeven. If there's a baby, then it's *our* baby. But it's my body."

"You will not kill the child?"

She shot him a glare. "No, I will not. Why would I abort a child who would be revered?" Her tone was unclear. He understood that she would give birth to the child, but he had no comprehension of why she all but sneered the word "revered."

"Janet—"

She rubbed a hand past her belly, pausing for a second before gesturing. "It's complicated, okay? I might not even be pregnant, but if I am, I want a say in how the child is raised." She swallowed. "In *where* it's raised."

"You want to take my child to heaven? You want to keep me from—"

"Stop! Keeven, just...no. You're the father. You have

rights. But I'm not going to just let you take my child and set it on an altar somewhere. Or shackle it to the Wall to keep the thing standing."

"What you say makes no sense!"

"The hell it doesn't!" She took a breath and then she took a step. She went nose to nose with him, her eyes steady and her words forceful. "I'm the mother, you're the father. We're going to figure this out, okay?"

"I cannot let you take my child away from me."

"And you can't keep me here, can you? You've blood sworn to get me back to my world."

It was true. He felt the weight of it on his shoulders. Yet another promise he was compelled to fulfill. But the idea of siring a child and not ever seeing it, of having it live in a place that did not cherish every life as a great gift...he couldn't abide it. The very idea was crushing him.

"I need you to swear something to me, Keeven. A...a blood thing like before."

"Janet, you have to listen—"

"You have to swear that we'll figure things out together. You and me."

"Of course—"

"No one else, Keeven. We'll decide together where and how the child lives. We'll agree, but I can't fight armies and magical compulsions and who knows what else the Goddess does to me. I can work with you, Keeven, but not all that."

He didn't understand her words. She was like a child who wanted things to be simple when life was anything but. "Divine gifts need to be honored. There are things the child must do."

"And if I disagree? What are you going to do then, Keeven? Lock me up? Keep me from my own child?"

"Of course not!"

"It's not 'of course!' What would have happened to you if you'd refused to re-build The Wall yesterday?"

"I would not do such a thing. Can you not see how

important our defense is? Do you want Aruckien running wild through our lands? Killing everything in sight?"

"Of course not! But that can't be the baby's whole life. I won't let my child be a slave to his country like—" She abruptly shut her mouth. She cut off her word, but his heartspace told him what she'd meant to say. He didn't need words to understand her.

"A slave like me," he said quietly. "You will not let our child become like me." The fury of that burned hotter than the pain in his throat. But beneath the fury was agony. She saw. She knew. His angel understood how he daily fought— and failed—to meet all his promises. And she would not let their child become as weak as he.

And while he struggled with the pain of that, she took a step forward. "You said it yourself, Keeven. You have no choices in your life. Everything is prescribed for you. What kind of life is that?"

"My life," he rasped. "My choice to honor the gift of my talents."

"And it's killing you."

A tide of emotions buried him, the feelings mashed together in unyielding conflict. Anger and resentment mixed inextricably with pride and patriotism. He served his people and found meaning in that. How could she think it was an evil way to live?

"You know nothing," he rasped. "You look at me and see sacrifice. Do you not understand what I do? Who I am?"

"You are a prince royale and a Knight that serves the Wall."

"I chose that."

"You were born to it. No one asked you what you wanted. They just told you."

"Of course I want it!"

"Really? What would you have if you could choose anything, Keeven? What would you do?"

He let his head drop back, his breath heavy in his lungs.

"Again with the child's games. Life cannot be lived in wishes."

She folded her arms. "My child gets to choose."

"No." He had not meant the word as anything more than an expression of frustration. He meant to say: no, she didn't understand his meaning. No, she cannot believe his life has been so regimented. But he saw immediately that she took his word badly. Her expression closed down and her shoulders squared in anger. Her hands splayed across her belly and she turned away from him. She didn't say a word, but every part of her rejected him.

With that one move, he felt her heartspace close down to him. He had not known it was possible for her to shut the door on their communication. Even when he'd put her in chains, she had not so cleanly separated herself from him. The change from last night's union was so abrupt and so complete that it cut at him. A bright slash of pain that left a raw emptiness in its wake.

He gasped at the agony of it, and in that moment, he forgot to moderate his breath. Were he healthy, he might simply have choked. But after all he had done yesterday, his lungs were at a delicate balance between pain and a crippling cough. That gasp tipped the balance. What began as a choke became a cough that tore at his throat. And with that pain, he could not prevent another gasp. Another cough. More and more until he felt his knees give out.

She was beside him at the first gasp, but when she could not support him, she started to cry out.

"Somebody help! Get a doctor!"

She'd forgotten that no one could hear her inside. His shoulders bunched as he inhaled through the restriction. The tubes to his lungs were thickening with the pain, the need to cough was overwhelming.

"Damn it!" She let go of him and rushed to the opening. "Somebody help!"

He didn't see if she went far enough to be heard. She must have because suddenly there were feet all around him. Hands supported him, though hers were the gentlest. He heard her curse and felt a pang of guilt for dying at such a bad time. They had not resolved anything…

If only he could get a breath.

If only he could stop coughing.

"Damn it, I'm an idiot," she said. She let go of him. He had managed a wheezing inhale, but there would not be many more. He could already tell that his throat was thick, the airway shrinking by the second.

"Keeven, I've got Marty's inhaler." She held something up before his eyes, but he could not make sense of it. He heard her curse again and then she pressed it to his mouth. "Put your mouth around it then breathe in."

He couldn't. Another cough racked at him.

"Damn it, Keeven. Seal your mouth around it!" She put her hands to his lips to help him. He was weakening, but he did what she wanted. And with his next inhale she squeezed it. He felt the movement in her hand and the puff of bitter air as it hit his tongue. He would have spit it out, but she held his face. "It's medicine, Keeven. You need to breathe it in."

Of course it was medicine. Nothing else could taste that foul. But he understood the principle. He had to time the puff of air with his breath. So while he fought to stop another cough, he put his hand around the device that she held to his lips. And when he next pushed himself to inhale, he did so through his mouth while they squeezed the thing together.

This time the medicine did not fall on his tongue. Or at least not as much. And while more people rushed into his room, a miracle happened. Instead of tightening, his breath eased. The effect was small at first, but rapidly growing. He took a breath and felt real air fill his lungs instead of the tiny whisper he'd been allowed. He did it again, and though it still burned, the wheeze was not so strong.

Oh to have sweet air in his chest again. He coughed, but not badly. Pain flashed in his throat, but it was brief. He could fight the urge to cough as he inhaled and exhaled in relief.

He looked to the small thing in his hand. It was her hand, actually, cradling a small metal canister with a white tube which he'd put in his mouth. He lifted it again, but she resisted.

"Easy there. Marty says only two puffs at a time. And, you know, it's meant for humans. We've got no idea how it works on you."

He looked at her, gratitude flooding him. "It makes it easy to breathe," he whispered.

She smiled, dropping her forehead against his. "Yeah, got that, big guy. But there could be side effects. Don't want you suddenly sprouting horns or twerking on the Wall."

He did not know her words, but the meaning was clear. No more medicine right then. It was more than enough. It was a miracle. He looked at her, seeing the worry on her face, and the relief that made her look at him with such love. He felt her heartspace open to him again, and the joy of that flooded him.

There was no choice then. He could not let her leave his world. He could not let her disappear from his land and his people, taking her medicines and her child with her. Neither could he sustain the pain of losing her in his heartspace. She filled him to overflowing, and he wondered how he could ever have existed before.

"I swear it," he said. "I swear that we will find an answer together."

She pressed her lips to his then. Swift and sure, but it was nothing to the happiness that flooded his heartspace from her. "I swear it too, Keeven. We'll figure it out."

It wasn't enough to bind them magically. There could not be any blood oath sworn on those words. They were too vague. But it didn't matter to him. She was too important for him to risk losing her. Child or not, she brought wonders to his world and joy to his heart. He would do everything in his power to keep her happy and safe. No cost was too great.

"So now that you can breathe again, let's go get your wife from Darth Vadar."

He looked at his angel and thought of all the myriad ways she could die in the attempt to rescue the princess. He also saw how absolutely determined Janet was to join in the endeavor. And right there, he made a decision.

In the future, he was going to pick easier vows.

CHAPTER 13

Wall City was a fascinating place. Sort of a mixture of army encampment and the Ewok tree village, if the Ewok built with see-thru force fields instead of wood and leaves. She could happily spend time here exploring, but instead she was chaffing under the days of waiting. She waited for Keeven to finish all the super-urgent, must-be-taken-care-of-now things that a commander had to handle. She waited to see if she was pregnant. She waited for her life to settle into some kind of order where she could function.

But there was the surprise. All her life, she had craved order and rules. Chaotic childhood plus academic mindset meant that she escaped into the steady, quiet pulse of an ivory tower. She loved it there.

Except now she kinda liked it here where there was a new surprise around every corner. It was as if her need to control her environment had simply given up the ghost. There was too much to understand, too much to try and fit into a neat rule of logic, so she just didn't. Frog people with super long fingers to climb trees? Not a problem. Magical stones to bring down fevers? Yawn. Super hot sex with Keeven every night? Now that was a benefit she could get into. And—added benefit—the condoms stayed together each night.

She continued to study their language every day with Meaghan. She also started looking into their medical practices. She was no doctor, but illness was their biggest problem, and it helped her study the range and possibilities of their magical stones. Ones to bring down fever, ones to immobilize a broken bone, ones to jump start a heart. Much easier than carting around a defibrillator.

They knew about basic hygiene. Hand washing was routine here. As was lifting the ill up as high as possible and allowing the breeze to clean the air around them. That seemed to be a cultural bias which she now understood if the ground held some sort of poison that burned through their lungs.

She also wondered about mosquitoes, and there were certainly insects around here. She explained what she knew to Meaghan who gave it to the doctors. Who knew if that was the problem here, but it was certainly another avenue to explore.

And she waited.

Until the morning when Alenth showed up carrying cold meat pies for breakfast. She opened the door quietly, trying to give Keeven an extra moment's rest. It didn't work because Mr. Always Working was pulling on a shirt before she'd even smiled. Alenth bowed deeply to her, his expression warm, but his skin was pale and there was an emptiness in his eyes. Whoever he'd lost to the zombies had certainly been important to him.

While she wolfed down the awesome, spicy falafel-like thing, Keeven looked at her with grave eyes.

"Are you still resolved to go?"

It took a moment for her to realize what he meant. And then a second more for her to swallow. "To the evil castle? Hell yes." Then she leaned forward, pitching her voice and her expression to mega-serious. "Keeven, I have to go."

She didn't want to explain why yet. She had an idea about their magic, a growing theory that she needed to explore. It began simply by noticing that all their most powerful stones, the ancient ones passed down through generations, were actually crystals. The evidence was pretty simple. Every magic stone was regular, beautiful, and way too perfect to be randomly discovered in a mine somewhere. Especially since there was no mining in this land because of the poisoned air in the ground.

Which meant they were manufactured. Probably by the same people who built the shuttlecraft. She had to find out more about those people, and she would bet her life that there were more clues in the castle. Then she shivered. She might literally be betting her life.

"It is extremely dangerous," Keeven said gravely. "I do not want you to go."

Talk about thought echo. "It's really important, Keeven."

"Why?" He grabbed her hand and pressed his mouth to her fingers. "Why risk everything?" By which he meant their possible child.

She shook her head. Even if he could understand what she was thinking, she had no proof. Only a hunch. Which meant she needed more data, and as far as she could figure out, the evil castle was the only place with a storehouse of stones.

"I'll stay out of the way until it's safe, but I have to go in."

He didn't argue further, though he wanted to. She could see it in his expression. But in the end, he simply nodded and pushed to his feet. "Then we leave now."

"Great." Meaghan had helped her put together a pack of essentials. She grabbed it and followed Alenth out the door. "So we taking the shuttlecraft?"

Keeven followed behind her, a warm hand on the small of her back. She had to admit it was nice to feel him there. All big and protective. "The transport is the fastest way," he said. "Once there, we will still have to walk. There is a hidden grove near enough to set down, but far enough away that the demonic force cannot see us."

She nodded, understanding the plan. But when she stepped into the transport, it was empty except for the three of them. She turned back to Keeven. "So are the ground troops meeting us there?"

He took a moment to process her words, but eventually

shook his head. "No ground troops."

"Oh. Air support?"

"Alenth will return to the grove at the same time every day."

"Um, not what I meant—" But it was too late. Keeven had already turned to Alenth and the men started discussing the details of when and where the pilot would wait and for how long. Meanwhile, Janet dredged up every military movie she'd ever seen and tried to piece things together. "So this is a secret infiltration. Slip in, slip out, all quiet."

Keeven nodded, his expression troubled. "There are secrets about this place that we cannot share. You are not to speak of it ever." Janet waited for him to explain, but he said nothing more. Great. They were back to stoic warrior.

"So who's your support? I mean, you're studly and everything, but you alone against a Magician? That doesn't sound smart."

He gestured to Alenth who nodded and settled down to do whatever pre-flight stuff he had to. That mostly involved buckling on the leather straps and putting his hands on the armrests. Janet wanted to study that a lot more closely, but she was too worried about Mr. Overconfident Prince who was about to take on the big baddy single-handedly.

"Keeven—"

"I have a way in that will open the door to the keep and also keep me hidden from the demonic creatures."

"Bilbo in the dragon cave. Got it." Though the idea that he had the One Ring to rule them all was a little unsettling in a vague kind of way. "But I need to search the castle," she said. "We've got to find—"

"I know what you seek," he interrupted, his voice tight. "I will make the demon sleep, and that will give us time to find what is needed." He gestured to his pouch and the stones there that induced a coma. Which would be lovely assuming the demon wasn't resistant in some way. And it wasn't a demonic *force* like he'd been saying before.

"Great idea, maybe. And for the record, I was going to say that I wanted to find some clues on how to recharge your stones." She had a dozen of the depleted ones in her pack in case she got an idea. "And while we're on the subject, there's no need to be so pissy."

It took a moment for her meaning to get through. He probably was stuck on the word pissy, but when he understood, his expression darkened to fury. He grabbed her arms and didn't drag her. No, he picked her up—as in bodily lifted her off her feet—and carried her not-so-gently to the back of the shuttlecraft. She hadn't thought the space all that large when she'd first been in here, but take out all the supplies, and it felt like he'd just hauled her across the Atlantic. Leaving Alenth—friendly Alenth—all the way back in the US with his attention on his controls as the transport lifted off.

Okay, so no help there.

She looked at Keeven who appeared even more pissed off then before and managed to say something really intelligent that sounded like "meep!"

Then he just stood there for a moment, radiating frustration and condemnation. On anyone else it would have looked menacing—and it was—but not in the usual way. This was a man pushed to the edge of sanity. And she very much feared she'd been the one shoving him there.

"No one speaks to me like that," he said, his voice low but throbbing with intensity. "No one but you."

She glared at him, doing her best not to let her temper run away with her. "Get used to it big, bad prince. I don't take shit from anyone." It was a lie, she abruptly realized. Back on Earth, she did take shit from just about everyone. She was a PhD student. Lowest man on the academic payroll and general minion to all. And she'd accepted it as the norm. She'd ducked her head and did everything she was told while praying that no one upset her applecart of a world.

Well something had upset it. A portal in the back of Marty's closet. And now she was here, squaring off with an angry Knight Prince, and she wasn't taking shit. She was smart and learning fast. She had things to offer this world beyond her womb, and he had to understand that.

"I'm not just some dumb baby-making machine," she snapped.

"And I give you every respect, Janet." He all but spat her name. "Why can't you give me a measure in return?"

She gaped at him, stunned by his words. "Of course I respect you. I wouldn't be doing everything I can to save you if I thought you were a dumb-ass."

"You challenge everything," he said his voice a low growl. "The air we breathe, the magic that keeps us alive—"

"The transport, the power source, the eco system. Yeah, I do. How else am I to learn how your world ticks? How else can I help you?"

He swallowed. He stared at her and in that moment, his expression was infinitely sad. "How can you not see what I want?"

She bit her lip. Okay, so she was missing something obvious. Take it apart logically, look at it from all sides. He was a leader of men. And she'd just challenged him in front of one of them. And not just a man, but a fellow royal. "Um, I probably shouldn't have called you pissy. But, in my defense, Alenth doesn't speak my language."

He all but rolled his eyes at that. "You have never had trouble being understood, even without the words."

Right. Tone would mean a lot. "Okay, so I'm sorry about that. I'll try not to call you names in public." That sounded a lot more grudging than she meant. Fortunately, he must have understood because he dipped his chin in acknowledgement.

Meanwhile, her brain was still churning. What else did he want? "I know you want babies, but I'm more than my womb. I have a brain—"

He bit off a curse of frustration, and she cut off her words as she studied his face. Wow. He was really pissed.

"Um, am I wrong?"

"Your children will be worshiped—"

"We've had this discussion—"

"But you are ten thousand times more valuable than any offspring."

She blinked. "What?"

"Every angel has brought new ideas to my people. Divine inspiration, heavenly concepts. Your every word is weighted with—"

"Oh shit." She could not express just how bad an idea that was. To take every word she spoke and make it divine? "I spit out nonsense all the time. It's kinda how I think."

His expression softened, but only a little. He was still pretty angry. "You cannot do that anymore. Not out loud and not in public."

Right. Inserting a filter between brain and mouth. Not going to be easy. "But you don't think that, right?" she said. "You know I'm just testing ideas, right? Testing—"

"Me."

He said it so quietly, she hadn't even realized he'd spoken at first. But she heard it in her heart, and she knew his meaning. He thought she'd been putting him through trials just for kicks.

"When will I prove worthy to you?" he asked softly. "What must I do? What trial must I pass?"

She shook her head, stunned that he understood so little of her. "I haven't been testing you. And even if I had, you've more than proven yourself, Keeven. I think you're incredible."

He waited, his gaze searching her face. And then he waited some more. It took her some time before she realized he wanted her to say something else.

"Uh…" She swallowed. She had no idea what he wanted and suddenly she felt incredibly inadequate. They were nose to nose at the very back of the transport. She was braced against the back wall and he was towering over her, his body stiffening more and more as he seemed to draw back from her.

She didn't want him to leave her. Not until she figured out the rules. Not just of his world, but of him. Of how they could manage a relationship when nothing around her felt safe or even sane.

"Keeven, don't abandon me yet."

He closed his eyes on a groan. "I have told you, I will never—"

"I'm not talking about your body. I'm talking about your heart." She dared to touch his chest. "Please don't leave me here."

He put his hand over hers, pressing down until her palm was flat and her fingers fully extended. She felt the warmth of him surround her there: the heat from his chest below her palm and the sheer size of his hand over hers. In that one small place, she felt him as completely as if he held her entire body cradled against him.

"I do not think I could even if I wanted it."

She gave him a weak smile. "Sure you can. All you have to do is stop talking to me."

He dropped his forehead to hers. "I do not use words well."

"So don't talk," she whispered. Then she raised her mouth to his. In this, they'd always communicated well.

Her lips molded to his and she pressed her tongue to the seam of his lips. He opened a second later, his tongue clashing with hers, the duel exciting even as she quickly lost ground to him. Soon he was pushing inside her mouth while his body grew hot around hers.

She was wearing the uniform of his troops. Loose shorts over leather boots. Her toolbelt because God knew something in there had to be useful. A simple shirt similar to a tee, though without any insignia. His outfit was similar, though he wore leather pants. And over the past few nights, she'd learned how to quickly get him naked. He'd mastered a bra equally fast.

But they were in public, and though Alenth had his

attention firmly focused ahead, Keeven probably didn't think a quick shag in the back of a transport an appropriately princely thing to do. And yet as his mouth devoured hers and his hands roved to all those wonderful places, she couldn't muster the strength to care. Not when he slipped his fingers beneath her shirt and let his hands caress up her belly. One hand quickly unfastened her bra while the other slipped up to cover her breast, thumbing her nipple with quick strokes that shot fire to her belly.

Then he had both hands on her breasts, shaping her in just the right way, pinching her nipples while she arched into him.

"Can we?" she gasped.

He lifted his head and growled out, "Quiet."

She thought he meant her, but a moment later, she realized it was a command to the transport. The back went dark and something dropped between them and Alenth. They had plenty of light from the few windows, but she couldn't see their pilot at all.

Then before she could ask, Keeven stripped her shirt and bra away.

"We are alone," he said before he began to suckle her breasts. One, then the other, while she writhed against the wall. He had her pinned there, his body hot and hard, and she ground her pelvis against his erection, knowing now his favorite rhythm.

Her orgasm was building quickly, the tightening in her belly exquisitely familiar. He always took her from zero to a zillion in seconds. Then while he still tongued her nipple, his hands dropped to her toolbelt. He unbuckled that, then her shorts. All of it pushed away before he left her breasts to kiss down her belly.

She gripped his shoulders, her breath coming in quick gasps as his thumbs slipped through her folds. He knew her so well now. He knew just how to open her, just how she liked to be rubbed. And she knew too that he intended to lick her to a screaming orgasm. He'd done it a dozen times already.

But she didn't want that this time. She didn't want him worshiping her without giving back. And so she took his face in her hands, lifting him up to look at her.

"Not like that," she said.

His expression was rueful. "No condom."

She gaped at him. Seriously? He hadn't thought to bring…

Then she quieted down. Her heart was still hammering, her breath less than steady, but in that space inside her mind where her thoughts and emotions collided, everything seemed to still. It was as if everything lined up neatly into two columns. The first was a long, long list of all the reasons why she shouldn't even consider sex without protection. In the other column were two things.

1. Keeven wanted a child.

2. She wanted to give him one.

It made no sense, and yet there it was. She knew the baby would be well cared for and much loved. And in a universe where she could step through a closet door and be in freaky land, this seemed like the most sane thing she could do. Give the man she loved what he wanted most in the world.

Because she loved him.

That's what solidified in the stillness of her heart: love. She loved him.

And so she smiled.

"We don't need one," she said.

There was a long pause and a growing shock on his face. He'd heard her. More than that, his heartspace was telling him what she truly meant: she would bear his child.

And while the awe of that infused his expression, she chuckled. "But you know, you're going to have to deal with whatever child comes out. She's likely to be just as mouthy as I am."

"Yes," he said as he slowly straightened in front of her. "With dark hair and eyes that see everything."

"And questions. If you think I never shut up, just you wait."

"He will be strong too," he said, as she helped him unfasten his pants. "I will teach him."

"Girls can be strong too."

His erection thrust forward, large and proud. She knew now that he fit her. That everything about him worked for her physically. She couldn't resist touching him, stroking the smooth head, gripping the shaft as he crowded forward.

"I know," he said. Then he touched her face, lifting it until she was looking into his eyes. "You want this? With me?"

"With only you. I will not do this with anyone else."

She felt him absorb her words. His body shuddered and his breath eased out of him as if he surrendered to her. But she didn't want capitulation.

"Tell me it has to be me," she said, echoing his words from their first kiss. "Tell me you want this with only me and no other."

He slid his hands down her body. From neck to shoulders, down her arms until he took both of her hands in his and lifted them up to his mouth, kissing her fingers.

"I want you, Janet. I have always wanted you."

"Because I'm an angel?"

"Because you're you."

There was more meaning behind his words. Flashes of emotions that burst through her consciousness before tangling with her own feelings. All of them came and went so fast, too fast and too complicated to label. But they all meant "her" to him. And he wanted "her."

She stretched up a leg, circling his hips before drawing him tight to her groin. He smiled as he let go of her hands to trail his hands down her ribs and hips until he gripped her bottom. Then he lifted as she pushed off.

A moment later he held her braced against the back wall while his erection pushed against her center. He held her carefully, his gaze trained on hers as she wrapped her legs around him. Then suddenly she stopped him. Suddenly, she remembered.

"What about your vows? Your promise to the princess?"

He swallowed, and she saw desperation in his eyes. "This cannot be wrong. The need, the desire. It must be fated."

Ah. Rationalization. She knew it well. "I will not be the cause of your fall, Keeven." And he would see it as a failure. In the cold light of day, he would think back on this and believe he had failed somehow.

"I choose this," he said firmly. "I choose you."

Then he thrust. She slid easily around him, stretching as she always did. He was large and she loved it. And he was hard in all the best ways.

And when he was fully embedded, he caught her gaze with his own. "You are right," he said. "Everything in my life is prescribed. Everything but you. So in this, I choose you."

"Okay," she whispered.

"Okay," he answered in her language.

He was leaning against her, his body holding her against the wall as surely as he pinioned her below. She tightened her arms around his shoulders, using her own strength to lever up enough to give him room to move.

He helped her, raising her enough that he slid out a little before pushing back home.

Then she pressed her lips to his face, kissing whatever she could reach. His hair, his temple, his nose, and eventually, his mouth.

His tongue met hers, and their kiss was deep and drugging. But still he didn't move inside her. He just kissed her.

Until she broke the kiss, needing air. So she clutched him tight and whispered against his ear.

"Love me." It wasn't a question so much as a hope. Or maybe it was a command because he answered.

"Yes."

Then he began to move.

A slow withdrawal, a steady thrust.

In and out, the tempo building slowly.

She gripped him, as best she could, but he was her sole

support. He held her in his hands and he braced her against the wall. And his thrust built inside her. Heavier, stronger, faster.

Harder.

His breath began to pulse.

Her own was ragged.

And every impact sent bright lightning bolts of sensation through her body.

Flash.

Flash.

Fire!

She arched and cried out. Her body gripped and convulsed around him. Ecstasy like a fireball of pleasure exploding within her.

"Yes!" he cried. Then he released.

Joy flooded their heartspace. His into hers and hers into his.

The worst thing about phenomenal sex is that eventually you have to return to reality. As much as Janet tried to stay in the sweeping ecstasy of epic sex, reality intruded. For one thing, Keeven was struggling to keep her high against the wall. In the wake of his own explosive release, he'd pushed her a good foot off the floor. But now she was sliding down the wall and taking him with her.

He steadied her, of course. She got the feeling he wanted nothing more than to always be there holding her up, helping her with whatever. But he had limits, and right now that meant he had to set her on her feet while he struggled to get his breath under control.

She could relate. Her heart was still jackhammering inside her.

But she had to stand or risk them both falling over. And the moment her feet hit the deck, she remembered that they were both in the back of a transport. And one glance out the window told her they'd already landed.

Huh. Wonder when that had happened.

She licked her lips then chuckled when she realized Keeven was watching the movement, his eyes dark and his nostrils flared. "Wow," she said. "You really are insatiable."

He had no answer except a dull flush to his cheeks.

Which made her laugh harder. "That's a compliment. I like it when my guy can't get enough of me."

"Then I shall make you very happy."

"Works for me," she quipped. Except of course, it didn't work right at that moment, because they had touched down. "Um…" she began, but he nodded.

"I know."

Then he took a deep breath and slid out of her. He groaned as he did it. She did as well, hating the sudden emptiness inside her. But they had a job to do.

They dressed quickly and in silence. He was fully suited up, complete with his sword and pack by the time she'd managed to get her pants and bra on. Keeven waited for her to finish, his expression growing more dour by the second. She looked at him in question, but he just looked back. A steady, long look, absolutely serious, and completely inscrutable.

"What?" she asked. Actually, she whispered it because a look that intense shouldn't be shattered with her normal voice.

He touched her face. A long, slow stroke of his thumb across her cheek and then over her lower lip.

"Keev—"

He kissed her. Slow and sweet. Drugging her into lethargy such that she melted against him.

And then he ended it.

Oh shit.

That was a good-bye kiss.

"Oh no—"

"Open," he commanded in his normal voice. The tone was loud enough to make her wince.

The door broke open with the pop and hiss of a hermetic seal. Then he pushed it aside before jogging out into the field.

She watched him dash into the trees, his speed faster than she thought possible for such a big guy. Everything in her wanted to call him back. There was no reason to risk himself right this second. She'd just agreed to have his baby. Perhaps he should wait to confront the demon until later. Like after their kid had gone to college.

But she held the words back. He wouldn't listen to them anyway. Her job right now was to wait. To sit with Alenth until he signaled that all was clear.

So with a sigh, she turned away from the hatch and looked to the front. Alenth was watching her with grave eyes. He knew better than she did exactly what Keeven risked running in there alone.

She swallowed, remember that she had to show confidence in him whatever her private fears were. "He's really good," she said aloud. "He'll be fine."

"Yes," Alenth answered, though she'd been speaking in English. He said more, but she wasn't fluent enough in the language to catch it all.

Ordering herself to get a grip, she headed for the cockpit. Might as well pass the time by getting her first good look at the dashboard. It was smooth and black, probably because the thing wasn't turned on.

"Can you...um..." She pointed to the dash.

He nodded, and then touched something on his armrest. She had no idea what, because it all looked like smooth plastic to her. But on the black dash multiple images and symbols appeared.

He pointed to a specific one—a view of the field in which they sat—and she guessed it was a camera view of what was in front. He touched it again, and the view changed to another area of the field. Ah. Back view.

"Can you show me more of the ground?" she asked. He

tilted his head, obviously not understanding her. Right. She searched through her memory to find the right words. "Show me the castle."

He nodded and a moment later the view changed.

She stared at it, her heart beating painfully in her throat. It couldn't be. It wasn't possible. And yet there it was.

"No. Nononononononononono."

She pressed a hand to her mouth to choke off her panic. Her mind was reeling from what was there stark and clear on the dash.

Then without a second thought, she grabbed her pack and ran out. She had to get to Keeven.

Right.

Now.

CHAPTER 14

Keeven heard her crashing through the underbrush long before he saw her. He cursed under his breath—this was supposed to be a silent approach—and moved to intercept her. It didn't take long. She rushed around a bush and he grabbed her arm, hauling her tight to his body.

She let out a startled cry, but he covered her mouth, doing his best to keep her silent and still allow her to breathe.

"It's me," he said. "Shhhh."

She nodded though she was breathing like a great racken.

"Is Alenth all right? Did something happen?"

She nodded, then shook her head. Thank the Goddess for the connection through his heartspace. At least he understood that she was agitated, but not terrified. And her gestures meant that something important had alarmed her, but it wasn't lethal.

So he waited, feeling her whole body gasp as she caught her breath. Naturally that brought to mind all the other times she had shuddered in his arms, and he stayed quiet just to appreciate the feel of her moving against him. She was merely breathing, but he would do a great deal to be the man she rested against every night and day of her life.

He set his cheek against her forehead, treasuring the seconds there even as he kept himself alert. She was still making too much noise and he did not know what type of creature the Magician had called to this place. His spies told him there never was any soldier or patrol, just the pulsing light of something evil surrounding the castle. But that made no sense. So he stayed alert and waited for—

"You can let go now, Keeven," she said, her voice quiet. "I can breathe."

"But you still rest at the edge of panic." Her heart was beating hard, her breath was short and quick, but mostly he felt the anxiety that stuttered through his heartspace from her.

"Um, yeah," she said. "It's because that's not a freaking castle out there."

He straightened, frowning down at her. "It's is—"

"Castles have turrets and moats and stuff. That's a massive pizza cutter with thrusters on either side."

He did not respond. He was trying to understand the images she sent him.

She huffed out a breath. "Listen to me. That's a crashed spaceship out there. And it explains how you have a shuttlecraft. How long has it been there?"

He tilted his head. "Centuries."

"And you've got a magic stone that opens a secret passageway into it?"

He nodded.

"Let me see it."

He pulled it out from the secret pouch in his pocket. It was a smooth black stone with a loop on one side. There were no markings, no contours. Just flat black—

"Christ, that's a keyfob."

"It's a secret magic—"

"Keyfob. Yes, I know." She leaned back against a tree trunk. "Keeven, there's a clear difference between your people—the royals—and the Freerik people. Is it possible that you're entirely different races?"

"Of course we are. There are enough similarities that we have had children together. But they are rare and in general, the races remain apart."

"That's because one race crash landed here from that spaceship. I'm guessing it's yours. The royals. Because you've got the technological superiority over the Freeriks."

He looked away. "That information is not generally shared," he said, keeping his voice soft.

She rolled her gaze back to his, her expression as close to horror as she'd ever shown him. "You know, I hate it when a society hides information. I find it beyond appalling."

"The royals know when they are old enough to mate."

"Because they need to propagate the species. The crashed spaceship species." She rubbed a hand over her face. "Wait a minute. The angels. You said they used to come out regularly."

He nodded. "A few every year for a while. And then fewer. You are the first in fifty years."

"Stasis pods. I'll bet anything there are stasis pods there spitting out people every so often. But you've either run out or something's changed."

"But you did not come from the castle."

"Exactly! I'm not part of your race. I'm human. From Earth. And… And…" She reached out and intertwined her fingers in with his. "And I don't know what else, but you're not going in there alone."

"It is not safe."

"Why? And why do you call it an evil castle, anyway?"

He shrugged. "It keeps the local populace away. And there is a protector."

"Like soldiers and stuff?"

He shook his head. "Not that I am aware, but I don't believe the castle is unprotected."

She frowned. "So is there a monster inside or not?"

He sighed. "I don't know."

"But…it's a spaceship."

"This is not my land. It is under the protection of the princess's family."

"You've never been here before?"

He shook his head.

"What about that glowing, throbbing energy field around it? Is that normal?"

He shook his head. "That is the demonic field. That is what traps the princess inside."

"And you're going to get around it how?"

"I have magic that may stop it or hide me from it."

"So we're working on hope. Great."

She stared at him, and he did his best to cover his worries. In truth, he had no idea if the stones he carried would work. He only prayed that he was clever enough to understand the Magician's evil before it killed him. "It is my task, Janet. No one else has the training or the skills to understand." The two others he had sent had never returned.

"But you don't understand," she stressed. "You're just guessing."

He shrugged. "That is the way one lives a life of service."

She grimaced. "I get it. You're the big high muckety-muck, so it's your job to take the risk, figure out the problem, save the princess. Whatever." She hefted her pack. "Okay, then. It's a good thing you've got me here."

He grabbed her arm. "You cannot go there. I do not know what I will face."

"Laser beams? Evil robots who scream exterminate?" She propped a hand on her hip. "Trust me, Keeven, I'm way more prepared than you are. You can't even imagine a trash compactor of doom."

He searched his heartspace but the images she showed him were too bizarre to comprehend. "I do not think you can either. Are you sure you are feeling well?"

She huffed out a breath. "Come on. Let's get your keyfob in range."

"Janet—"

She turned on him. "Trust me, okay? I can help."

He looked at her, his heart sinking. "This will be the way with you always. You will say things that make no sense and then ask me to trust you."

She arched a brow. "You got a problem with that?"

Yes. No. Maybe. But he found that he was smiling. "My life has gotten infinitely more strange since meeting you."

She snorted. "Tell me about it."

And so they began to walk.

Janet was about to enter a freaking spaceship. Every time she'd thought she'd seen everything this planet had to offer, something else appeared and made her question her sanity again. But oddly enough, this sudden appearance made sense.

They started climbing to the demon's "castle" while she kept staring at the massive size of the thing. It wasn't quite the Enterprise, but it was close. The disc was on its end like a pizza cutter, and there were two long cylinder things on either side. Or rather, one long cylinder angled up in the air and the remains of the other one smashed against the mountain.

It looked like the ship had crashed into the mountainside forever ago. The dirt and the vegetation had grown up along it, but the thing was so huge that the bulk of it was still visible.

"So if we come across any eggs, don't go close to them, okay? Just stay back." She'd seen *Alien* too young, and now had a terror of Easter eggs.

Keeven didn't answer. He just shot her an odd look and shrugged. She liked that in a man. One who understood her babbling as a nervous reaction and was completely unfazed by it. In truth, she saw his lips quirk into a slight smile, and she knew he was laughing at the images she was shooting them through their mystical link.

If she ever got him to Earth, he was in for an entire week of science fiction movies. Meanwhile, they just kept climbing toward the base.

"So do you know where the front door is? Or are we going to be climbing through the smashed reactor core?" If they had to rappel down a silo to churning fanblades, she was going to…well, she was just going to say, I told you so!

He didn't speak except to gesture to the smashed cylinder. It was hard to see details given the glow that surrounded he ship, but it looked like an area of the pizza cutter that was stories deep into the mountain. The ship seemed to have cleaved a many-mile furrow into the ground before coming to a stop. There were certainly crumpled sections, but that part was relatively intact. They'd probably get there in another hour's worth of heavy hiking.

Fortunately, she was way more fit now than at any other time in her life. Part of it had been the enforced slimming diet of eggs and lake water. But it was also the lifting and carrying while Keeven was sick, the walking all around the Wall, and of course the hot sex she'd been having. She was able to keep up without collapsing, which was a wonderful thing.

Meanwhile, Keeven was constantly on the alert. He stood protectively between her and the ship. He moved quickly through what shadows there were, and he spoke not at all. He was being all big protective warrior, and she loved him for it. She just doubted that the defenses here would be anything like what he expected.

Which held true until she stepped into a snare.

She'd been stupid, wandering off a bit from following Keeven because she wanted to get a better look at the spaceship. Then whip bang, and suddenly she's caught in a massive net and hanging from a tree.

She cried out. Hard not to when suddenly the ground lifts up and enfolds you in its ropey arms. It happened so fast, she couldn't even believe it. She was lucky she hadn't gotten whiplash while her feet suddenly ended up near her shoulders and her head dropped back against the thick net.

She was still spitting out dirt that had somehow gotten into her mouth when Keeven straightened up beside her. His eyes were dancing as he looked at her, apparently having satisfied himself that there was no danger. Damn, he was even sheathing his sword.

How humiliating after her big show of: I-can-help. Trust me.

"Yeah, okay, I got caught in a game net," she groused. "But at least I'm not covered in bird vomit."

"I thought I told you to stay behind me," he said quietly. He was keeping his voice low as part of his plan to sneak up on the big crashed spaceship.

"Yeah. I got distracted," she said, her face heating. Just because they were facing a high-tech castle didn't mean there weren't low-tech problems. Like a game snare that hung her from the nearest tree. "I'll listen to you now. Promise."

The look he gave her spoke volumes about how much he believed that. But he didn't argue. He simply traced the origins of the trap and unbound it. She was dumped unceremoniously on the ground before he grabbed her arm and helped her stand.

"Thank you," she said.

He brushed dirt off her cheek, his touch tender. "Will you listen to me now? There could have been spears in that trap. You could have broken something."

Oh hell. She hadn't even thought about that. Every jungle movie she'd ever seen flashed through her mind. Not to mention the opening of the first Indiana Jones movie, big rolling boulder and all.

"I swear I'll do better."

"I'd rather you go back."

"Not a chance."

He nodded, obviously expecting that answer, and then turned back toward the ship. She was about to fall in beside him when she saw the flash.

It was a little bit of light, only seen because Keeven happened to be standing near it and his shadow made the flash all the brighter. She never would have noticed it otherwise.

"Wait a second," she said. Then she walked closer to it. It

was a metal disk set in a rock with a dull red stone in the top. And the red light was flashing. "Have you ever seen anything like this before?"

"No." Keeven peered down at it. She didn't dare touch it and she made sure he didn't either, but given its position and angle compared to the trap, she had a pretty good guess as to its purpose.

"I'll bet it's a perimeter sensor adapted to tell somebody that the hunting trap has been sprung."

He frowned. "It is a communication stone?"

She arched a brow. As far as she could tell there had been no phone-stones anywhere. Apparently, she just hadn't noticed them.

"Kinda," she answered. "But it's just one way. It will tell whoever's on the inside—"

"The monster."

"—that something triggered the snare. And I thought you said the monster was just a fiction told to keep people away."

He shrugged. "So some say. Others swear the opposite."

"But you're royal. You're from the spaceship. Don't you know what its defenses are?"

"I have told you. Those are the secrets held by the princess's family."

"Well, now that the two of you are married, you'd think she'd let you in on a few of them." Her tone was acerbic. Not intentionally, but she still got pissy whenever she remembered he was married.

He didn't answer. Instead, he looked down at the blinking metal disk. "Is it safe to proceed?"

"Sure. You've got the magic keyfob, remember?" She had no idea if it was safe, but she liked holding on to whatever reassurance she could muster.

He nodded as if that made sense and then turned to go, his steps quiets and careful. They were on the edge of the wood, and Janet was looking forward to crossing into sunshine even if it made them way more exposed.

She started to follow when the sound came. Compared to Keeven's near silence, this was the sound of an elephant trundling through the forest. Keeven heard it first, of course, stepping between her and the deeper trees. She thought for a moment about climbing up one, but frankly, she never been that nimble even as a kid. So she just stood there, cringing behind a tree trunk and feeling like an idiot. As soon as she got home, she was signing up for a self defense class.

Meanwhile, Keeven drew his sword, stepped around the disabled trap, and waited. He was as hidden as such a big guy could be behind a tree, and he appeared so calm it was zen. He was listening, his balance was poised a little bit forward, and every part of him seemed happily relaxed. She, on the other hand, was gripping her tree trunk hard enough to dig the bark painfully into her hands.

And all the while whatever it was came clomping through the woods. Thud. Thud. Thud. Jesus, she was going to scream.

The first part of it she saw was its legs. Big harry knee connected down to a hoary foot. She had to clap her hand over her mouth to keep herself from squeaking in alarm. She knew that kind of body. It still featured in her nightmares, and this one was bigger. But she held her breath, praying she was wrong but a second later, there it was. A gool and his rucksack of doom held loosely in his massive fist.

Keeven didn't give it time to fully step into the narrow clearing. He was swinging his sword with deadly ease. But there wasn't a lot of space for a big man and his sword, much less Keeven and a gool.

The blow that should have severed the thing's head, dug deep into the controlling collar and set off those lightning shocks. Both of them went sprawling, their bodies twitching like live eels.

But good news: the collar was severed. Or mostly gone. Which meant the biggest danger was from the rucksack. She'd be damned if she sat here watching while those imp shits attacked. She might not have taken a self defense class, but she sure as hell could run. So that's what she did.

She ran forward and grabbed the sack. Huh. Not that heavy. In fact, it looked at first glance just like an ordinary smelly sack. Whatever. She knotted it tightly closed then turned to the beastmonster.

The gool was still twitching and looking rather singed. She knew the feeling. So did Keeven who was doing much the same thing. So while the ugly thing was still defenseless, she grabbed hold of the collar and pulled.

She knew what was coming. With luck, the thing had already discharged much of its power in the first blow.

ZAP.

Not so much.

She flew backwards, but the force of it did one good thing. She ripped the collar apart and was still gripping the thing even as she was thrown backwards out of the little clearing. And then she just kept rolling because she had no control, and it was the only way to hopefully dislodge the damned thing from her fist. It didn't work, but she did manage to bounce off a tree trunk, tumble sideways away from a raised root, and sort of slide-flop onto the grass just clear of the woods. All in all, an impressive distance. Also...*ow.*

And then the damn thing zapped her again.

Ow!

It was still discharging random shots of electricity even as she lay in the grass. Damnation. Why the hell couldn't she let go? Electricity. Duh. But...*ow!*

Okay, so this was—d

Ow.

Going to take—d

Ow.

A bit.

Ow. Ow. Ow.

Odd how she could still think while being randomly zapped.

Then she frowned. Or tried to. Her vision was getting

weird. Was the air turning white gold?

Ow.

Longer pause between the shocks. Had it finally run out of juice?

Not just white gold but vaguely body shaped? Did this world have ghosts? A steady stream of them coalescing around her. It was kinda pretty.

One seemed to dive at the collar. She would have flinched away if she had the control, but she didn't. Instead, she just lay there and felt a tingly kind of cold.

There was a zap too—kind of bright in the overall white gold—but she only vaguely felt it. Nothing like what the thing discharged before. Then the ghosty thing seemed to expand or diffuse or something like that, only to be replaced by another thing.

Okay, so they were freaky.

And she wasn't seeing things, so it was time to back away. All she managed—

Cold. *Zing.*

Not even a zap, but a fizzle of energy as another of those ghosty things dove at the collar.

Time to let go of the collar. It took concentrated focus, but she managed it. She opened her fingers and twisted her hand such that the collar fell to the dirt.

Damn her hand was cold. More than her hand. Her whole arm.

She heard a roar. The gool of course, and gathered the energy to roll to her side. Shit, it was cold.

And more of those ghosty things were diving through the collar which was sparking and spitting like a fourth of July sparkler.

She saw the gool stumbling to his feet. Well good. Maybe he could help. Keeven was getting up too, though unsteadily. So much for his zen poise, she saw him grit his teeth as he lurched for the support of the nearest tree.

But the gool wasn't stopping. He wasn't acting like the

other guy. The one who'd become an ally. Nope. This guy was bellowing and stumbling about. And he was pissed. His fists were flailing, his eyes were wild, and...

Oh shit. Out of control gool.

This is what Keeven had feared when she'd pulled the collar off the other one. That he'd go rampaging nuts.

She had to get moving. She had to help. At least until Keeven recovered enough to fight. It shouldn't be hard. All she had to do was gain Ugly's attention then outrun him.

No problemo, except she could barely push herself upright. And the ghosty things were getting thick. The air seemed to tingle as she breathed. And she was so damned cold. The least she could do was scream at it.

"Ungh," she managed. Not so much a scream as a groan. It hadn't been loud enough to draw anyone's attention, but she saw Keeven look around for her.

No, no. She was fine, assuming she didn't freeze to death in this sunlit field of ghosts.

Ghosts. Wait. No way.

She couldn't possibly be having the life sucked out of her by ghosts. That was just too much.

She narrowed her eyes, focusing on the golden white things as they zipped through the collar. Every time they one through it, the thing sparked energy. Less and less, she realized. Holy shit, they were draining it.

She found enough coordination to turn to look at the crashed space ship. Oh hell. That was the glow around it. It was these things, only most of them were over here eating up the gool's collar.

Ghosts that ate power. Got it. They'd been sucking from the spaceship, but now were chomping down on the collar. But once the collar was drained...

Oh hell. It might just go for her. Was she more powerful than a crashed spaceship? One that had been inert for thousands of years? Who the hell knew, but she didn't really want to hang around to find out.

And bonus, while she'd been peering at the power sucking ghosts, she'd gotten some feeling back into her legs. She managed to push up to her knees which was real progress. And looking over at Keeven, he was standing upright as well, sword up, if not exactly zipping around at light saber speeds.

Big and Ugly was doing the best of all three of them, but he was just crashing about alternately pummeling things and clutching his head.

"Janet?" Keeven called. "Are you all right?"

"Peachy," she lied. "Pay attention to crazy pants over there. I'll be there in a second."

"Stay back."

And get drained by the ghosts? Hell no. But that didn't mean she wanted to wander into the gool's sights either. She made it to her feet just in time to have a ghost pass through her chest.

Oh shit.

Like a wave of ice through the center of her body. Not good. Not good at all.

She gasped and fell to her knees. Just how long did she have until that collar was dead as a doornail? She had to get moving. But before she pushed up, she tried to time it with a break in the ghosts.

No such luck. They were swirling all around her now, vague impressions of mouths gaping wide as they dove through the collar. Which meant she just had to suck it up and move. There wasn't going to be a break in the damned things.

She pushed to her feet, choking on her breath as another went through her shoulder on its way to the collar. She had to get away from the collar, toward the trees.

She stumbled forward feeling only two more icy waves through her body. A few more steps. A few more. She'd picked out a tree that would be a good brace for her. Big enough to hold her up and be a block from the psycho gool who had focused on Keeven as his target.

Thank God, Keeven seemed to be getting his strength back. His feet were moving fluidly now. His sword dipped and parried smoothly now too, but there wasn't a lot of room to swing. Not with Ugly flailing his arms like meat cleavers.

"Get him to come this way!" she called. Let the ghosties have him. "Come on Ugly!" she said, waving her arm. "Come get me!"

Didn't work. The gool was focused on Keeven. So she picked up a rock. She might be freezing to death, but she still had some dexterity. With as much of a bellow as she could manage, she threw the rock straight for Ugly's forehead.

Great throw. Solid aim. She was pleased with herself until it stopped just short of the trees and thunked to the ground.

WTF?

She lurched forward toward her tree. She was stopped a foot short of the bark. A solid, invisible wall. Not painful. Not sparking light. Nothing. Just a barrier she couldn't cross.

But it hadn't stopped her from rolling through it before. She knelt down, trying to feel if it stopped before the ground.

Nope. It was solid all the way down. Which meant it was a one way door either to trap ghost prey or keep the hungry buggers focused on the ship. Either way, she was screwed. She didn't have to look back at the collar to know it was losing juice fast. The sparks weren't popping like they were before. Plus, the air was getting thicker around her and the cold was getting worse. Which meant that the ghosts were getting bored with the collar and coming for her.

Hell. She pushed back upright, feeling her way, trying to find any weaknesses in the field. Nothing. Well, this sucked.

At least Keeven was getting control of the big bad. Except he was backing her way, drawing the gool down toward her. Great, except then he would be trapped too.

"No!" she bellowed. At least she had gotten her voice back, if the hoarse croak she emitted could be counted as a voice. "Don't cross the tree line! You can't get back."

He had just whacked at the creature, numbing its right arm which now hung limply from its side. Apparently gool hide was pretty thick. Ugly howled and lunged forward, but thanks to her bellow, Keeven stepped sideways instead of backwards. Then instead of continuing the attack, Keeven looked at her.

She pressed her hand hard against the force field. "It's blocking me from going back."

Then his gaze travelled behind her to the dimly sparking collar and the ghosts. She saw his eyes widen and his skin go sickly pale. Okay, so in one glance, he'd figured out the situation and was scared shitless. Not a good sign for her. If she ever got through this, she was going sit him down and have him explain in detail all the big bads in this world, so she'd know exactly when to crap her pants. Not a helpful thought, but there it was.

And right then, as if to bring her back to her present disaster, a ghost whipped through her chest. Ugh! Like being pole axed by an icicle.

She looked back at the collar. Dead. As in Dr. McCoy, "He's dead, Jim." Which meant she was the only tasty morsel here. Well, her and the gool who was just now turning on Keeven. Because if she couldn't save herself, at least she could keep Keeven from being pummeled.

"Oh no you don't, buddy," she bellowed. Apparently, Ugly liked throaty croak voices. Great. She ran toward it as far as the force field allowed. Then she screamed and jumped up and down as much as she could, given that her extremities were going numb.

Ugly turned toward her and roared.

"Come and get me! I'm right here!"

And then, right when his attention was wavering, Keeven did a really impressive thing. He planted his sword into the ground to use as a kind of pole and as he jumped both feet up and slammed them both straight into Ugly's side. Probably not the best use of a sword, but it worked.

Ugly wasn't looking and was probably a little off balance.

Keeven's shove sent the creature tumbling forward, very much like what Janet had done not two minutes before. He stumbled, then tripped, then did an ungainly roll.

Right at her.

Oh shit.

He was coming through and would be trapped on this side with her. Step one: get out of his way.

She stumbled aside. She'd meant to do an impressive leap, but she was beginning to shiver. This was really bad. Especially as she'd stopped feeling poleaxed. Though her eyes could see movement in the ghosts, they no longer seemed to be flying through her. It felt more like an all over ice blanket.

Beside her, Ugly roared. Loud and pissed like before, but this time she heard the undercurrent of terror in it. This wasn't, I'm pissed and going to kill you. This was, Oh shit, I'm about to die.

She glanced back and shuddered—or shivered harder.

She might be in a ghost fog, but he was buried beneath a gold white avalanche of ghosts. Okay, so they liked him.

"Janet!"

She turned. Keeven was standing at the treeline. Had he been trying to get her attention? Shit, she was losing focus.

"Janet!" he repeated.

"Stay back."

"Find the source. Find the source of the wall."

He pointed along the line of the force field, left and right. She squinted.

"Can you see the source of it? I can destroy it from this side, but which way?"

Good question. She narrowed her eyes, choosing to walk left simply because it was further away from the gool. In part, because he was flailing and she didn't want to get accidentally kicked. Also, she hoped the ghosts would prefer him to her.

She started moving, Keeven pacing her on the other side.

"Stay back," she repeated.

"Do you see the source?"

"What does a source look like?"

"Blue stones."

She didn't see any. Twisting around, she looked back along the field the other way. Nope. Nothing there either. Just rocks and trees, none of them blue.

Well, the one thing she did know was that it wasn't here. And given that the field was keeping the ghosts around the ship, she extrapolated a rough geometric line. A barrier that kept the things over the ship. Kind of like a funnel with this being one side. Which would put the source roughly ahead.

"This way," she guessed. Then she started lurching forward again. Fortunately, she had this handy dandy force field beside her to keep her upright. All she had to do was lean a shoulder against it—or a numb hand—and whammo, instant assistance.

Keeven rushed ahead. Not out of sight, but far enough ahead of her that he was clearly scouting. And she was obviously slowing.

Then somewhere in her brain, a neuron fired. It began with a question or maybe it was more of a complaint. It went something like, what the hell did these things find so tasty in her? She thought it was simple heat. Body temperature, and all that, but then why would the ghosts love the collar more than her?

Energy. Duh. Or maybe electrical energy.

Which meant that anything with batteries would keep them from munching on her. At least for a little while longer.

Ugly wasn't making a lot of noise anymore. He was still bellowing in a moaning kind of way. So they were still attracted to him, but she had enough of the white creatures around her to be a problem.

She looked down in her pack. The halogen flashlight might help. It was hard to flip it on with frozen fingers, but she manage. And right then, her hand went dead. As in frozen stiff.

Okay, the ghosties like that. So when the thing dropped from her numb fingers, she kicked it as hard as she could away from her.

Better. Off they zipped after it leaving her to lurch along the force field for another few yards. Progress. But where the hell was the source?

Then she saw it. Not blue stones. This was like a closet door hanging out at the edge of the clearing. For a moment her heart soared. Home! Finally, she could get back to triple mochas and YouTube videos. Pajamas and pizza and...

No Keeven.

Well that was sad enough to make her slow down. She didn't want to leave him. In truth, she wasn't even sure she wanted to leave this nutso world, but she didn't belong here. She had no idea how things worked here. And she...

Wait a moment. That didn't look like Marty's closet there. No tabards or slut boots. As she stumbled closer, she saw scarred wood tables and a guy in chains being hauled forward by thugs. Turns out throughout the universe, thugs look kinda the same. Big guys with weapons and no sense of humor, especially for the sobbing, starving guy in chains dropped at the front of the closet.

"There!" Keeven bellowed, pointing to the doorway. Or maybe not. Were there blue stones at the corners of the thing? She didn't know. She couldn't really see well because...

She looked behind her. Flashlight was dead. Ghosties were back munching on her.

"I don't think that's a good place to go," she mumbled. Her lips were numb so it made it hard for her to form words.

Keeven didn't hear her. Or if he did, he was distracted by the pretty glowing crystals. She half walked, half slid closer, her eyes on the inside of the door.

Chained guy was begging, probably for his life. He was on his knees, he was sobbing, he was looking with hopeless eyes up at someone Janet couldn't see.

Hell. After a lifetime of TV addiction, Janet had seen a full range of emotions—or so she thought. But even though this looked like it was being played out in a tableau, it was more real than that. The despair in sobbing guy's face was real. Hope, desperation, and the certain knowledge that he was about to die.

Oh God, it was awful.

"Close it," she grunted to Keeven. She couldn't bear to see any more. She ought to just look away, but she couldn't.

Which is when she saw Darth Vader. For being the really evil baddie, he looked strangely normal for this world. Brown leather pants, loose linen shirt. He was even balding and with a paunch. He looked like her Uncle Joey, the one who had let her jump on his back as he roared around. But this guy wasn't laughing. He was barely even smiling. It might have been easier to handle if there was evil laughter or something. But no, it was like he was pulling on his socks or something.

He just gestured to the thugs to restrain chained guy. Not so hard, given that chained guy was naked and clearly starving. Then Not-Uncle-Joey stepped over and wrapped something around sobbing guy's neck.

Janet knew what it was before he stepped back. She knew what was about to happen and still couldn't force herself to look away.

Poor starving guy had a control collar on him. It looked absurdly loose on his thin neck for about ten seconds. And then he began to thicken. She couldn't see the power that went into his metamorphosis. No glowing light, but she could feel the waves of energy. Or maybe it was that it got the ghosts' attention and they started peeling off of her to zip toward the closet.

But even with lots of ghosts diving through the door, it made no difference to the chained guy. He was growing larger, his spine lengthening and his chest barreling outward. His tunic split. It was probably a good thing he hadn't had any pants on.

Oh God, it was awful. Sure she'd seen Bruce Banner hulk out dozens of times, not to mention several awesome werewolf transformations. But this didn't match any of them. It was a heaving, pulsing, heartbeat-like expansion of agony. Because if the guy's face and screams were anything to judge by, it was a painful, hideous process.

And weirdest of all was the way his high pitched scream kept dropping in pitch. *Aieeeee* became *Eeeee* became *Errrrr*. Not in a smooth slide, but in a pulsing drop that made her want to vomit.

And all the while, Not-Uncle-Joey just stood there watching with an almost bored look on his face. Even when the ghosts started diving in straight for the new gool during his birth pains.

Oh hell. He couldn't have just created the guy as food for the ghosts. That would be awful. Probably not because as she looked, the things seemed to have difficulty going through the door. Not impossible, but they weren't zipping through like they had with her.

She looked over to Keeven. He had maneuvered himself around enough that he could see inside, and his expression was even more grim than before. Without looking at her, he pulled out a stone from his pocket.

It was huge in terms of gemstones. Bright red and the size of a plum, though rough in texture. More rock-like than crystal.

He concentrated on it and she watched it grow bright. Strobe light bright, though it wasn't pulsing so much as vibrating. Then he caught her eye.

"Hold this as long as you can. Gather as many of the Suckers as you can and then throw them—"

"At Vader. Got it."

"Throw it hard."

"Not a problem." She wanted to chuck that thing straight at Vader for poisoning her memory of her favorite uncle. And for being a generally evil douche.

Keeven's stone was getting almost too bright to look at, and it was still ramping up. He tossed it underhand to her, and she failed to catch it. Too bright to see plus numb fingers did not make her a good outfielder.

Fortunately it didn't matter. She was better at kicking than throwing anyway.

Gold white ghosties streaked toward it. She ended up ducking down as things from the spaceship joined them. Holy shit, there were a lot of them. The air was dropping to sub zero in seconds. If she didn't kick that thing soon, she was going to be too frozen to move.

She looked at Keeven. He was poised with his sword pointed upward. Or rather, pommel down above a blue stone. Planning to smash it, obviously.

Meanwhile, Not-Uncle-Joey must have noticed what was going on. She heard the new gool roar as the evil Magician pointed toward her. Orders to attack, obviously.

"Hell no," she said. It came out more like *ee oo,* but whatever.

Gathering every ounce of energy she had, she aimed and kicked with the top of her foot. Thank you, summer soccer for teaching her how to do that.

And score!

Right through the center of the door to clang off of new gool and thunk at Vader's feet. Yes!

Ghosties flew in afterwards. A steady stream of gold white that warmed the cockles of her heart, if not her fingertips.

She might have done a little dance of joy, except that she'd lost the last of her strength with that mega kick. Somehow she was on her knees and listing slowly sideways while new gool started to come out.

Well, that was quite the collision of magical creatures. Ghosts and gool. Someone ought to do a rap about that. But what happened to Not-Uncle-Joey? She couldn't see, but she hoped he was a dead pop-sickle.

And she toppled.

Sideways, thank God, but she'd given out. Lucky for her, she got to look at Keeven as she fell. He was very impressive with his bulging muscles as he slammed down the pommel of his sword. Wham.

Once was all it took.

The blue stone shattered.

Whoosh. Felt, not heard. Though there had been a funky popping sound.

Then he ran to the other side and another blue stone there. Bam. That one was gone now too.

The gool was halfway way out. Apparently the collision of him and the ghosts had made the pathway too thick for him to cross easily. But he'd get through pretty soon. And when he did, she was a sitting duck. Or a lying duck.

And then Keeven did it again. The pommel of his sword smashed down. Except there weren't any more blue stones that she could see. Was there a clear one? With red speckles?

She couldn't tell.

Apparently, this crystal was harder to crack. Diamond, maybe? Bummer. Didn't matter how studly his muscles were, he wasn't going to shatter a diamond like that. Not with the ground to absorb some of the impact.

Apparently, he came to the same conclusion. So with a grim expression, he reached into his pack and pulled out a small tube. She didn't see what it was. Only that whatever he poured out of it was thick, slow as molasses, and black. And either it stank or the gool did. Who was three quarters of the way out, by the by.

She tried to move. At a minimum, she ought to be able to roll sideways or something.

No such luck. She was still too cold.

And then Keeven did it again. Bulging muscles, rippling chest, and the slam of the pommel of his sword down.

Crack.

Fizz. Like a TV turning off, the closet wavered and then disappeared. As did a quarter of the gool. The rest fell oozing onto the ground.

Ew.

She closed her eyes.

A moment later she felt Keeven, all hot and manly as he gathered her close. Hot was the main thing this time. The heat of his body was like a furnace, and she yearned for it. This was probably how ice cream felt when the hot fudge went dripping over it.

He didn't say anything, he just pulled her tight and if she'd had the strength she would have grinned. She didn't, so she just lay still, letting him hold her.

Yes.

Especially when he pressed kisses to her forehead.

Yes, when he chaffed her arms.

And especially yes when he began to murmur against her skin.

"Don't leave me, Janet. I cannot do this alone. Please don't leave."

She had no intention of going anywhere. Well, except for back home. Oh hell, that was the choice, wasn't it? Him or home? Him or home?

She passed out before she could make a decision.

CHAPTER 15

Keeven felt the moment when his angel lost consciousness. She wasn't dead, thank the Goddess. Merely drained of her magic.

When he had seen the Suckers around her, his heart had failed him. Why hadn't he realized that the glow around the castle was the evil creatures and not something inherent to the structure itself?

Idiot! She had nearly died and the horror of that stole the strength from his body even now.

To fail at the Wall was bad enough. To lose the princess to the Magician, to see his realm fall to the evil from the north was nearly unthinkable. But to lose Janet? Not the angel who had come to save his people, but the woman she insisted he name her. Janet the fierce. Janet the questioning. Janet his lover.

All those words tumbled through his mind like rocks grinding against one another. She was beyond definition in his mind, all words failing to encompass all that she was to him.

He had nearly lost her. He stroked a finger across her pale cheek, thanking the Goddess for the blush of life slowly returning to her body. He looked over his shoulder to the structure behind him. Without the Suckers surrounding it, it appeared almost mundane. An aging, oddly shaped thing that was his people's greatest treasure and darkest mystery.

He should go there now, assure himself that the princess still lived, and finish his business quickly before returning to the Wall.

He should, but he could not force himself to move. The closer he went to the castle, the sooner he would have to return Janet to heaven. He would have to face the way he had betrayed his vows to his wife. He would have to watch as Janet left, taking with her any child that she might bear. And most devastating of all, he would then face the rest of his life as it was prescribed by duty and responsibility.

How had this happened? All the woman had done was make him smile when he ought to be serious. She'd pestered him with endless questions, and then held him tenderly at the end of each day when he thought the weight of his responsibilities would break him. She had steadfastly pushed him out of his normal habits and into her world of questions. Why this? Why not? Why must you?

And so he had. Why must he marry a woman not of his choosing? Why did he think that all creatures born of the Magician's magic were evil? Why did his mother send him to seal bargains and save all the secrecy to herself?

Endless questions that he fought in his mind, weaving and wrestling endlessly as he tried to pin down the answers. He had none. And so he looked at his angel and wondered if she had been sent not to give him a child, but to wake him from his obedient daze.

But how to give her back? How did he face the doubts that she had instilled in his mind without her at his side? And how did he part with her when he had given his blood oath to do so?

He gritted his teeth. He could not answer these things now. What he had to do was find shelter for them, heat for her, and food for when she woke. In many ways it was a return to those first nights when they were caught near the birdbeasts, and he thanked the Goddess for one more night such as that.

He leaned forward, gently gathering her lush body in his arms. Then he carried her carefully away from the castle. He did not know what awaited them inside the structure. For now, he would guard his angel's rest and glory one more night by holding her close.

She woke some hours later. Her skin had long since returned to normal temperature, thanks in part to the roaring fire he built beside her. She stirred, then blinked, her luminous brown eyes at her.

"Keeven?"

He was already moving, bringing her hot soup to drink. "Rest now. The Suckers are gone and you are safe."

She smiled. "Of course I am. I'm with you."

She did not know how her words eased his heart, even knowing how many ways he could fail her. But that she could have such faith in him, spurred him on as nothing else.

"Drink," he said.

She did with his help. Though when the cup was empty, she passed it back to him with a grimace. "Not hot chocolate, but surprisingly tasty."

"How do you feel?"

"Better." Then she looked around at the campsite. The firepit, the protection stones, even a tarp beneath her to keep her dry. "You've been busy. How long was I out?"

"You rested only a few hours. I built up the fire to heat you. Everything else is as normal."

She waved a weak hand at him. "Have you eaten?"

He nodded.

"Set the traps?"

"Yes."

"All safe until the morning when we storm the castle?"

"I do not think an assault will be necessary."

She smiled. "Great. So come hold me. I'm feeling chilled."

Alarmed, he touched her skin. Did she have a fever? She felt cool to the touch, but—

"I was teasing. I'm fine."

"But—"

"I want you to lie with me, Keeven. And not just in the wrap your arms around me and make like a toaster oven way."

He smiled. As usual, he did not understand near enough of her words, but he knew her meaning. "You are still weak."

"So make me feel better."

He could not resist her. Not on this last night before he faced his wife. But he could make sure that Janet's every moment was steeped in pleasure before a healing rest. He smiled at her, slowly tracing the curve of her jaw and then the sweep of her collarbone before slipping his hand lower to cup her breasts.

"Perhaps I should check your skin to see that you are not feverish."

"Perhaps I should get naked so you can check me everywhere."

His glorious angel. How she made him smile.

The morning came too soon for Janet, but the excitement returned the minute she looked through the trees to the space ship. Today she would get inside. And it was even more appealing now that the ghostie glow was gone. Of course, that made it look all the more derelict as she began to see the clear signs of wear, but whatever. Crashed, old spaceships were still awesome.

Keeven seemed pensive, but he did what was necessary to get them moving. He always did what was necessary, and she did her best to make him smile as he did it. She even got him to chuckle once, and that just made the day even brighter. And then, finally, they were moving stealthily toward the ship. And in time, they made it to the entrance point. And stood there.

"Um, Keeven? What now?"

He shook his head. "I don't know. My instructions said to come here."

"Ah. Right." She looked around the crumpled metal that might have been plastic because it wasn't rusting. "Where's the keyfob?"

He offered her the stone. There was no place to press it, no twisting to open it. Perhaps she had to put it against something. She tried touching it to the wall. Even banged it a couple times.

"I have no idea," she huffed as she offered him the stone back. "Try saying open sesame or something."

He took the stone. "Why would I want to open seeds?"

"What? Oh. Never mind. Look, it's your genetic history. Just, you know, activate it."

He arched a brow. "I have already tried that."

Then a voice cut in from beside them. Female, irritated, and definitely bitchy.

"Say your name, idiot."

Keeven whirled around, his sword raised. But there was no one around. Probably because the voice came from a speaker somewhere in the wall.

"Open the door, Princess."

"You open it."

He glowered as he looked at the wall. He held his sword in a relaxed grip, but it was definitely at the ready. And then he spoke. "Open the door. I am Prince Keeven Gudtundsdor, Knight of Askel."

And just like that, a panel slid open revealing perhaps the most beautiful woman Janet had ever seen. She had emerald green eyes, dark curly auburn hair, and a petite body that made her look like a lusty, luscious fairy.

And she was holding a laser gun aimed directly at Janet's heart.

"Um…" Janet said.

"And who is this?" the woman said, her voice all sing-songy.

Keeven tensed. Janet tensed. Hell, it felt like the entire mountain side drew up tight. "Um, we're here to rescue you," Janet tried.

"Silence, demon," the woman spat.

Demon?

Keeven glared at his wife. "She is Angel Janet who rescued me from—"

"She's not an angel."

Janet huffed. "I keep trying to tell him—"

The bitch pulled the trigger.

Keeven felt the power hit Janet and responded without thought. He caught her before she collapsed on the rock, setting her as quickly as he could on the ground before he turned to his wife. His black-hearted wife who had just killed his angel.

But before he could put voice to the fury inside him, she held up her hand—and the weapon—to the sky in surrender. "Calm down. She's only stopped."

"Stopped?" It's possible he snarled the word.

"Her heart beats. She breathes. She lives, but she cannot move."

The relief that flooded his system was dizzying, but he kept himself crouched and his sword at the ready. He didn't even remember bringing it to bear, but it was before him and trained on the princess. Where it would remain until she gave him some answers.

"Explain why you would do this? Quickly, before the monster comes."

She actually rolled her eyes at him. "There is no monster. Not like that."

A grim quiet settled into his gut. "So you lied to me." It was not a surprise, and yet it hurt. This woman was his *wife*.

"No," she snorted. "My mother lied to you. And her mother before that." She shrugged. "There are monster-like defenses. It makes it easier to just say monster."

"I am not some peasant—"

"No. You're the thick-headed puppet of your mother."

He glared at her. Odd how he'd once thought her dark hair and thick curls alluring. As all of the women of the Bodil, she had mysterious sloping eyes and the body of a temptress.

As a boy, it had been no hardship to think that one day she would be his wife.

But now he looked at her and thought her looks overblown and her attitude childish. She was not a woman who could walk through a birdbeast colony. She had not the patience required to tend a sick man or even learn a new language. She wanted what she wanted now and had no care who she hurt to get it. Her childhood was littered with the victims of her petulance. But he was no child, and he would not tolerate such actions in his wife.

So he sheathed his sword with a swift stroke. The only monster to face here was her. Her sigh of relief seemed to echo in his head.

"Good," she said. "Now that—"

He slapped away her weapon then charged forward, hand to her throat, pinning her against the interior wall. He did not like leaving Janet exposed and helpless on the ground, but he judged the greater danger was this evil creature he'd married.

"You will be silent and listen, Princess." He all but spat her title. "You will cease this petulance and you will act befitting your station as my wife."

"I will not—" Her voice ended on a squeak as he pushed harder against her throat.

"I have tried to be patient. I thought you were taken by a monster. I came here to save you."

"I wasn't attacked," she rasped with what little air he allowed her. "But I escaped here."

"So I guessed. Your mother said—"

She abruptly twisted, shoving his hands away in a move that many of his soldiers couldn't master. He hadn't expected it, so he was too slow in the counter, and suddenly she was free from his hold. "Will you listen now? Goddess, if I'd known running away was what it took, I'd have done it back when we were kids!"

This time he was the one who rolled his eyes. "All you needed to do was send me a message. I would have responded as quickly as my duties allowed."

"What are you talking about?" she said. "I sent you letters until I was sixteen, then messages through the stones, then through couriers. I have been trying to talk with you for years. Not once have you responded."

He frowned at her. She did not have the appearance of one who lied. But how could this be possible? He took a breath. "You know I am a Knight of the Askel."

"Of course. My mother reminds me of it daily." Her voice took a mocking tone. "He is a prince and a knight. Any woman would be proud to have such a fine man to bed. Think of babes he will sire."

He did not know whether to be pleased by the praise or insulted by her mockery of it. He chose to ignore it completely. "Then you know I do not lie. Therefore I say to you, I have never received a direct communication from you. Ever."

She stared at him, and he returned the look. "Not one?" she finally whispered.

He shook his head. "Not one. But as my wife, we will have ample opportunity to speak. In truth…" He glance uneasily back at Janet. "We must speak of the angel."

The princess held up her hand, counting off her points on her fingers. "First off, she's not an angel."

"She is a truer angel than you can possibly know."

"Second, we are not married. We have never been married and are not ever going to be wed."

"Of course we are. I stood there and vowed myself to you. I heard your words in response."

"You heard a spell. My mother forced me to comply. Didn't you notice my eyes were flat? My face devoid of expression?"

He shifted uncomfortably on his feet. "I thought you disliked this as much as I did but had chosen to honor—"

"No. A thousand times no. I will not vow myself to you ever. Mother forced me."

He blinked. "This is possible?"

She simply stared at him, her expression saying everything he needed to hear. Of course it was possible. Her mother was the greatest sorceress they had.

"Then how did you come here? If she put you under a spell—"

"I'm not completely absent of training. Just obedience."

That part he knew too well.

"I was able to break it. There are ways."

"You should have come to me—"

"You would have bedded me! And then I'd be pregnant and…" She threw up her arms. "This is like talking to a stone."

"No. It is like talking to a child who refuses to explain. Or admit her mistake."

Her eyes flashed fury at that, but she squared her shoulders. "I ran. I was headed here to find an answer when…" Her voice trailed away and her eyes took on a haunted look. He didn't speak, but waited with as much patience as he could muster for her to continue. Eventually she did. "Aruckien. I didn't think my mother would do such a thing to me, but…" Tears made her eyes bright. "She can get very angry."

"It was not her. It was bad timing."

She looked up, hope sparking in her eyes. "Are you sure?"

He nodded, though inside, he wondered. That the Princess could suspect the Queen of such perfidy was unthinkable. To consort with the Magician to attack her own daughter? Ridiculous! And yet, a daughter often knew her mother best, and he had to consider the possibility. But not at the moment. "How did you escape?"

"I ran very, very fast."

He arched a brow at her, but she refused to be daunted.

"Don't you think that I had prepared ways to get away? There is a way to travel very, very fast. I had it. And I came here."

"But the Aruckien followed?"

She nodded. "And when that did not work, they left and the Suckers appeared."

"Trapping you inside."

"Yes." She took a deep breath. "How did you find me?"

"Your mother gave me your token." He held up the stone that Janet called a keyfob. "She said you had been abducted by the monster."

"My mother lies." Then she huffed out a breath. "You have no idea how good it is to say that. She has a spell on the palace preventing such words." Then she straightened. "Look, I don't care what your mother said or what vows we swore. I'm not going to be your wife. That's why I left. And if you think I'm just going to lay down and breed babies because our mothers said so, then you are beyond stupid."

He stared at her, his breath smoothing out. Her words should have infuriated him, but they did not. They completely absolved him of his guilt for his consort with Janet. And so he leaned back against the wall, his breath flowing from him in both defeat and gratitude.

"All my life I have served the realm. Yours and mine."

"More idiot you."

Her glared at her, knowing this was the crux of their differences. "It is an honor that I cherish."

"That's because you get to be useful. You protect the Wall, you get to swing that big scary sword, and you command our people."

He nodded. "That is—"

"I get to breed babies."

He sighed. It was a normal female complaint among the royals, so he did not debate it. "There are a thousand ways to be fulfilled as a woman. To serve with honor."

"But I still have to have your babies? No. I. Will. Not." She straightened up, gesturing behind her to the monster's castle. "There is an answer to our people's problems here. I know it. I just have to find it." A pleading expression flitted across her face. "You have to let me keep working."

He looked behind her. There was nothing but dimly illuminated walls. "Your family has protected this castle for generations. What do you think is here that they do not already know?"

"A way to power the stones," she said simply.

He sighed. "Your kind has tried to make mine unimportant for hundreds of years. It will not happen. You need my kind to power the stones. There is no other way."

"There used to be."

He shook his head. "You chase pipe dreams."

"No—"

"You have shamed your family, shown the royals to be petty children, and wasted my time when I am needed at the Wall." Of all of those things, it was the last one that bothered him the most. The royals would always have their squabbles. The populace seemed to glory in retelling their every childish folly. Indeed, they seemed to grow restless if there was not some new scandal to report.

So that shame was a petty one compared to the loss of his time in the search for her. In the worry that the land had lost another powerful royal. And in the guilty knowledge that he had hoped she was gone forever so that he could be free to stay with Janet. That was the true source of his fury, and he let the full heat of that lash out at his no-more-wife.

"While I was gone searching for you, the Wall was breached." He spoke coldly, the words bitter on his tongue as she paled from the blow of what he said.

"Breached?"

"Fourteen times, Princess." Again he spat her title. He wanted her to know that she was a leader who had failed her people.

"Oh, Goddess."

"Aruckien invaded and I was not there to stop it. To see it. Because I was searching for you."

She pressed a hand against the wall. She knew as well as

he what that meant. "Who? How many?"

"Four at this count. Three more are missing." Then he took a breath, speaking the names of the dead with cold finality. She flinched at every name. She had known them as well as he. Better, actually, because while he had been focused on learning to defend the land, she had been with the women arranging all the rest. She and the girl Sewen had once been inseparable.

"Sewen?" she whispered. "Oh, Goddess. How is Alenth?"

"Grieving."

She put a hand to her mouth, and he saw tears spill from her eyes. But he did not compromise his stance. He laid this all at her feet, and he would see that she faced the consequences of her actions.

"Keeven," she whispered. "I'm so sorry."

"I do not want your apologies. You will return with me now to Bodil Citadel. You will choose another husband from the roster, and you will marry him. Our children will grow up together and we will raise them to avoid your folly."

She didn't speak. She just shook her head, denying his words. But in this he would not be defied. She was a princess and the most powerful Bodil witch short of her mother. She had a responsibility to bear the next generation. The people needed it. They needed more royals, especially since she had just cost them four of their kind.

"You will obey," he said sternly.

"I can help our people other ways."

"You cannot. This is the only way."

To which she simply looked away. She was fighting the struggle, the burden of a female royal. Only a few of them went happily into breeding. Most of the females fought it throughout their childhood, but it was a necessity. All bowed to it eventually. It was only because she was a cosseted princess that she had thought she could be different. But in this, she was more chained than others. He knew. If it were not for Angel Janet, then he would be as tied to her as she was to whatever man who would be her mate.

He saw the agony in her eyes and felt a stirring of sympathy. The female did have it harder, but in this he could not compromise. He watched as acceptance came into her eyes along with fresh tears. But her head bowed, and the curls of her rich dark hair fell forward to shield her face.

Dark. Mysterious. And so ill suited to rule.

Then a voice cut through the silence. It was as familiar to him now as his breathing, and yet Janet's words—as always—confused him.

"She's right, and you're being a jerk."

He looked back to his angel where she was levering herself up on her elbows.

"Janet, do not give her false hope."

"I'm not, you moron. I'm telling her she's right. There's another way to power your stones." She gestured weakly to the castle. "Whoever built this had a way to power those stones without you doing your mumbo-jumbo over it."

"I do not…what?"

"There's a way. Look, you can't blame her for the zombie attack any more than you can blame yourself. So cut her a break and help me up. I'm going into my first real live spaceship, and I'm going to find what you need."

"The world doesn't work that way," he said.

She blinked. "I can't believe you just said that. Like your freaking world has rules."

"It does. And our most sacred is—"

"Babies. Propagation of the magic. Got it. But there is another way." And with that she started to stand. He moved quickly to help her, but was too slow. It was the Princess who was there, gripping her arms as she helped the angel to her feet.

"Do you know of something?"

Janet gave her a lopsided grin. "I know a lot of things. And if you promise not to shoot me again with your paralyzing ray, I promise to do everything I can to keep you from being a brood mare."

"Agreed!" cried the Princess, and she lifted her hand to her mouth to tear open her skin for a blood bond.

Janet held up her hand. "No. No need for any blood. Just get me into the Dead Star, okay?"

And so it was done. Turning their backs on him, both women hobbled inside the monster's castle, completely in accord. And he—a knight and a prince—the one with right on his side, was forced to shuffle along behind while they vowed to make him completely obsolete.

And then they made it worse. They had the gall to laugh when he began to curse.

Janet had one goal: to learn everything she possibly could about the spaceship. A spaceship! Her entire soul sang to the word. She was the first human to ever get to explore an interstellar vehicle of alien origin. She felt like the first ape who touched an obelisk in the movie *2001*.

And sadly, ape was the operative word. Because she was ill equipped to explore the place. She had no tools of her own. Nothing to measure or scan with. No way to study without poking into places that might cause more harm than good. So before she started flipping switches that were going to blow up on her, she settled for a basic orientation.

That meant talking to Princess Has-A-Point. Yeah, because as much as Janet hated agreeing with anything Miss Stunningly Gorgeous said, she absolutely understood where the woman was coming from. No one wanted to be just a baby-making machine. And that, apparently, was what her lineage had doomed her to.

So with an attempt at civility—even though the woman had freaking shot her—she smiled as warmly as possible as they lumbered down the hallway.

"My name is Janet, by the way. I'm not an angel in any way shape or form. At least not what this planet means as an angel. So if I'm going to help, we need to start talking."

The princess had already warmed up to her, so she

returned the smile. "I am named Crissanna. And if you did not come from the sleeping chambers here, where did you come from?"

"A planet called Earth. Or a delusion of massive proportions." She chuckled to show that she was joking, except there was always that niggle of worry that she was insane. "And, by the way, how come we can communicate? I know you're not speaking English. Your lips aren't forming the right shapes, but I can understand you."

The woman's eyes widened and she nodded. "You are not speaking Cichen."

As one, they turned back to Keeven who was following them with glowering looks. Behind him, the door was closing with a near silent hiss, and so the sunlight behind him disappeared. That left only the dim half light that accented the shadows on his face as he pouted. Well, maybe not a full pout, but the man was definitely brooding. He didn't like being away from the Wall for any longer than necessary, and given the breaches lately, she couldn't really blame him. But this was important. And more than that, it was a freaking spaceship. If there were answers anywhere on this world, it would be here.

"Cheer up, Keeven. I swear I'll do this as fast as possible."

He nodded, his expression softening only by the smallest margin. And then he sighed. "I do not know why you two can understand each other. It must be part of the magic of this place."

Could be. Janet added it to the list of mysteries she wanted answered. "Okay. So let's start with how this place is laid out. Give me the basic overview."

That took about ten minutes, mostly because that's how long it took to walk to the central elevator. Once there, a handy dandy little plaque map gave her the whole outline complete with a little dot that indicated YOU ARE HERE.

With Crissanna's help, she learned that most of the pizza cutter part had stasis pods but nearly all of them were black. Probably dead. The side tubes were thrusters, just as she'd guessed. There was a shuttlecraft bay, mostly intact and what had to be the bridge, completely gone. Flattened when they crashed into the mountain.

Crissanna had been doing most of her work in a middle section toward the back of the pizza cutter, and it was to that space that she led them.

"I spent many hours studying that map," she told them as they walked the back corridor. "This room was on it, but not opened. I thought if there was something no one had found before, it would be in here."

Janet nodded. "Sounds logical enough."

Then they entered it. It was a strange room, as space ships go. Janet pulled on all her vast experience of science fiction television and film to deduce that it was a room in a spaceship. That's about as far as she got.

Big and filled with lots of stones. Some were black, some glowing, some just sitting there looking pretty. And all of them were lined up on huge shelves labeled clearly with numbers. Or at least that's what Crissanna said. Janet couldn't read them.

So, a library of stones? There was a desk with a notched protruding arm and a blank wall. And some equipment that Crissanna said she'd taken from other places. She'd hoped that it would recharge the black stones, but it had done nothing but explode a few.

Oops. Except, oddly enough, Crissanna didn't seem to be at all embarrassed about that. Janet would be curled up in the corner of the lab in horror, but Crissanna seemed to take such a disaster in stride. Janet rather admired that in her.

The explanations continued. Keeven settled down on the floor and began to eat something jerky-like from his pack and Janet did her best to not notice that he looked good in a relaxed-warrior kind of way. On the upside, Crissanna didn't seem to notice at all, which reassured Janet a thousand fold. There didn't seem to be any love lost between the two not-actually-married people. Assuming, of course, that vows spoken under duress didn't count.

So Janet settled deeper into learning everything, pleased that she had enough to keep her happy for two lifetimes or more.

Which is why, after just a couple more hours, she was dismayed to discover exactly what she was looking for.

CHAPTER 16

Janet didn't know what gave her the idea. Maybe it was the old *Star Trek* episode where Spock went through a portal to the ice age and got it on with a fur covered hottie. She wasn't a big fan of the classics, but her parents were, so she'd seen the episode a time or three. Or maybe it was simply that she wanted to take the room back to its original state with its original equipment to get a mental baseline. Or perhaps there really was some divinity guiding her hand.

Whatever it was, she set a crystal in one of the notches obviously made to hold crystals. She dropped it in and suddenly the blank wall behind Keeven began to hum. Thankfully, his reflexes were good. He leaped away before he was dropped into the swampland that appeared behind him.

It started out bright, but then rapidly dimmed, holding at a kind of opaque half light that might have been a bad projection of an old film. Ten seconds more and it began to fade, dimming to a waver that looked so familiar until it disappeared with a barely there pop. But Janet had felt the blast of humidity and heard the distant boom of thunder in that swamp image. She knew it was a portal, opened for viewing by crystals that were losing their charge.

Or rather she guessed. But part of her knew.

After all, the portal back into Marty's closet had looked just like that before it had disappeared. This was a portal machine. It had to be.

And maybe Marty's closet was in there too. Assuming she could find it. And assuming the power maintained long enough for her to find it.

"How many crystals were in this room?" she asked.

"What was that?" asked Keeven.

Crissanna answered Janet. "I have not taken any rocks from this room. These I have brought here." She gestured to a pile in her work area.

Janet looked around the room, focusing on the neat rows of rocks on the shelves. "Have you seen that happen before?"

Crissanna crossed to a shelf nearest the open wall that Janet now knew was a portal. "These here produce pictures. Different ones but they fade quickly."

"Because it takes a lot of energy." She said, her belly tightening in excitement. She could go home. If the right portal was there, she could go home!

"Do you remember one of a closet? Of shoes and dresses and stuff?"

Crissanna shook her head. "I did not look at many of them."

Of course not. She'd been trying to re-power the stones, not drain them. Janet rapidly counted the stones. There were just under fifty. If there was a portal to Earth anywhere on this spaceship, then it would be here.

She moved with rapid speed, dropping the stones into the slot one after another. She saw a desert landscape under a white sky. Nope.

Then rocks, as in the inside of a mountain or something. Nope.

Next came darkness that sucked the air out of the room. Definitely not.

Then a bunch that didn't seem to work at all before one that opened out on the middle of an ocean. Water spilled through, making Crissanna squeak, but the portal shut rapidly.

Very rapidly, Janet realized. Because with each successive stone, the portal worked slower and for less time.

She glanced at Crissanna. "It's running out of power."

"Yes. Tomorrow it will be better."

"So it recharges on its own."

She nodded. "That was how I got the idea to come here. I thought there was something about this room that might re-power the stones."

Ah. "It's not likely in the air. It's probably pulling energy from some other place."

She saw frustration flash across the woman's face and Janet reached out to touch her hand.

"Don't worry. I have some ideas. But first, I need to get home and grab some tools."

Keeven stepped closer. "You have your belt. Are there other—"

"Big tools," she interrupted. "Way better than a hammer and some duct tape."

He nodded, but she could see that he didn't like what she was doing.

"I'm trying to help, you know," she said, her voice tight. "Some basic electronics will help narrow everything down. I mean, I don't have a tricorder or anything, but even a volt meter will help." She stopped babbling the moment she realized they had no understanding of anything she said. "Never mind. Let's just see if I can get home."

She went back to flipping in stones, one after another. No one spoke. At least Crissanna helped pass her the crystals. Keeven just watched them and glowered. And then it was there. Marty's closet. One stiletto boot on the floor and ugly tabards galore. Plus Marty standing there in a bra and skinny jeans with her mouth hanging open.

Janet cried out as it disappeared, the portal up for barely a second. Home. Earth. She could get out of whack-a-doodle land.

Odd how that made her chest clench even more.

She looked back at Keeven. He must have seen the closet. He must know...

She watched him swallow then nod, his expression blank.

"We will rest here tonight and then tomorrow you can leave." He held up his hand. "You have helped me rescue the princess, as you swore." He cast a single disdainful glance at Crissanna which she returned in equal measure. "And now you have found your path home. Our vow to each other is fulfilled."

She opened her mouth to say something smart ass. It was on the tip of her tongue when she felt the magic of their vow lift off her shoulders. She hadn't even realized it was there, but between the space of one breath and the next, the weight suddenly lifted. The compulsion to remain with Keeven was gone. She felt it dissolve such that she even swayed backwards once the pressure was gone. It was that tangible and that ephemeral.

"What was that?" She didn't really need to ask, but she felt like she had to fill the sudden emptiness between them somehow and all she had were words.

"Our bond to each other is gone," he said.

"Just like that?" That wasn't what she wanted to ask. She meant to say, bull shit our bond is gone. Except those words stuck in her throat.

Meanwhile, he looked equally sour. "Yes." Then he turned to Crissanna. "Is there food in this castle? A place to wash and rest for the night?"

The woman spoke coolly. "What food stores I had are gone. With the Suckers outside, I could not catch game."

"The danger is gone. I can catch and cook what we need. And there is at least one snare easily mended."

Right. The snare that had pulled her up into a net.

"But what of rest?" he asked.

She shrugged. "There are many rooms in this place. Pick one."

Brilliant conversationalists, all of them. Not. Meanwhile,

Janet distracted herself by thinking of all the things that she still wanted to learn here. "Um, hey..." She began, feeling awkward with Keeven and hating it. "There's a ton of things I still want to explore. Would you mind taking care of food and stuff?" she asked him. "While Crissanna shows me around some more?"

He dipped his head, every movement looking stiff and formal. "I will prepare food and bed for you, Angel. Please, if you could teach us anything, we would be most grateful."

Lord, he sounded like he was using the royal "we." Worse still is that he had gone back to calling her "Angel." But before she could express how heartsick that made her, Crissanna touched her arm.

"What can you explain?"

Janet nearly laughed, but there was no humor in her anywhere. "Very little, I'm afraid. But let's start in the engine room."

Crissanna frowned. "Which is—"

"The place that attaches to the cylinder that isn't destroyed."

"Ah. Yes. The place of light but no noise."

"Uh...yeah. Lead on."

And so the timed passed without Janet thinking of Keeven more than once every twenty seconds or so. Fortunately, she had everything else distracting her until her eyes were so scratchy, they burned whenever she opened them.

Still, she would have kept working if Keeven hadn't forced her to look up from an incomprehensible collection of crystals in what might be a motherboard.. "You are too tired to make sense of this."

"Just a few more minutes while I—"

"Accidentally touch the wrong stone and damage what little we have left?"

She looked up startled into semi-alertness by his words. "You're talking like this is a spaceship and not a monster castle."

His chin dipped the tiniest fraction. "While you have been here, I have been studying some of the stones. I forced Crissanna to show me."

"Stones?"

"Records. Of my people when they crashed here."

"Holy shit, you've got working records? Where?"

She was wide awake now, but he shook his head. "It is not in your language."

"But I understand Crissanna. There's a translation field or something. It's something—"

"Tomorrow, Janet."

"I'm leaving tomorrow."

He was silent a long time. Long enough for her to realize how devastating those words were to him. And maybe to her.

"I will come back," she said.

"Then you will go sleep now."

And with a firm hand, he led her to a room. It looked like it might once have been a lounge of some sort. Or maybe an office. Mostly it was an empty space where he'd laid out bedrolls. He'd stacked the debris of what could have been chairs and a desk into a corner.

Two bedrolls as well as a plate of food, now cold. She hadn't thought she was starving until that moment. Then suddenly hunger roared through her, and she went straight for it.

"Thank you for this," she said.

He didn't respond except to settle on top of his bedroll to watch her eat. He offered her water even before she asked and then escorted her outside to wash up. It was full dark, but they walked together to a tiny stream where she cleaned off her hands and face. Then she ducked around a rock to pee.

She'd gotten over the embarrassment of doing this days ago. Modern plumbing was something this place sorely lacked. But she might as well wash a bit as she did this. So she stripped out of her boots and pants then stepped into the chill stream to relieve herself. It wasn't until she began to wash that she saw the truth, and the shock hit her with more bite than the chill water.

She was bleeding. It was her period, which meant she wasn't pregnant.

No baby.

She must have cried out. She must have made some sort of sound because Keeven appeared around the rock, his sword drawn and his gaze snapping to her even as he rapidly scanned everything else.

She swallowed and tried to talk. It took two attempts, but eventually she spoke with some semblance of calm. "It's okay, Keeven. I just...I mean...I..." What? She'd already gotten used to the idea that she was pregnant. She'd believed she carried Keeven's baby by divine, broken condom decree.

But she wasn't pregnant, and that was a good thing, she told herself. The last thing she needed was a child, especially if she was going back to Earth. And yet she was crying. Big fat ugly tears that blurred her vision before streaming down her cheeks.

He closed the distance between them, stepping fully into the stream despite his boots. "Angel," he whispered as he wrapped her in one arm. His other still held his sword, but down and away.

She snorted, and it wasn't a pretty sound. "That's just it, Keeven. I'm not your angel. I never have been." No divinity. No baby. Nothing but her ignorant, failed PhD self. She tried to pull away, but he held her tight. She resisted for less than a second, then pressed herself tightly against him, letting the tears flow.

He held her while she sobbed, pressing his lips to her forehead, before whispering her name. "Janet, Janet, Janet." Over and over until her heartbreak eased. The tears stopped, and she pushed away to clean herself up.

He let her go. The cold water was bracing on her face and downright freezing on her feet. And while she washed, he took a step out of the stream to continually scan their surroundings. She wasn't exactly sure why. It was night, the only illumination coming from the three moons. Then again, perhaps there was a lot to see, she thought as she looked out over the vista.

She knew she was distracting herself. Thinking nonsense instead of the truth. She was devastated that she wasn't pregnant. And if that wasn't a kick in the gut. Not because of the lack of fertility, but because that meant something else entirely.

She was in love with Keeven. Deeply enough that she wanted to have his child. To watch the little bugger grow into his or her powers. To see Keeven as a father and then a grandfather. She wanted to grow old with him because she loved him. And that was the stupidest damn thing ever. Because he lived for his duty. To make children and grandchilden with someone of his race.

Which she wasn't.

A couple hours before, she'd had Crissanna take her to the stasis pods. That's what they were. Frozen people asleep in some suspended state. And since Earth had never developed that technology, his race and hers were entirely different. Which meant he needed to mate with one of his own kind to get a child of power. A human wouldn't do it. It had to be one of his own.

She sighed, doing her best to choke off the sound. He heard her, of course, and she saw his gaze cut hard back to her. She was out of the stream now, drying off on a rag he offered her. Lord, he knew what she wanted even before she did. And didn't that just dig the knife in deeper?

"Can you tell me what has upset you now?"

His voice was quiet, his tone gentle. She knew he was patient too, so if she didn't tell him, he would accept her decision and wait.

"You know I'm not an angel, right?"

He shrugged. "You did not come from the pods, but that doesn't mean—"

"I'm not of your race, Keeven. I'm not from your planet—neither this one nor wherever you came from. I'm human and you're...I don't know. You're not."

He frowned. "It doesn't matter."

"It does matter. Keeven, I'm not pregnant." She took a deep breath. "We may look the same but we're different species. It's very possible that I can't get pregnant by you. And even if I did..." She looked at her hands. "The child won't be magical except from you. It won't be the powerhouse of talent you're expecting because it's a dilution of your genetics."

He didn't speak at all, and she didn't dare look at him. She'd just killed all his hopes. Every damn one of them. He was stuck back with the princess whom he obviously hated. And she was completely useless to him unless she could figure out the technology behind his stones. Which, let's be honest, wouldn't happen for years, if ever. It's not like she could plug in a laptop to their spaceship and see the tutorial.

She'd come up short, and the weight of that failure had her dropping down onto the rock with her head on her knees.

"And I thought getting kicked out of the PhD program was the worst thing that could happen to me," she said.

She felt his hand then. A touch on her shoulder, warm and comforting. She knew the width of his fingers, the sweet scrape of every one of his calluses and the gentleness of his quiet presence. She knew what he was worth, and that she couldn't be equal to him was the hardest thing she'd ever had to bear.

"I'm so sorry, Keeven. I really tried."

"We are not done yet, Angel."

She felt her hands clench and if she'd had more strength, she would have hit him. "God damn it, I am not an angel!"

He caught her fist in his hand. She hadn't done more than lift it in his direction, but he caught it and held it cradled in his palm. "You are to me, Janet."

And then he kissed her. Not with passion, not with anger,

but with a simple shared caress of kindness. Of comfort. Of…

Of passion now. Because the more he stroked his lips across hers, the more she felt the sweet press of his tongue, the more her blood heated. The more she wanted him inside her, pumping hard, creating the child that wasn't ever going to be. If she had any wish for any god or goddess listening, it was that she give this man everything he wanted. And failing that, she would give him herself.

So she kissed him deeply. She wrapped her arms around him and flattened her hands across his broad back. And then she murmured into his mouth, "Make love to me, Keeven."

He pressed a kiss to her cheek, nibbling up to her ear before he whispered, "Always."

He made her a bed. The bank of the stream was rocky, but he made a blanket from his clothing. He lay her upon his pants and his shirt and the smell of him surrounded her. She pulled off the rest of her clothes, shivering in the cold mountain air, but she didn't remain chilled for long.

He pressed his mouth to her tight nipple, sucking her as she clutched him. He continued to lave her, nipping her in just the right way. Soon she was crying out, grasping for purchase on his wide shoulders.

He could have built her to orgasm right like that. He'd done it before. But she didn't want that for him tonight. She is the one who had failed him, so she wrenched herself away. Gasping for breath, she pulled his face up to hers. "Let me show you," she said. And in her heart, she thought, let me show you how much I love you.

He didn't understand what she meant, so she pushed him to lie down. There wasn't room on their clothes, but with the addition of her pants and tunic, he had a space to lie down. Then she began to kiss him, stroking her tongue across his flat male nipple much as he had teased hers. And while he groaned beneath her, she reach for his penis. She wrapped it with her fist, stroking him until he jerked his hips toward her.

"No, Janet. Let me—"

She silenced him with a kiss. All this time, she'd been sucked and kissed and adored to orgasm. It was about time she returned the favor. He was close, she knew, so she stopped what she was doing, squeezing the head to hold him off. And then she looked at him.

"It's always been you," she said. "And it will always be you for me."

Then she straddled him. He thrust into her easily, and yet she still felt the stretch of his organ inside her. He was so big, and she adored the full feeling. He was thrusting harder inside her, holding himself back until she was ready. But she did not want him so controlled. So she leaned down, supporting herself on her hands as she bent to whisper into his ear.

"I love you," she said.

She felt her words hit him in the jerk of his hips, the sudden mad ram of his body. He was wild as he slammed into her, and she arched, feeling him go deep, feeling all his power thrusting into her. His hands held her hips in a fierce grip, keeping her steady as he slammed into her one more time.

And then he exploded. She felt the power of his ejaculation in her whole body. And it was enough to throw her over the edge into orgasm. A sudden explosion of sensation as pleasure subsumed her whole body. Pleasure and something else...

Love.

Keeven cradled her close, calling her every beautiful, tender, adoring name he knew. His mind was filled with such words even as his body held her resting on top of him.

And in the silent beauty of their union, he made his decision.

CHAPTER 17

The plan was simple. She would put the Earth crystal in and dive through the portal before it collapsed. Keeven and Crissanna were to wait two days to re-open it. Day length wouldn't be the same between the two planets. Hell, it was possible that time itself worked differently, but in the absence of proof, she assumed everything was on the same basis. Meaning sixty seconds on Earth would be sixty seconds here.

After all, travel between dimensions had to require way more power than between distances, so she guessed that they were on the same temporal wavelength or whatever. Which meant that since she'd been here over a week, she'd been gone that long from Earth.

A week gone from home. She wondered if anyone noticed.

Anyway, the plan was to dive through, start whatever tests she could, and then be back at Marty's closet for the rendezvous. She figured she'd need at least a couple days to do some initial tests and grab some equipment. Then she'd camp out in Marty's closet until the portal re-opened and she could come back, hopefully with fully recharged stones. And some equipment. And a how-to book on flush toilets.

Simple plan.

Set to execute now.

She swallowed and looked at Keeven. After everything they had done last night, after she'd told him she loved him, he'd said nothing. Sure he'd been the perfect lover, but that wasn't the same thing. She wanted the words. She wanted the feeling. She wanted to be his one and only. But he wanted a baby, and since she couldn't be the womb he needed, she needed to leave. And yet, it was so damn hard.

He smiled and touched her face. "We will work this out," he said. "Together."

Then he took the Earth stone from her hand and with a gentle grip on her arm, ushered her to the portal. He glanced once at Crissanna, silently telling the woman something—he had no idea what—then dropped the stone into the slot.

Marty's closet appeared: grainy, well-lit, and with lots of clothes on either side but not directly in front. Plus there was Marty with a bag of chips and the empties of a half dozen frappuccinos sitting in the door. Weird, but Janet didn't have time to think of that. She just leaped.

Or rather, she was partly pulled because Keeven leaped first.

Oh shit. Shitshitshitshitshit! But there was no way to stop it. They landed with a stumble. Or rather he landed solid, she stumbled. And Marty nearly choked to death on a potato chip.

The moment she gained her feet, she spun around. The portal was gone. It was the back of the closet, stiletto boot and all.

"Are you crazy?" she screeched at Keeven. "I don't know that I can get you back. I mean I hope. I think it'll work. But damn it, we might have just hosed all the power!"

He still gripped her arm, tighter now since he was keeping her from tripping over Marty's zillion pairs of shoes, but at her words, his hands actually softened, stroking her skin in the way that always seemed to calm her down. Even when she wanted to be rip roaring mad.

"I told you we would find an answer together. So I am here to find that answer."

"What answer?" she cried, throwing up her hands. "I still

can't have your baby." To which Marty—who had just recovered from gagging—slapped a hand over her mouth.

"It is not a baby I want, Janet. It's you."

Lies, lies, lies. She wanted to scream the word at him. But it wouldn't come out. Instead, her eyes teared up even as she thumped him in the chest. "It's not going to work."

"It will work." Three words. Rock solid in his faith. And she just shook her head.

"You're insane."

He shrugged. "Perhaps you should introduce me to the protector of this portal."

Yeah, because Marty looked so much like a protector with her hair in a messy ponytail and chip remains scattered all over her tee shirt. Still, the woman was her best friend. And she'd missed her this last week. So she gestured while Marty pushed awkwardly to her feet.

"Marty, meet Keeven, a really stupid prince. Keeven, this is Marty, my best friend. Don't worry. She cleans up well."

To which Marty simply laughed before wrapping Janet in a bear hug. It was tight and filled with the smell of frappuccino and french onion chips, and it was undeniably her best friend.

"Jesus, I'm so glad I'm not insane," Marty said against her hair. "You're alive. You're here. And I'm not losing it."

Janet laughed. "Hold onto that thought because it's about to get a lot weirder."

"No, it couldn't," Marty said, not letting go. "Everyone said you'd just skipped. End of PhD meltdown. But you left your phone and purse behind, so I didn't know what had happened. You were just gone. And then I saw you, and I thought I was going insane. I mean I'd been worrying myself sick for days, but you were there. I saw you. And who the hell is he?"

It was impossible not to love her friend for this. She laughed even as she was wiping away her tears. Damn. She was home. A home with Marty and chips and frappuccinos, and she couldn't be happier. Except, of course, for the amazingly selfless man beside her who might have just given up everything for her.

"Um," she said finally pulling back, "so he takes some explanation. As I said, his name is Keeven. Or rather Prince Keeven Gunden-something of Askel."

Marty's eyebrows raised as her gaze hopped between Keeven and Janet. "A prince? Should I bow?"

Janet tried and failed to cover her laughter. "I didn't, but you can if you want." Then she turned to Keeven. "Can you understand a word of what she's saying?"

He shook his head. "Not a word."

"She is asking if she should bow to you. Because you're a prince."

Oddly enough, he didn't laugh. "It is our custom to open the hands and lower the head in greeting." He demonstrated, and Marty mimicked the gesture.

Janet watched with a renewed feeling that her life was surreal. And when they were done, she looked at Keeven. "So that's great and all, but don't expect anyone else to do that." Then she glanced at her friend. "Marty's special."

Her friend shot her a look. "If you say special ed, I'm going to hit you."

Janet grinned, but her thoughts were already on what she had to do. They had three days, give or take, and a lot to accomplish. "So, how long have I been gone? And are there any more frappuccinos."

Marty nodded. "Downstairs. And since last Friday."

Janet rolled her eyes. "I know when I left. I want to know what day it is." She sobered as she gestured to Marty's closet. "Did you know you've got a portal back there?"

Marty's face paled. "Like…um…Narnia or something?"

"Yeah. Exactly like that. Only no lion or witch. Just tiny zombies that eat you and big gools who don't. Plus birds the size of a Volvo."

Marty didn't answer. She just stared, her eyes narrowing.

But then her gaze hopped to the closet and Keeven and back. Obviously this was not processing well. Which shouldn't have been a surprise. After all, she'd lived through it, and it had taken her days.

"Let's start with what day is it? And a frappuccino."

They headed out to the kitchen, Keeven trailing behind, his gaze taking in everything. "Wednesday. Ten days after you…left. Your dad's freaking out, by the way. You need to call him."

She would. In a minute. "So I'm out of the physics program."

"That butthead Dr. Jettison claimed that you freaked and ran."

Of course he did. "He can bite me," she said firmly. "I've never run in my life. Except from zombies and birdbeasts, but those don't count." Then she giggled. "I even fought an gool—an ogre. And won!"

Marty shook her head. "I don't know which one of us in insane, but—"

"Yeah, get used to it. Okay, first things first." She opened the refrigerator and grabbed a frappuccino. One sip and she was in caffeine heaven. It actually gave her shivers of delight. Then with a grin, she passed it over to Keeven. "Go on. You'll like it."

He took a swig…then gagged. "Is this what you drink here?"

So maybe not. Still, she stuck out her tongue at the man before swiping the bottle back. Then after she'd drained half of the coffee heaven, she gestured to Marty. "Next I need a shower and real clothes." Tunic and leggings was an awesome look, but she was missing her jeans and tee. Not to mention a clean bra. "Then he needs decent clothes—"

"Nah," Marty drawled, being much too obvious about her inspection of him. "He's good."

"He's mine," Janet said loudly before her friend held up her hands in surrender.

"No harm in looking."

"Yeah, there is. I've declared that there is." Then she sobered. "Okay, Miss Engineer, I'm going to show you something that I need your help with." She drew out the pile of dead stones. "These need to be recharged."

"Rocks?"

"Magic rocks."

The look Marty gave her went beyond skeptical into call-the-men-in-white-coats.

"You've got a portal to another world in your closet, and you won't work with magic rocks?"

Marty grimaced as she picked up a rock. "Fair point. So how do we recharge them?"

"That's the question." She picked up a dead fire rock and handed it to Keeven. "Can you charge this?"

He shrugged. "I do not know the rules of your world."

"Right. Let's find out." She turned it over in his palm. It was a basic fire starter stone. One of the easiest to charge. She watched him concentrate. Marty too was looking with her skeptical face. And then they waited. And waited. Janet had seen Keeven recharge a stone like this in seconds, but this time, his breath was labored and his eyes seemed to glaze. She saw perspiration dot his forehead and felt anguish seep through their link.

This was wrong. This was bad. "Stop—"

He gasped as he set the stone down, his whole body contracting into itself.

"Keeven!"

"I am fine," he said, though his voice sounded thready. "Try it."

She looked at the stone. She hadn't seen any magic seep into it, and she usually got a hint of something. A feeling if nothing else. "You know I can't turn it on."

He nodded. "Get something to burn."

"Right. Where's the mail?" She didn't wait for Marty to answer, but grabbed a stack of junk mail from near the door.

Then she set the stone on top of two Victoria Secrets catalogues plus an ad for cheap car insurance. She was about to throw in the breadstick coupon from the nearest delivery pizza place, but Marty grabbed it right back.

"Don't you dare."

Janet nodded, making sure she had on her serious face. "Right. My bad." Then she looked at Keeven. "Okay. Light 'er up."

She'd seen him do it with barely a thought. At most a flick of his hand. But this time he had to focus and speak a word. She couldn't even follow the word in his language, but their link translated it to, "*Now.*"

And all three catalogues plus some of the table burst into flame.

Marty squeaked and jumped back, but no more than Janet. Even Keeven looked startled. This time Janet was the first to recover as she peered down at the smoking pile of ash.

"Shit. The rock's gone. Not to mention some of my table."

"Your world is unexpectedly flammable," Keeven commented.

She laughed, having no idea how to respond to that. Then Marty eased forward.

"How'd you do that?"

Janet shrugged. "That's what we're trying to figure out." She pulled out her bag of stones. "I have stones in here for fire, a bunch for a big ass force field, one for holding back stink—that was a personal favorite—and a few that I have no clue what they were but I grabbed them because they were pretty. Only one crystal though. They're kinda protective of those."

Marty stared at her. "You're joking, right?"

"Narnia. In your closet."

Marty nodded. "Right. Okay."

"So…think these will get me accepted into the engineering department? Full ride?"

Her best friend stared at her. It took about two very long

minutes, but eventually her smile grew, then broadened, then left her laughing silently as tears rolled down her cheek.

"I know just who you need to talk to."

Janet grinned. "Cool. Because I'm kinda holding the whole spaceship thing in reserve."

Marty laughed even harder. "Spaceship. Right."

"Right. With stasis pods and everything."

It took less time this round. But then her friend suddenly froze. Her eyes widened and she stared. "Wait. Really?"

"I'm thinking of calling it Aslan. You know. Code word when we're in public and all."

Marty just stared at her, and then she abruptly dropped down into a chair right next to the smoking pile of ash. "Narnia. In my closet." Then she suddenly gasped. "Oh my God!" She stared at Janet. "We've got to buy this house, like *now*."

Keeven decided it was time to take a stand. Janet had been going non-stop since they entered her world. She and her friend Marty had negotiated her entrance into a new form of study, she had met with her father and a banker to buy the home they lived in, and then she had taken him to a lab where they had worked through the night. Now it was midday and she had rubbed her eyes for the hundredth time.

"It is time to rest," he said to her.

She looked up from a device she called her laptop, blinking her eyes at him. "I can't quit. There's so much more—"

"I did not say quit. I said rest."

She straightened up from her seat, groaning as she pressed a hand to her back. He adjusted to help her, rubbing the ache from her muscles and allowing her to rest her head back against him. The warmth of her body invaded his senses as did the scent of her hair and the erotic groan she released.

"Don't stop," she said, her voice creating a low throb in his belly.

He didn't answer, the need for her cutting off any words. He just kept touching her, his hands spanning her lower back, his body tight to hers. It was all he could do to keep himself from thrusting against her, but they were in public. There were others working in this lab, constantly eyeing him with puzzled frowns even though he did his best to fit in. He wore their jean clothes and ate their cold pizza, but they could tell he wasn't an engineer like them. He would never be like any of them, and that thought caused him infinite pain. Because that meant he could never be worthy of her.

"You're awful quiet," Janet said as she turned in his arms. "Tired?"

He looked away. "Yes, I am tired."

"But that's not why you're so quiet, is it?"

She knew him well and so he shrugged, choosing to divert her attention rather than answer. "You need to rest. You cannot solve my world's problems in a day."

She thought about it, yawned once more, then gave him a tired smile. "You're right, as always." She pushed up from her stool then glanced at her friend. "I'm wiped. Gonna crash for a couple hours. Hey Marty, can you call me if—"

Her friend responded without looking up from her machine. Janet grinned and grabbed Keeven's hand. Then she looked over at another woman in the lab. One who had been looking at him quite often. "Sorry. I'm taking the eye candy home with me."

The other woman flushed and looked away.

Outside was ugly. Cloudy with a humidity that made his clothing stick to his body. Janet had told him that her world did not run on magic stones, but on electricity that powered just about everything. The end result was much the same as in his world: housing that kept the elements away, cool air when it was hot, warm heat when it was cold. But there were other things that were night and day different.

The machines that roared or clicked or beeped in her world were beyond his comprehension. Cars and planes were the least of what terrified him here. He had watched their videos, listened to her phone device, even looked at pictures of what appeared to be fashionable. All if it showed him a world of color and noise that made his head hurt. He longed for even the chaotic chatter of the creatures who shared space with them in Wall City. That was a noisy place for him, but her world seemed to be all chaos all the time. It was beyond him, and yet, she obviously adored it.

"You need to start talking to me, O Stoic Prince. Otherwise I'm going to think you want to ditch me and go out with Nancy."

"Who is Nancy?"

"The girl in the lab who couldn't keep her eyes off of you."

"Oh. She is a lovely woman." Then he looked down at her. "But I cannot see anyone but you."

Instead of being pleased, Janet narrowed her eyes, hesitating before she spoke. "I'm not sure what that means, Keeven. Does that mean you are honor-bound to me? Or that—"

A vehicle screeched beside them, its metal front coming perilously close to them. Janet spun on it and banged on the hood.

"Pay attention, moron! A stop sign means stop!"

Gestures were exchanged between both the person in the car and Janet, but she kept walking, her expression growing brighter by the second. Which truly confused him. He was woefully unprepared to protect her in this strange place. He hadn't even seen the vehicle coming.

Meanwhile, Janet began to chuckle. "I know I shouldn't be pleased about giving someone the finger. We really don't need more rudeness in this world, but..." She turned to look at him. "Before I would have cringed and rushed away, thinking that it was my fault. Or even if I knew it was the dickhead's fault, I would have been too shy to talk back. But what is one driver compared to a colony of birdbeasts? I feel so much stronger now. So much more me." She flashed him a warm smile. "I feel like I'm standing tall for the first time in my life."

"You have always been tall in my eyes."

"I know," she said with a laugh. "That's what makes me love you."

He winced at her words. He felt the truth of it in his heartspace, but he also knew her doubt. There was anxiety in her words, fear that underpinned the emotion. And that was not love. Not true love, so he looked away, not knowing what to do to fix their separation.

He heard her sigh beside him. "You know what? For a guy who made a very impulsive leap into my world, you're acting very much like a guy who regrets he ever met me."

His gaze whipped back to hers. "No, Janet. Never—"

She held up her hand. "Let me remind you that your vow of honesty holds here too."

He stiffened, insulted to his core. "Of course it does."

"And that I can feel it when you lie." When he opened his mouth to object, she immediately moderated his words. "Or at least when you're not telling the full truth."

He stopped walking, feeling frustration in every part of his body. "I came here for exactly the reasons I told you. So that we could find the answers together."

She nodded. "And we are."

"You are," he corrected. "I am useless here." He gestured to the cars that moved at incredible speeds behind them, to the lights on buildings that burned bright enough to hurt his eyes. And in his mind he thought of the other things he had seen on her laptop, each more fantastic than the last.

She grabbed his hand and pressed a kiss to his fingers. "You told me it would take some time for me to understand the rules of your world. Why would you think it would be any different here?"

He huffed. Because he was a man. Because he was accounted very smart. Because of a thousand other things that were egotistical and very wrong. So he focused on the other answer. "Even in my world, you were brave and smart. You faced the enemy without flinching and gave us magic to ease my cough from the tunnels."

"I did flinch. A lot. And the only reason I wasn't completely bonkers was because I was relying on you." She grabbed handfulls of his shirt and tugged him closer. "Do you seriously think I need you to comprehend modern electronics? That I think you should face down an idiot driver in a Mustang for me? Damn it, Keeven, I need you to love me, not protect me. Not worship me. Not do any of those other things." She touched his lips. "I want you to love me."

And there it was. The secret wish of her heart, spoken aloud to him. He knew it was the truth, knew even that it was what she had always longed for. It was what all young women spoke of, including Crissanna and the girls of his childhood. But it was not a man's lot. It certainly wasn't a possibility for a prince.

"Janet," he said with a sigh.

"It's okay, Keeven. I know you can't force yourself to love me."

Did she understand nothing? "I cannot love anyone. I…" He took her arm and led her to the nearest tree. The bark was rough and somewhat sticky, the shadows here barely enough to cut the heat, but he still put her there and he still touched her face as gently as he could even with fingers tainted with sap.

"You misunderstand me," he said. She waited, her eyes open and her heartspace all but screaming at him to love her. But he had no words. Nothing he could say to explain. So he kissed her. He pressed himself against her, he possessed her mouth, and he put every bit of desire into the way he caressed her hips and waist. He wanted her. He desired her with a madness well beyond reason. And for him, that was as much a declaration as he could make. And when they separated, he was gratified to see her looking dazed, her eyes sleepy with pleasure, her nipples tight with desire.

"Do you want me or the baby?" she whispered.

"If I wanted a child, I would have stayed behind with

Crissanna and forced her to honor our arrangement."

Her eyes widened. "So you want me?"

"Have I not demonstrated that on numerous occasions?" For emphasis, he thrust against her, letting her feel the hunger in his erection.

She flushed, her cheeks red. "Well, that part I know."

He was silent a long moment, at last feeling his way through her confusion. "You think I can do this with a woman I do not want? That I bed women without...without..."

"Love, Keeven. You can't even say the word."

And now it was time for the truth. She would make him say it baldly. "I do not know what that is, Janet. How can I say it without that understanding?"

"Because you feel it?"

"Listen to your heartspace. Do I feel it?"

She was silent. Quiet enough that she closed her eyes and let her head drop back against the tree. Around them the machines made noises, people chattered, and he heard a few birds lost amid the clatter. But he didn't move. And he tried to open his heartspace to her. And he waited.

And waited.

In the end, she lifted her hand and pressed it hard against the flat of his chest. "I feel confusion inside you. Longing. Loneliness. And a need for me."

"Is any of that love?"

She frowned. "Maybe. Kinda." Then she shook her head. "You'll know it's love when you do something completely out of character, against all logic, even though it costs you something."

He blinked at her. "You wish me to act insane."

She chuckled. "Yeah, I guess. I started to fall in love with you when I stepped through the portal in the first place. Narnia at the back of Marty's closet? Impossible. But when I really knew I loved you? That came when I agreed to have your baby. Against everything that made sense to me, against my independence and even the plan of returning here, I still wanted to give you what you wanted most."

"But you cannot have my child. You said—"

"I didn't know that then. Which is how I knew I love you."

She was silent for a long moment, looking at him and obviously waiting for something. All he could think was that he could not do that. He had too many responsibilities to sacrifice others. And everything he had to give was already hers.

"Keeven," she said softly. "Why did you jump through the portal?"

"Because you would not be able to find the answer to magic without me."

She nodded slowly. "Wasn't it a little because you wanted to be with me? That you couldn't bear to be without me?"

He stroked her arms, seeing where her thoughts had taken her. But he was a knight. He couldn't lie to her. "Of course I wanted to be with you. But I came because I need a way to recharge the stones. Without that, my land is lost."

He saw the disappointment in her eyes. Worse, he felt it wash like icy water through his heartspace. "So it was a calculated risk." A statement, not a question. He answered it anyway.

"Yes, Janet. A risk. A choice that I thought about most of the night before." Then in case she did not understand his meaning, he forced himself to say it. He forced himself to crush her completely. "Angel, I cannot sacrifice my people for you. I owe my people too much for that. Which means I cannot love you. Not how you want."

He felt the words hit her, felt the understanding of what he'd said settle painfully into her soul. And he saw her blink away her tears.

"Janet—"

"I get it. And even if I didn't, I can feel it." Her voice was thick, but the agony washing through his heartspace said even more. "It's weird. I found another world in a closet. I've discovered a spaceship and magic crystals. It's probably the greatest discovery since the new world. But it turns out I just want you to love me." She touched his face. "That's called irony."

He closed his eyes, savoring her caress while he wished he had the words to ease her pain. He didn't.

Eventually her hand dropped and she pushed off the tree. "Come on. I'm too tired to deal with this now."

He didn't speak. He had done enough damage, and so he followed her to her home. He protected her back as best he could as they crossed through the maze of pathways that led to her building. One that was on the ground and closed off to the air. And he went with her to the top floor where she rested, but he didn't go in.

"Janet, should I rest elsewhere?"

She spun back to her, her eyes bright with unshed tears. "I—" Her word choked off and then she looked away. "Rip off the Band-Aid, right?"

He did not know what that meant.

"Well fuck that. You're here right now, and I want…I want…" She broke down, the tears flowing freely.

Nothing could stop him then. He entered her room, enfolded her in his arms, and carried her to bed.

CHAPTER 18

Keeven loved her in every way he was capable of. They had only hours left before Crissanna opened the portal again. Hours left before he had to take whatever magic she could re-install in his stones back to the Wall. Whatever knowledge she had gained would be with him then as he left her. Because he could afford no more time apart from his defense of the realm.

So he loved her every way he knew how. And as her body rippled in pleasure around him, he released himself into her. His seed, his wishes, and his only pleasure—all these he gave to her. Because when he returned to Bodil, he would have to be a prince again.

When she settled into sleep beside him, he whispered the closest words he could manage. "If I could love anyone," he said. "It would be you."

And with that, they both had to be content.

Keeven was fast asleep when Janet's device chimed. Musical notes that had them both rapidly disentangling legs and arms. She reached for the small machine while Keeven grabbed his sword. But his weapon wasn't needed here. Especially when he heard Janet croak a hoarse, "Hello?" and then Marty's tiny voice responded. Even without understanding the language, he could hear the excitement in the words. And then Janet's face blossomed into a grin.

"What has happened?" he asked, unfocused worry knotting his muscles.

"Marty did it. She's powered the stones. We just need to test them."

Fierce joy burst through him. Janet had done it. She had solved everything, and he couldn't be more proud of her. But then she looked at a bracelet on her arm and began to curse.

"What?"

"We've slept too long. Crap, the portal's going to open soon. Shit, shit, shit."

There were more sounds from the device while Janet scrambled out of bed, her naked flesh pink and beautiful in the sunlight that filtered through her heavy curtains.

"Yeah," she was saying. "Just bring them to your closet. There isn't time. We'll test them over there." A longer pause while she was shaking her head. "I don't know. It's working now, but I don't know how long that portal will last. We have to recharge *those* stones." Another pause and then she laughed. "Damn it, *I don't know*. Just come here. Bring equipment. We'll figure it out. Bye."

Then she pulled the device away from her ear and grinned at Keeven. "Two weeks ago, I thought my life was over. Then you appeared in the closet and I'm excited about every day. I have a purpose and a hot guy in my bed. And..." She reached over to kiss him deeply and quickly. He held what he could catch of her body—her arm, her shoulder—but then she pulled back. "Look I know things are not quite right between us. I know there are problems, but we can figure them out, right?"

He didn't know what to say, but he tried anyway. "Back home, things will be different. I have to return to the Wall. I have—"

"I know. But let's take this one step at a time, okay?"

He smiled at her because she wished it. And because his heart was aching at separating from her, he answered in her own language. "Okay."

She straightened up with a grin. "Look at you. Learning English and everything. I'm gonna shower. Oh, I'll text Marty to grab me a latte and muffins for everyone, and then we'll set up in front of the closet."

She dashed into their water room—a marvel he fully intended to copy somehow—while he set his sword back into its scabbard. Had he just lied to her? Or as close to one as he had ever allowed?

Once back in his world, he would need to become a prince again. He could not live without children. He had a duty to his people to pass on his magic. But the idea of lying with another woman made him want to retch and then kill things.

He looked at the sunlight through the window. Was there time? One last…

He stood up and stripped off his clothes. He had learned about showers yesterday. But now he would experience one with Janet.

Keeven could not suppress a dark sense of dread. He didn't know why, but the feeling was real and nearly overwhelming. He tried to reason it away. He tried to think that it was merely because he was returning to his duties in his world. But this darkness went beyond that. And it was ugly as it gripped his gut.

Janet felt it too. She was pacing just beyond the closet entrance. She had calculated the time of the portal's opening, and yet she kept muttering and figuring on her fingers while Keeven stood in taut awareness by the back of the closet. The more he tried to reassure her that Crissanna would be prompt, the more the woman fretted about time and dimensions and portal dilations. He had no understanding of these words, and so he simply smiled to reassure her, knowing that the gesture wouldn't work.

Of the three of them, Marty was the only happy one. She was nearly hopping in her excitement as she stood near Janet.

"We're clear on everything we're carrying, right?" Janet

asked for the third time. "The portal won't stay open long. Nine or ten seconds, by my guess. We should time it."

Keeven didn't answer. He wore the backpack she had given him. It was heavy beyond anything he had carried before and he didn't know how the thing didn't split apart from the weight. Beyond that, he had his sword in one hand and the bag of recharged stones—they hoped—attached to his belt. They'd not had time to test them. He could only say that the stones held magic that he hoped was shaped to the spell as designed. It did not feel like the power he gave to a stone, but it wasn't exactly different either. They would simply have to pray it would work.

But what about this feeling he had? Something evil—

The closet flickered. He felt the surge of magic, now familiar in its power and shape. Like a thousand tiny pinpricks without pain. Just pressure and the growing awareness of—

Bad.

Something was very wrong on the other side. He knew the scent, felt the power, even tasted the vileness of Aruckien on the air. He didn't stop the think, but acted as he had been trained. He was a warrior, and this was something he did very well.

He leaped through. The portal wasn't even finished forming, but he leaped, half afraid he would splinter apart.

He didn't. He landed on steady feet, his sword raised and his senses on full alert.

They were here. The Aruckien so thick in this room that they crowded his feet and climbed the walls. And beyond them, the Controller. Not just a gool with a sack, but the full Magician. Dark eyed, smooth black hair, and slitted eyes half closed as he muttered his spells.

Keeven turned to see Crissanna, screaming as she was buried by the Aruckien. She was beside the mechanical arm that held the earth stone. In an instant, he understood what had happened. She had stayed behind. Instead of running or hiding, Crissanna had waited here to open the portal. She had waited while the Aruckien attacked, dropping the stone in place just before being overwhelmed. And now he was here, but it was too late. There were too many of them, and he could not fight them all.

And in that moment, he realized something else. If he was overrun, who would save Janet?

The choice appeared before him in that split second of absolute clarity. He might survive. He had a mostly defensible position. His sword was already up and a quick throw straight into the heart of the magician would end this quickly. If he had enough time. If he didn't miss. And if the evil creature had no defenses.

But if he failed, no one would protect Janet.

And he could not risk that.

So he saved her. He exposed his flank, he gave up all hope of survival, and he used his split second of advantage to swing his sword down across the machine that held the Earth stone. With one blow, he severed the arm and smashed the stone.

The portal winked out with a tangible pop.

Janet was safe.

He and Crissanna were lost.

And if the Magician gained control of this castle, then the realm might be lost as well.

The Aruckien swarmed him. He felt them everywhere, biting through his clothing while the poison seeped like ice through his body.

And in his last moments of life, he realized something startling. He had just given up everything for Janet. His life, his world, his everything to save her.

He almost laughed.

This was what it was to love.

CHAPTER 19

"Keeven!"

Janet saw it flash before her eyes. The portal, the fucking zombie shits, and the Controller. Not a hulking gool this time, but Not-Uncle-Joey with a boatload of eyeliner-like tats that bled all over his skin.

And then she saw Keeven swing. She hadn't realized what he was doing. Not at first. Not until the portal winked out with an audible pop. And she slammed face first into the back of Marty's closet.

"No, no, no, no, no," she cried as she banged her whole body against the drywall. Then she slid down, too agonized to do more than just lean against the wall.

She had no way to re-open the portal. The machinery was all on the other side. And if what she remembered of the room was right, then Keeven had just destroyed the portal device. Smashed it to smithereens from the looks of his swing.

"What the hell is that?" screamed Marty from behind her. "And that? And that!"

Janet turned to see three of the aruckien standing there dazed. Right. Because the portal to the Magician was closed. "They're zombie shits."

"What?" screeched Marty.

"Actually, they're called Aruckien, but in either language they're shits. Land piranhas might be a better description." With quick, deadly movements, she used the dagger that

Keeven had given her to end them while Marty continued to squeak in horror. Not really surprising since the black blood was oozing over her shoes.

"So...um..." Marty asked as she grabbed a roll of paper towels. Like that was going to be enough. "What happened to the portal?"

"Gone," Janet said.

"But it'll come back tomorrow, right? Or in two days?"

Janet shrugged, the weight of the movement almost too much for her. "It has to be done from the other side."

"But Keeven will do it, right? When it's re-powered?"

Janet tried to answer. She wanted to say something positive. There was still hope somewhere. Keeven could survive, right? He'd survived those things before. But that was when he had help and room to fight.

And even if he survived the fight, he'd destroyed the portal. She knew it to the depths of her soul. Hadn't she felt the decision in her heartspace? In that split second before he swung, she felt the decision and the knowledge.

That's what made it all worse. She hadn't thought she could possibly feel more wretched, but she knew it was true. The more she thought about that moment, the more she felt the message in her heart.

He loved her. And so he had destroyed the portal to protect her.

She started to cry. Thick, heavy tears that pissed her off even as they felt like the inevitable expression of her situation.

"No," she said through the thick knot in her throat. "No," she repeated louder. "This is not going to end like this." A few weeks ago, she would have crumpled into a sobbing ball of despair, but a few weeks ago she hadn't trotted through a colony of birdbeasts, faced zombie shits and ghosts, or fallen in love. She had now, and the man she adored was not going to sacrifice himself for her.

"Quit whimpering and think!" she screamed at herself.

"I wasn't whimpering," Marty shot back.

Janet turned to her best friend. "I wasn't talking to you." Though of course, Marty had certainly been whimpering. "I need to figure this out. I need to…"

Except it was all pretty simple, wasn't it? Something she hadn't even considered before, but seemed to loom huge in her brain. All this time, she'd been thinking that she'd been brought to Keeven's world to introduce him to science. To teach him things like electricity and flush toilets. But what if it went the other way around? What if she was supposed to *learn* something? Not just how to fight down evil baddies, but how to have faith. Faith in herself, sure, but also faith in something larger than herself. Call it magic or the Goddess or the power of love. It didn't matter.

After all, Keeven didn't have a portal when he opened the doorway to Earth at the very beginning. He'd just had prayer and his magic stones. Well, if he could do it, so could she. Genetics, science, and naysayers be damned. The universe was a mystery, and this was all she had.

She quickly gathered all the stones she had and poured them at the base of the closet wall. Then she looked at the wall and prayed to get back to Keeven. She wasn't willing it to happen. She wasn't bartering or begging, even. She just surrendered everything she was to Keeven's goddess. Her knowledge and her confusion, the power in the stones, and the overwhelming love in her heart. She gave it all up to Keeven's goddess and waited in hope, in faith, and most especially, in love.

It took a long time. Long enough for her heart to quail, for her eyes to water, and her breath to stutter not once but three times. But she kept at it, giving even her fears to the Goddess.

The first inkling she had that it worked was Marty's gasp of shock. Janet hadn't even realized she'd closed her eyes, but at that sound her eyes flew open and she saw the battle. She had a moment to process flames. As in a screaming, burning inferno.

Then she leaped into it.

* * *

Keeven felt the shift in the power. He knew Janet had opened the portal again—though not in front of him. His heartspace told him she was behind him, in a space behind the arm that had controlled the portal.

So she was here, in a room filled with Aruckien, the Magician, and the fire he prayed would kill them all. How fitting that his last act would be in the midst of knowing he had utterly failed. He had not kept Janet safe. He had not kept the Magician from invading his realm. And he had not protected the secrets of the castle.

And yet, even knowing all that, he did not stay his hand. One firestone had not been enough. Even through the heat and the blaze, he could see the Magician with runes black across his skin keeping the danger away from him. They would all be burned alive except for that one bastard. Unless Keeven first cut the runes from the bastard's face.

That meant abandoning Janet and Crissanna to their fates. He had done all he could for them, sacrificed in every way he knew how. It had not been enough. All that was left to him was his duty, and everything in him urged him down this path.

So he attacked with his sword flying while his skin blistered. He ignored the Aruckien still driven to bite him despite the flames that consumed them. And he pressed to the Magician. The man was not a fighter. He relied on his magics and his minions to defend him. If he could just cut him once on the face. Once.

He couldn't get close.

The man had his hands upraised, creating a field that deflected every blow from Keeven's sword.

Then he heard Janet scream. It was raw and filled with fury as she began throwing things at the bastard. He saw first her dagger, then crystals. Thing after thing pelted at the Magician, while Keeven redoubled his own attack.

And then he did it. He swung fast enough to get through. Not a lethal strike, but enough to bloody the Magician's cheek. Enough, thank the Goddess, to tear the rune apart.

Done.

So he grabbed the last of his firestones and threw it with all his strength. He aimed straight for the villain's eyes and activated it with a curse. And with his last breath, he spun around and launched himself at Janet. If they were to die, then he would do so protecting her.

CHAPTER 20

"Come on big guy. I know being bald sucks, but you gotta face it sometime. Come on, Keevan. Wake up."

Janet.

He answered her call. He struggled to wake merely because she asked it. And in the end, he was able to blink his eyes open only to see the floor. Huh. He was on his stomach, looking through a window on the table, and the rest of his body was completely numb.

Alarm flashed through him despite his groggy state. He could not lie here on his belly—

"Whoa there, big guy. Relax. Don't move. Everything's fine."

Janet sounded so relieved, she calmed his panic.

"I cannot move," he croaked, only now realizing it was true as he said the words.

"You can, just very, very slowly." Crissanna's voice. "But let me suggest you don't. At least not for a few days."

He flexed his arm and found out it was true. It would move, but the numbness alarmed him almost as much as the unrecognizable gray floor. "Where are we?"

"Med bay," Janet answered. "Or what used to be their medical area. Turns out Crissanna is quite the doctor."

"Of course she is," he said, trying to gather his thoughts. "It is what is expected of the women of her lineage."

"That and babies," Crissanna said, her voice excruciatingly

dry. "Bodily functions are our greatest joy." Clearly not, but he did not want to think about her. Instead, he fumbled through his thoughts, trying to remember.

Fire. The Magician. Aruckien. "What happened?"

Janet chuckled. "Exactly what should happen on a spaceship." Then he saw her face, more of his panic easing as he saw that she was well. She settled down on the floor in front of him, and her smile was so beautiful it brought tears to his eyes.

"Janet," he whispered.

"That's me. And do you know who you are? The hero of the day."

His lips curved—slowly—into a smile. It felt so good to just look at her. "What happened?"

"You fried the evil baddy. Good thinking with those firestones. Or should I call them little hand grenades? You blew his face off and then..." She took a breath, obviously for dramatic effect. "Fire suppression system."

He took a moment to understand. In his heartspace, he saw fire dying down to nothing. In seconds, everything was out.

"I don't understand."

"Me either. Don't know why it didn't kick in at the beginning. Probably because this place is hundreds of years old. Or maybe it's because I used up a bunch of the power. Whatever the reason, I'm grateful. After the big boom, the air was abruptly sucked out of the room. Starved of oxygen, the fire dies, then with a big ear popping hiss, all the air comes back and we don't asphyxiate."

He took a moment to follow this, his heartspace telling him that the castle's magic destroyed the fire, thank the Goddess. "The Magician?"

"Kaboom. No head."

"The Aruckien?"

"Burned or easy to kill without the Magician's mojo."

He nodded. Then slowly, he gathered his strength before pushing himself up enough to look about him. He needed to see this place and see that they were safe. She followed him, her expression cautious.

"Everything's fine, Keeven. The portal room has major damage and we'll be a long time figuring stuff out there, if ever. But we're safe. The realm is safe. Big bad Magician is dead."

He looked at her, seeing the earnestness in her expression and the honesty as well. She was safe. He was alive. It was a miracle.

Then Crissanna stepped into his field of view. "Really dumb to be up and about, Keeven. But then I never thought you particularly bright."

He ignored her jab in order to study her wounds. She had bandages all over her body, half her hair had been burned away, and her eyes were haunted, but she seemed healthy. A lot more healthy than she ought to be.

"How did you survive?" he rasped.

"I was covered in Aruckien. I never thought I'd be thankful for that, but they took the brunt of the explosion."

His gaze went to her wounds. "But the poison. How are you still alive?"

She flushed and looked away, clearly embarrassed. It was Janet who answered.

"She's immune to their poison."

Keeven's eyes widened. "What? Is this magic?"

Janet shook her head. "She did it the old fashioned way, taking a little every day until she built up a tolerance. Cumbersome, probably made her childhood a nightmare of yuck, but apparently her mother made sure she was immune to a lot of this world's poisons."

That explains why he'd thought her a sickly child when she was young. "So you are well?"

She nodded slowly. "Thank you for rescuing me, Prince Keeven."

Formal address. A thanks that came from not just a woman to a man, but a nation to another. "It is my honor to serve,

Princess Crissanna."

"I'm still not marrying you. That ceremony we had was completely invalid. Our laws nullify any contracts formed under compulsion."

Yes, he realized, she was indeed well. "Yes, I know. And so I hereby dissolve our vows as invalid."

Two women exhaled their relief. Keeven found that he too felt better than he had in years. His whole life perhaps. Especially as he was now free to turn to his angel.

"Janet." Nothing more. Just her name.

She touched his face, a slow stroke that he could barely feel. Whatever medicines numbed him made everything feel as if it came through a thick cloth. And yet looking into her eyes, he felt her touch all the way to his soul.

"Listen here, big guy, I think that your goddess has done a hell of a lot to get us together. So I say we stick with divine faith. You're not to go marrying anyone else and—"

"Marry me, Janet. Be my wife and let me serve you until my dying breath."

She smiled, the look radiant and somewhat chagrinned. "How about we agree to love, honor, and cherish, okay?"

"Okay," he said in her language.

Then she hesitated. "Even if I can't have babies with you?"

"You bring much more than your womb, Janet. You bring love. You make me strong. And I love you."

"I love you, too."

He felt it then. Love. Deep in his heartspace, flowing out like a never ending river. She loved him and all was well. So he moved—with excruciating slowness—until he cupped her face in his hands and could kiss her lips. And then he spent a very long time being sure that she was well served. It was, after all, his sacred duty as her prince and her mate.

She was the one to break the kiss, drawing back as she caressed his face. "Slow down, big guy. You're not up to the big stuff yet."

Certain throbbing parts of him wished to argue, but he

knew better. He could not do what he wanted as thoroughly as he wanted just then. So he let her push him back down onto the bed, face down because his back was still raw from burns he was just now beginning to sense.

"You just rest there," she said as she settled onto the floor beneath him. "Rest while I tell you all the thousands of ways I'm going to study this here magic castle."

"You are happy to do that?" he asked.

"There's only one thing on this planet that I like better."

His eyebrows rose in query.

"You, big guy. Loving you in every possible way."

His heartspace flushed again with that river of love, and he returned it a thousand fold. Meanwhile, her words continued to flow as if she had not just given him the answer to all his prayers.

"First off there's the engine room. I know it's smashed, but come on. There's got to be a Nobel prize somewhere there. And don't get me started on those stasis pods. Oh my God, the things I want to look at there...."

EPILOGUE

Go! Go now! *Move!*

Marty was mentally screaming at herself before she managed to unstick her feet and lurch forward. She'd just seen Keeven first, then Janet dive through the portal at the back of her closet.

It was her turn now, but God she was slow. This was why she sucked at sports because no matter how much her brain told her to move, her feet were sluggish at best. She could plant herself like an oak, but she rarely managed to leap into the path of the ball or avoid the attack. In this case, all she had to do was run through the flames of doom at the back of her closet and she'd be in a real live spaceship.

Come on, go! She was not going to be left behind again.

She did it. She closed her eyes, held her breath, then barreled through all the while praying that she didn't burn to death. It actually helped that she had thirty pounds of equipment on her back because the momentum kept her moving when she would have flinched back.

There was a moment of heat, a second when she prayed she didn't burn down their house while they were running around the spaceship, and then everything was dark and cool.

She stopped, her feet thudding onto stone as she stood hunched with her eyes slitting open. Her heartbeat was pounding loud in her ears, but what she saw was nothing. As in near total darkness.

Then she felt a hand on her arm, firm and insistent. It was tugging her to the side. She squeaked in alarm, but the hand didn't let go.

"This way," a man's voice said.

"Janet? Where are you?" No answer. And worse, this guy didn't sound like Keevan. Which meant she had no guide in this Nothing-Like-Narnia world."This way, angel. Quickly."

She took an unsteady step toward him, more because his grip was insistent. But she was still getting her bearings, and she hated moving blindly through the dark.

"What happened to the fire?" It was good she wasn't burning to death, but her voice was echoing weirdly.

"Shh." It wasn't a soothing hush noise. It was short and clipped. The kind of sound you make when you didn't have time to explain.

She took another step forward, mostly because she didn't have a choice, but then she planted her feet. She wasn't just wandering off in the dark with a strange guy. She'd seen too many episodes of *Buffy* to think that was a good idea.

"Where's Janet?" she demanded.

She felt him shift, simultaneously moving around her and inching her forward a bit more. She felt his breath by her ear, then smelled leather and man. His hand pressed gently against her lips. She felt hard callouses on his fingers then he shifted again, bumping against her backpack.

"You travel heavy. No wonder you are slow."

"So tell me—"

His hand pressed hard against her mouth. She would have objected but at that moment she heard a sound somewhere ahead. A murmur maybe? A thud? She felt the man beside her go taut, but he didn't do more than that. He didn't seem to want to hurt her, so for the moment she decided to give him the benefit of the doubt. She stood silent until…nothing. All was quiet.

She felt him exhale, the heat of his breath curving

erotically around her ear. Not what she meant to feel right then, but there was no reasoning with hormones. Then she felt him prod her gently forward. Fortunately her eyes had adjusted now, and she could make out slivers of light gray around a rough door directly ahead of her. Two steps further and she saw it was heavy oak, rough-hewn and braced with iron just like those found in medieval castles and every D&D cartoon she'd ever seen.

She stopped moving, looking about her with a weird feeling of déjà vu. Why did this feel exactly like her walk-in closet, done medieval? Minus the tabards and shoes and stuff. It was bare stone and this guy, but the shape was the same. Not that closets were shaped all that different, but still.

"This is not a spaceship," she whispered, summing up the obvious fact first. "So where am I? Who are you and—"

"I'm Antone, and I'm rescuing you," he interrupted. "Now be quiet."

How very sexy Italian he sounded, but he still hadn't answered her question. "Where's Janet?"

"I don't know," he said, then he released her to step up to the door and peer through a crack. She didn't know how he could see anything, but whatever he saw must have reassured him, because he eased the door back open.

This time she saw muted gray light cupped in the hands of a young boy with big eyes. He stood sentry by the door in a hallway that would fit perfectly in any dungeon or evil subterranean lair.

The boy nodded once then scampered up a stone staircase, taking the light with him. Big guy next to her went less quickly, mostly because he still had a hand on her arm and was trying to pull her after him. But before she started hoofing it upstairs while carrying thirty pounds on her back, she was going to get some answers.

"Antone—" she began.

He huffed out a breath, sounding very frustrated male. "You are in my home," he said in a low undertone.

His home? "Well good—"

"But it has been taken over by thieves and brigands."

Thieves and brigands? Now this really sounded like a D&D game come to life. Which could have been fun if she knew the rules.

"How did I get here?"

"You came through the wall just as predicted by the Crazy Woman."

That was reassuring—not.

"Now will you come quietly, or do you wish to be killed where you stand? I cannot tarry here longer."

"Where are you going?"

"To safety," he snapped, and apparently that was all she was going to get as he turned and sprinted up the steps to where another oak door stood partially open. He moved incredibly fast with a lightness that was almost eerie. If only he were blonde, she might have thought him elven. But he had dark curly hair clubbed back into a ponytail, and his clothes made him look more like Inigo Montoya of *The Princess Bride*—leather boots, pants, vest, plus a flowing light gray shirt. She also now saw the outline of bow and arrows and maybe a sword. All he needed to say was, "Prepare to die," and she would have totally applauded.

Instead, she bit her lip trying to decide. In the end, there really was no question. Go with the cute guy in leather or wander around in the dark alone? She chose cute guy and huffed it up the stairs.

He gave her a nod, then pressed his finger to his lip. *Well excuse her* for not being used to carting around thirty pounds of generator on her back. If she had a moment, she'd grab her inhaler and take a puff, but he was easing through the doorway and she guessed there wasn't time.

Sure enough, he stepped into the hallway beyond while motioning her to follow. She did her best to slip through the half-open door, but the backpack was really big. Stealth wasn't so easy. But she made it, only wincing when her pack banged against the door with a dull thunk. She saw his shoulders tense, but he didn't shoot her a glare or anything.

And now that she'd decided she was going with him, she did her best to enter into the spirit of sneaking through a castle. Thank God she'd chosen to wear her cross trainers. Her sandals would totally have clip-clopped on the stone floor.

They were in a hallway on the ground floor, judging by the sunlight pooling on the floor down a ways. She saw tapestries on the wall, a braided run on the floor, and two guys with swords stepping around the corner.

Oh shit.

Antone grabbed her wrist and spun around, but there were three more guys on the other side. Two big sword guys flanking another leather clad Inigo type, though this time with shorter, blonder hair and no weaponry that she could see.

Marty reached for the door back to the dungeon, but one of the sword guys slammed his boot against it, banging it shut. Which meant that they were well and truly trapped. And then everyone drew their swords, Antone included.

"So this is the rescue part?" she asked, her voice unnaturally high.

Antone glanced back at her, his expression rueful. Oh hell, she knew that look. It was a "sorry, we're screwed look." And then there was no more time to think as the guards attacked.

The End

There's more coming from Janet and Marty. Look for
Accidental Angels Book 2, Christmas 2016.

Children of mixed races have their own set of rules. As the daughter of a Shanghai native and a staunch Indiana Hoosier, *USA TODAY* bestselling author Kathy Lyons, who also writes as Jade Lee, struggled to find her own identity somewhere between America and China. Her search took her throughout Asia and the United States. In the end, the answer was found in writing fiction and the amazing power of love.

For the latest news on Jade or Kathy, visit them on the web at

www.jadeleeauthor.com
www.kathylyons.com
www.facebook.com/JadeLeeBooks
www.twitter.com/JadeLeeAuthor